A FAMILIAR STRANGER

MCGARVEY BLACK

BLOODHOUND
— BOOKS —

ALSO BY MCGARVEY BLACK

This book is dedicated to my sister Diane McGarvey who has tirelessly read and critiqued my books. How lucky to have a sister who is also a best friend. I guess she forgot about all the times I tortured her when we were kids.

"You see George, you really had a wonderful life. Don't you see what a mistake it would be to throw it away?"

— **Clarence the Angel,** *It's a Wonderful Life*

1

―――――

When a person is hit by a train, they don't bounce off and fly through the air. A lot of people think they do, but they don't. Their body gets caught up in the wheels and then ground into a thousand pieces. Arms here, legs there, sections of torso strewn across the tracks. It can take days to find all the pieces. It's a messy business.

On a cold winter afternoon, a little black-and-white dog with lopsided ears followed a stranger down the main street of a small town in New Jersey. Oblivious to his canine companion, Eddie Gamble took deliberate steps along the busy road. Icy gusts blew his remaining strands of gray hair straight up revealing patches of pink scalp. Snow flurries seemed almost suspended in the air as he got closer to the orange neon lights of an old donut shop on the far corner.

Only fifty-two, he looked ten years older but moved steadily like a horse with blinders, eyes fixed on the finish line. The small stray dog cheerfully kept pace behind him. When Eddie entered the bakery, the animal sat outside and waited as the lights on the street flickered on all at once.

Walking to the counter, Eddie looked at the display of

donuts on the wall. They all looked old, like they'd been sitting there for the better part of the day, because they had. He looked in each metal basket until he found the kind he was looking for —cinnamon, his favorite.

"You know what you want?" said the disinterested teenaged girl behind the counter, a silver bullring in her nose. Eddie looked at her nose and wondered if it hurt when she got it pierced. *Does she take it out when she has a cold? My daughter pierced her eyebrow but at least it wasn't her nose.*

"Let me have half a dozen of the cinnamon and sugar," said Eddie pointing to a wire rack with his chin.

"If you buy twelve, you'll get one free," said the girl texting, not looking up from her phone.

"I don't want twelve," said Eddie glancing at his watch. He still had a little time before his appointment.

"You don't want any with sprinkles? Cinnamon is kind of boring. That's what the old ladies get," said the girl, her eyes still glued to her screen.

"I want six cinnamon," he repeated.

The girl let out a sigh, rolled her eyes and reached for a sheet of white waxed paper and placed donuts into a brown paper bag.

"That'll be five dollars," she said.

Eddie fumbled through his gray overcoat pockets and pulled out a small wad of disorganized, crumpled bills consisting of a ten, and five singles. He unfurled each one and handed five dollars to the teenager.

"Have a good one," she said, not looking at him while handing him the receipt. "They said on the news we might get a lot of snow tonight. If we have a blizzard, I won't have to come to work in this crappy place tomorrow."

Eddie nodded and handed the girl his last ten-dollar bill. "Keep it," he said.

"The whole thing?" said the girl in disbelief looking up at his face for first time. "No one ever gives us tips here. Thanks," she said, flashing a big smile and tucking the money quickly into her pocket in case he changed his mind. Looking out the front window at the snowfall she noticed the little dog sitting outside the door. "That your dog out there?"

"I don't have a dog," said Eddie not turning around to follow her gaze.

"I thought I saw him walk up with you when you came in," said the girl. "There are loads of street dogs around here because of all the restaurants. Plenty for them to eat, I guess. I thought maybe that one was yours though. He's kind of cute."

"Not mine," said Eddie eating a donut.

The girl's phone vibrated and she walked away into the back room.

As Eddie chewed he was vaguely aware the donuts were stale and hard but still tasted good—sweet and greasy. He finished his second trying to remember the last time he had eaten one and guessed it was probably in college. *Never worried about anything then. Coffee, beer, burgers and pizza. Never gained an ounce. That was nearly thirty years ago. Everything was so easy then.* Standing alone at the counter finishing another donut, he didn't turn his head when the front door opened and two older people walked in. The teenaged girl heard the door open and cut her call short to wait on the new customers.

Eddie looked down at his watch again. *Time to go,* he thought. Folding up the remainder of his donuts in the paper bag, he tucked it into the large pocket of his coat. The weather forecast predicted temperatures going below twenty degrees that night. He buttoned his collar all the way up and walked to the door bracing himself for the cold outside.

I should have moved to Mexico or Hawaii, he thought. *I could have opened a little surf shop in Costa Rica. That would have been a nice life.*

Pushing open the door of the shop, he stepped outside into the cold night. Frosty air enveloped him and within seconds he felt the little hairs inside his nose freeze up, like hard, tiny spikes. The small dog stood ready to move.

Still unaware he had a shadow, Eddie continued his trek down the main street. A block or two further on, he sensed a presence and turned around. The mixed breed looked up at him quizzically with expectation. Eddie could see the dog was nothing but skin and bones so he dug into his coat pocket and pulled out the brown paper bag.

"Hungry?" he said, leaning over giving the scraggly mutt a piece of donut. The dog jumped for the treat and devoured it in seconds.

"I guess you are hungry." He placed another piece on the ground and patted the dog on the head. Wagging his tail, the dog gobbled it up and looked to Eddie for more. Emptying the contents of the greasy bag onto the sidewalk, the weary man walked away leaving the dog eating happily on the curb. Eddie looked at his watch again. *I need to move faster or I'll miss it.*

Two blocks further down, he walked past his own battered silver Jeep Cherokee parked on the street. Exhaling, he watched the vapor from his lungs hang in the freezing air. On the sidewalk, people rushed from the stores to their cars hoping to outrun the snow and cold and not slip on the black ice. Eddie didn't notice any of that, he stayed focused and continued to walk.

Across the road, two teenaged boys hurled snowballs at passing cars. When one landed on the sidewalk several feet in front of Eddie, he barely noticed it. At another time in his life, he would have laughed, bent down and packed his own snowball and hurled it back. But not this day: he had somewhere to be and no more time left.

The snowflakes floated down faster and heavier now. It was only a little before six, but the downtown streets were nearly empty. Everyone wanted to get home to lock their doors and put on a fire before the big storm hit.

He passed signs for the train station and checked his watch —right on time. Turning the corner, he walked through an empty lot filled with remnants of an old building, now only piles of bricks. It had grown darker since leaving the lights of the street and Eddie took out a flashlight from his coat pocket. He flicked it on and off. Satisfied it was functioning properly, he reached into another pocket for an envelope—it was still there.

A thick coating of snow covered the ground as he tramped through the deep, empty lot. Now far from the street and stores, he turned on the flashlight to continue his journey across the dark, flat, open field. With no buildings or trees to shield him, the wind nearly blew him over, but he kept going.

A train whistle sounded in the distance reassuring him that he was going in the right direction. Minutes passed and a second whistle blew, louder and closer. He figured the trains were filled with thousands of commuters from Philadelphia trying to get home to their families before the storm.

Marching towards a distant flickering light, an image of Eddie's younger self flashed in front of his eyes. He was twelve, riding his bicycle alongside his father as the older man walked home from the train station at the end of a workday. Eddie's dog, Checkers, half lab, half who knows what, ran happily alongside the bike. When the three arrived at their house, his mother, Marian was in the kitchen making a meatloaf—Eddie's favorite. She looked young and attractive. He had forgotten how pretty his mother was then.

The snow had stopped but Eddie kept walking. As the

clouds cleared in one spot, a bright yellow crescent appeared in the sky. The white ground sparkled as the moonlight bounced off the frosty blanket that covered it. *You can't screw this up, not this time. Follow the light.*

Several steps further, he tripped over something hard and pointed his flashlight at the ground beneath his feet. Hidden under all the white powder was what he had been searching for —railroad tracks.

Still distant, the train whistle howled again, but now it was more emphatic and impending. Trudging methodically alongside the metal rails he finally stopped. He had arrived at his destination. Planting his feet firmly between the two rows of steel, he licked his cold, dry, chapped lips and tasted tiny bits of leftover sugar. The sweet cinnamon flavor triggered an onslaught of scattered images.

He visualized his friends stealing empty soda bottles from a church basement and cashing them in for the bottle deposit money. Timmy Tierney, all freckles and teeth, bought chips and Twinkies with his money. Eddie bought a couple of fresh cinnamon donuts from Elmer's Bakery with his cut. He saw kids clapping and cheering, when they voted him MVP of the high school baseball team. Then an image of winter, he was twelve in a snow fort. He and his friends were throwing snowballs at some girls making them scream. Everything was so easy then.

Bursts of arctic air made Eddie's eyes tear. He closed them for a moment and saw Timmy Tierney again. He hadn't thought about him in years, not since Timmy went off to law school. Eddie smiled ruefully. *Everyone thought Timmy would end up in jail, not defending the people trying to stay out.*

The train's warning sound blew one more time and Eddie opened his eyes. The approaching light grew bigger. He couldn't look directly at it, that would be too hard. Slowly, he turned around putting his back to the oncoming light. Still holding his flashlight, he braced himself. Looking down he saw two red eyes right in front of him.

Startled, Eddie cried out and stumbled backwards nearly falling. Steadying himself, he pointed the flashlight where he had seen the two eyes. There, sitting on the tracks was the little black-and-white stray with the lopsided floppy ears. The dog's tail wagged when the loud horn blared again three times in rapid succession.

"What are you doing here?" shouted Eddie kicking snow at the dog to move the animal off the tracks. "Get out of here, now. Go! Get the fuck out of here, you stupid dog," he pleaded. The little dog put his head down on the metal near Eddie's feet.

"Get away from me. Please!" screamed Eddie. The dog only looked up at Eddie as two more deafening whistles blasted out. "Get off the tracks." He desperately tried to shove the animal away from him and out of the path of the coming train. A final ear-splitting warning from the engineer pierced the air causing Eddie to whip his head around. The train was now only 200 feet away and coming fast. He looked back at the dog and their eyes locked as the bright light overwhelmed them both.

2

SIXTEEN YEARS EARLIER

W henever people met thirty-six-year-old Eddie Gamble, they walked away smiling and thinking, *What a great guy*. Eddie possessed everything a man could want. He had it all except for one elusive thing, and he could never figure out what that was. Capable of grand gestures of kindness and compassion he could also turn on a dime and react with selfishness and anger. If he was charged up about a new business idea, he'd easily get everyone around him on board. Eddie Gamble had heaps of charisma which turned out to be a blessing and a curse.

When he was down, your heart broke for him because you didn't know why, only that something was off. People didn't know what to do with him when he was like that. No one wanted sad, low-energy Eddie, someone who couldn't make decisions. They wanted high-flying, electric Eddie, the man who was on fire. He knew it too, so he kept up the façade. When the pressure to be "Eddie Gamble, rainmaker" was too overwhelming, he'd fake a smile or tell a joke pretending he had it all together. With a smile that often had a "cat who had eaten the canary" quality to it, he disarmed people which only added to his charm. You couldn't help but smile when that devilish grin spread across his handsome face and triggered his dimples. There was something wildly exciting about him and most people wanted to go for a ride on his rollercoaster. Eddie was fun. A smile or a wink from him could make your day. But, if he turned on you, it could be devastating.

Most people who live large don't usually go very deep. In that respect, Eddie Gamble was unique. Always the first one to reach out if someone was in trouble, he'd eagerly give a hand to a person down on their luck with no expectation of reciprocity. That's what endeared him to so many, a humongous streak of empathy at his core, possibly because he understood pain. When he did things that were wrong or unethical, most people eventually forgave him. It was probably that empathetic streak that kept Eddie Gamble this side of being a sociopath.

As Eddie pushed through the revolving doors of Andover Media, one of the largest and most prestigious consumer media companies in the United States, he smiled. It was his first day as the new associate publisher of *Vacation.com* and *Vacation* magazine, the second largest travel brand in North America.

He didn't know it then, but in two years' time, he would make a fateful decision that would change the trajectory of his career and ultimately his life. Until then, he continued to believe his own press: he was the golden boy—capable of anything. That mindset would ultimately be his undoing. Once his fall started, there would be no way to stop it. The media industry is small. If you screw someone on your way up, they'll be at the front of the line to help you start your journey downward.

Eddie got his job at Andover Media the way he won most things—impeccable timing. With a knack for being in the right place at the right time, good things seemed to happen to him without him doing much at all. Friends often joked that he had done a deal with the devil, that he led a "charmed life". Deep down, Eddie kind of agreed with them. Still, no matter what he did, the good stuff always came his way. Even his new job at Andover Media, that had been a huge step up, was just another one of the lucky things he'd fallen into. That's the way it always was and he never questioned it.

His leap over to Andover started at a media industry cocktail party at the New York Public Library. He had run into a few colleagues and within minutes had the group laughing until they cried, each person privately thinking, *that Eddie Gamble is one terrific guy.*

From a distance, a woman in her early forties with short red hair wearing an expensive navy-blue suit and heels carefully watched him entertain the crowd. When the group dispersed, the red-haired woman approached Eddie and introduced herself as Julia Bowman, publisher of *Vacation* magazine. *Vacation* was owned by Andover Media, the crème de la crème of all media companies. After exchanging business cards, Julia got right to the point. She was looking for a number two to run her national advertising sales team and wondered if he might be interested in discussing it. She confided they were about to fire her current associate publisher, and she needed to replace him—yesterday.

"I've heard your name bandied around as someone to watch. I saw you back there," said Julia sizing him up. "You handle yourself extremely well. People instinctually like you. I could use some of what you've got in my sales organization."

"That's very kind of you," said Eddie flashing the Gamble grin with just the right amount of humility. "I know a few jokes."

"It's not the jokes," continued Julia shaking her head and leaning in closer. "You've got natural talent. You're smart and charismatic. The loser I have in there now is a total disaster. He's incapable and wooden and the salespeople detest him. Not to mention there have been some sexual harassment complaints. I need to make a change quickly."

At the time, Eddie was the eastern sales manager for a small but well-regarded music magazine and website called *Drake's Downbeat* or *DDB* by the trade. He managed four east coast salespeople and carried a small account list of his own. He'd been there less than a year, and considered *DDB* a short stopover on his long-term career path. Fifth in the music category in terms of audience size, *DDB* had a stagnant circulation and advertisers did not automatically think to buy space in its pages. Eddie only took the job because he thought it would be a strategic stepping stone to bigger and better positions. In a short amount of time, he realized the monthly uphill battle to secure ad dollars was a nearly impossible feat. *DDB* was never going to turn a profit in the crowded music space. *Rolling Stone* and a few of the other larger players garnered the lion's share of ad budgets leaving only crumbs for publications like his.

Julia Bowman described her team and the positive environment she hoped to create at *Vacation* with the right management partner by her side. With Eddie's always perfect timing, this job would be the lucky break he had been waiting for to move on up. Being the associate publisher at *Vacation* would propel him into the limelight. It was the big time. He could leave his current rinky-dink company with only a single title and go to one of the most prestigious consumer media companies in the world with eighteen national publications and websites.

"At *Vacation* you'd manage seventeen salespeople across the United States," said Julia.

"I'm flattered," said Eddie smiling sheepishly at her, "but I don't know..."

"Just come in and talk to me. You can spare one hour, can't you?" said Julia. "It might change your life."

Eddie took a deep breath but didn't reply.

"Come on, Eddie, you have nothing to lose and everything to gain. If after an hour you decide it's not the right move for you, walk away. We'll part friends. I'm willing to waste an hour. What do you say?"

The following Tuesday at 9am, he met with Julia in the Andover offices on West 59th Street. Entering the building he looked around. The lobby was new and modern with lots of glass and natural light. A steady stream of employees filed through the turnstiles using their electronic security badges to gain entrance. Andover was the top of the media heap. *Doesn't get much better than this*, Eddie thought as he noticed how well-dressed all the employees were and that most of them were extremely attractive women.

His meeting that day with Julia Bowman and three senior members on her team went extremely well. They all thought Eddie was amazing and after he left they unilaterally agreed he would make an excellent associate publisher. The rest happened fast and within two weeks a generous offer was extended that included a luxury company car lease, a golf club and gym membership, and a town car and driver at his disposal, seven days a week.

The night he got the offer, an excited Eddie discussed the opportunity with his wife, Clare, in their small New Jersey kitchen. While she was thrilled to hear about her husband's new opportunity, at the same time she was concerned about him not honoring his commitment to his current employer.

"Don't you think you might be jumping jobs too soon?" said Clare. "You've only been at *DDB* for ten months."

He had been at each of his last three jobs barely a year before he left for a bigger and better one. Now that their daughter Sarah was three and a half and another baby was on the way, Clare acknowledged they could use the additional money and second car. Still, she was concerned things were moving too fast and that Eddie's jumping around would come back to haunt him.

"I've got to grab for that gold ring, if I'm going to get anywhere," said Eddie. "You're too cautious."

"You made a commitment to *Drake's Downbeat*. Can't you just enjoy the ride you're on for a while?" said Clare. "You're always distracted by any new shiny object."

"It's how I'm wired."

"We have a great life right now. I love you, you love me and we have a beautiful little girl. We can pay our bills and take a vacation every summer. We don't need more. The more we get, something will be sacrificed."

Eddie only half-listened because he had already made his decision. Clare knew that before she opened her mouth but she wanted to have her say anyway. He made a point of talking important things over with her, but in the end he always did exactly what he wanted. Now, the die had been cast.

Two weeks, one resignation and a last-minute Gamble family vacation later, Eddie started his job at *Vacation*. Walking up to the building that first morning, he noticed a homeless man, dressed in old clothes with long gray hair sitting on the ground in front of the Andover offices. Something about the juxtaposition of the man and the building that published the most affluent brands made Eddie stop. He looked to his left and saw a coffee cart on the corner, walked over to it and ordered a coffee and a bagel with butter. Breakfast in hand, he walked back to the homeless man and introduced himself.

"Hi, I'm Eddie and today's my first day of work in this building," he said to the homeless man. "Would you help me celebrate my new job by having a breakfast on me."

The homeless man looked up suspiciously. "What you got?"

"Coffee and a bagel."

"I take milk and three sugars in my coffee."

"I got it covered," said Eddie chuckling as he handed the man the coffee cup and bag. "There's extra sugar and a container of milk inside."

"Cause I don't drink coffee without three sugars," said the homeless man as he greedily took the food. "You put cream cheese on the bagel? I like bagels with cream cheese."

"Sorry, I got butter."

"Butter's all right."

"Next time I'll get you one with cream cheese. See you tomorrow," said Eddie with a warm smile followed by a little salute.

Entering the lobby he showed his driver's license to the security guard. "Go to the ninth floor, they'll take your picture and give you an Andover ID," said the guard. "After that, you'll go to the new employee orientation across the hall and then you're to report to the twenty-second floor. That's where the *Vacation* offices are."

For the next hour, Eddie was efficiently handled and processed by the fine-tuned Andover Media on-boarding team. Coffee and bagels were served at a short Q&A with a human resources director and within ninety minutes Eddie had his ID, was briefed on all company benefits, got the keys to his company car and signed his family up for the healthcare plan. *This place is total class. It's where I belong,* Eddie thought as he shook hands with the HR woman who officially welcomed him into the Andover Media family.

When he resigned from *DDB* two weeks earlier, his boss hadn't taken it very well. The boss had gone way out on a limb in order to hire Eddie.

"I know Gamble doesn't have that much experience," his old

boss had told the owner of the company, "but I have a good feeling about him. He's got game." When Eddie resigned after only ten months on the job, *DDB*'s owner was livid.

Eddie knew his move kind of screwed the guy that hired him, but what could he do? *I wasn't looking for a job but when opportunity knocks, you have to open the freakin' door,* he told himself. It wasn't his fault Julia Bowman offered him an amazing job. Whenever he had a pang of guilt, he rationalized it, reminding himself that he had a growing family to support. *It would be wrong, irresponsible even, for me to turn down this new job making great money. I'll be running a national sales team for one of the biggest media companies in America.*

Silently humming a happy tune, Eddie took the elevator up to the twenty-second floor to begin his upward climb in the New York media world. He had already decided, Andover was where he'd make his mark. Within two years, he promised himself, he would take *Vacation* from number two to number one in the travel category and make it the "must buy" for advertisers. His personal goal was to knock their main competitor, *American Traveler,* the number-one book, off its throne. That's what he had told Julia when she made him the offer. Completely confident in his aspirations, he was certain he would make it happen because everything always went his way.

Growing up, Eddie was picked for every sports team and was usually the standout. In college, he dated the prettiest girls, serenading them with his acoustic guitar, ran the biggest parties on campus and still somehow managed to pull out decent grades with a minimum of effort. On the few occasions his final grades were abysmal, he'd sweet-talk a professor and they'd eventually agree to raise his grade or give him a chance to do extra credit to bring it up. In the end, Eddie's powers of persuasion prevailed. His smile, his dimples, the way he cocked his head, squinted his eyes and laid on the bullshit worked on almost everyone.

Walking through the hallowed halls of Andover Media that first day, Eddie's body tingled. Only thirty-six, he was one of the youngest associate publishers in the company and in the media business. When he called his parents to tell them about his new job, Frank and Marian Gamble were ecstatic. His father said things like "outstanding" and "well done" and that he was "proud of him". His mother squealed that now she finally had something to brag about to all her friends at the club.

"Will your name actually be in the magazine, Eddie?" asked his mother. "That would be so nice to show my friends. Helen Fitzgibbons might finally shut up about her daughter who was appointed a judge. Your job is so much more exciting and glamorous."

"Sure, Ma," said Eddie, "my name will be in there, right up front on the masthead."

"Then I'm going to keep a copy of *Vacation* in my purse at all times so I can whip it out when the other women start yammering about their kids," his mother had said.

The elevator doors opened on the twenty-second floor and Eddie got off. He approached the young, cute, dark-haired receptionist and his eyes widened. *Even the receptionists here are gorgeous. I love this place.*

"May I help you?" the receptionist asked politely blinking her big sultry brown eyes.

"I'm Eddie Gamble. Here for a meeting with Julia Bowman," said Eddie smiling broadly, dimples on full display. "Actually, I'm the new associate publisher."

When the woman heard Eddie's name and title, she sat up a little straighter and gave him her full attention. "Julia made the announcement about you in last week's sales meeting. Welcome to *Vacation*," she said, pouting her lips slightly for effect. "Go straight down that hall and make a right at the end. Julia's assistant sits around the corner. You know what we say here, right?"

Eddie shook his head.

"It's not a job, it's a vacation," she said, laughing.

He grinned and gave her a wink that made her blush a deep pink. Walking down the long hallway he passed through what appeared to be the inner hub of the *Vacation* organization. He went by the marketing and promotion departments, and spotted the art department down another hallway. Coming upon a bunch of cubicles, he guessed he was in the sales department— home of his new team. Everyone appeared busy and he made a mental note of that as he walked on.

"You must be Eddie Gamble," said a middle-aged blonde woman with her hand outstretched. "I'm Tracy, Julia's admin. Welcome to your first day. Here we always say, it's not a job it's a..."

"Vacation," said Eddie with his signature wink, "so I've heard."

Julia was on the phone when Eddie appeared in her doorway. She smiled and waved him in. While she finished her call Eddie sat and looked around at everything in her extraordinarily large corner office. He had been there during his interview but had been focused on impressing everyone and hadn't noticed his new boss's spectacular digs. Now that he was an official member of the Andover Media club, he relaxed a little, and absorbed the surroundings.

With white marble floors, Julia's office had two walls of glass with unfettered northern and western views of Manhattan. A large blond wood and glass mid-century modern desk with three chairs facing it sat at the center. To the right a modern leather sectional couch was flanked by an oversized white marble coffee table. In the center of the table was an enormous glass bowl filled with peanut M&M's. He later learned that Julia's assistant had strict instructions to keep the giant candy bowl filled at all times. Julia had learned early in her career that meetings went much smoother and creative input increased dramatically if there was an endless supply of candy around. She had selected peanut M&M's for two reasons. They appeared to be everyone's favorite but more importantly she was allergic to nuts and wouldn't be tempted. A connecting doorway on the other side of the room led to a private bathroom, shower and dressing room. As he took it all in, Eddie decided he wanted an office with his own bathroom and bottomless bowl of candy.

Still on the phone, Eddie listened to Julia as she cut a deal with a major hotel chain to exchange advertising barter dollars for hotel rooms. If she could make this happen, the *Vacation* sales team would hold their annual meeting at a resort for zero cash. Eddie listened to the way Julia handled herself. *She's impressive.* One of the youngest publishers in the media business, Julia was barely forty and had been the publisher of *Vacation* for nearly three years. She was beautiful, fierce and played for keeps. Eddie figured he could learn a lot from her. His goal was to be a publisher before he was forty, like Julia. He planned to study her every move.

Trying to wrap up her call, Julia made little circular movements with her fingers and crossed her eyes slightly, making Eddie laugh. Thirty seconds later, the deal was done. With a satisfied smile she beamed at Eddie as she ended the call. "Guess whose sales team is going to have their meeting in the Bahamas?" said Julia, her eyes on fire.

"Seriously?" said Eddie visibly astonished. "You hold your sales meetings in other countries?"

"Welcome to Andover Media. We do things BBF: bigger, better and faster," said Julia.

When Eddie flashed his signature smile, she was enchanted

and it reminded her why she had hired him. If *Vacation* was going to eclipse *American Traveler* as the top US travel brand, she needed the whole sales team functioning at a higher level. Everyone knew *Vacation* was a better editorial product than *American Traveler* and *Vacation's* circulation numbers exceeded their competitor. Her brand's only problem—they had been outsold. *American Traveler* had become predictable and stale. *Vacation* was contemporary and fresh and focused on experiential travel for modern affluent travelers. Julia had committed to the Andover Media brass that they would overtake their competition in advertising revenue within twenty-four months. She believed Eddie was her secret weapon to make that happen.

After exchanging a few pleasantries, she walked Eddie through his first day's itinerary of back-to-back meetings with various department heads. He had one hour free in his office to meet with his new assistant before his string of meetings commenced. After work, Julia was taking him and the sales team out for drinks so everyone could get to know the new sheriff.

Walking Eddie down the hall to the sales department, Julia led him into a normal-sized office with one wall of north-facing windows. It was about one tenth the size of Julia's but it was still pretty damn nice and had a great northern Manhattan view. When Julia left him, he sat in his brand-new leather chair at his brand-new desk and swiveled around to look out of the window. *This is where I was meant to be.*

Minutes later, Eddie's assistant walked him through the Andover basics while making a list of everything he would need to make his office feel like home. She'd order paintings, plants, and personalized stationery, and promised his mini fridge under the wood credenza would be replenished with designer bottled water daily.

"You think you can get me a large bowl with some M&M's

like Julia?" said Eddie. His assistant smiled and nodded enthusiastically as she left.

Eddie sat back in his chair looking out the window. *In two years, I'm going to have a big corner office with walls of glass, marble floors and my own private bathroom.*

3

With only another month until the new baby arrived, an exhausted Clare Gamble moved around the kitchen more slowly than usual. The baby boy growing in her belly had recently quieted down and Clare had joked he must be "getting some rest before his debut". Seated at the kitchen table in their Manalapan, NJ colonial home, four-year-old Sarah drew in her Disney Princess coloring book. The little girl's nursery school was closed for the Jewish holidays and it was up to her mother armed with a pile of activities and crafts to keep her busy. Bloated and tired, Clare hoped her husband would be home early to give her a much needed break.

Since starting his all-encompassing new job at *Vacation,* Eddie hadn't been home much. Clare was feeling a bit like a single mother and was slightly resentful. Sure, they had discussed his long hours and frequent travel before he accepted the job, but that didn't make her day-to-day reality any easier.

"I'll have to be on the road a lot and there will be a fair amount of late nights in New York entertaining clients," said Eddie. Taking clients out for lunches, dinners, evenings at the theater, spinning classes and even spa nights with wine and hors d'oeuvres was expected.

"I don't understand why *you* have to be out at every single event?" Clare had complained only a week before. "You're out every night. There's got to be other people who could attend some of these functions besides you?"

"I'm the associate publisher, the buck stops with me," said an exasperated Eddie. "The company expects me to be out with my salespeople and their clients. That's my job. We talked about this before I accepted. Since you're in a mood, now's probably not the time to mention this but I have several trips coming up. I'm doing a tour of the *Vacation* remote offices in California, Chicago and Florida over the next few weeks."

Clare let out a disgruntled sigh.

"I work at a travel magazine," Eddie said as he walked across the room and put his arms around her. "That means I've got to travel. Walk the walk. At some point, I'll have to go to Europe and Asia, too. It's my job but I promise, it won't be like this forever."

Clare sighed again as she lowered her very pregnant body onto a kitchen chair.

"I need to make my mark in the media business. After I do that, I'll be home every night. You'll be sick of looking at my face," he said with a laugh. Noticing how tired she looked he massaged her neck and she eventually relaxed. "Once I establish myself, someone else will do all the entertaining. Then, I'll be home by six while still collecting a big fat paycheck. That's what Julia Bowman's doing right now. She paid her dues and hired me to do the grunt work so she doesn't have to."

Clare knew Julia's whole backstory. Julia had hired Eddie to wine and dine clients so she could step back and take a more strategic role and get home at a decent hour. For years, Julia had been the one flying all over the world doing the meetings. Now, she had passed the baton to Eddie.

"You think I like taking clients out every night?" he said with a sardonic smile as he sat down next to her. "I'd much rather be home. I'm doing all this for you, for us, for our family. You and the kids will have everything you deserve."

"We don't need things," said Clare, quickly looking away because her eyes started to fill with tears, "we need you."

Eddie put his arms around his pregnant wife again and gave her a hug. "I think some of this weepiness are your hormones talking."

"No, it's not."

"This is a whole different ball game from my other jobs. Andover Media is the big time. Pretty soon, everyone in the business will know who I am and we'll have enough money to do whatever we want."

Much of what he said was true. The money he was making at *Vacation* was more than double what he had earned at *DDB,* not to mention the company car, the country club and the other perks. Soon, Eddie told her, they could afford a bigger house. They'd be able to pay for the kid's college educations and he could easily retire in his fifties. When that happened he figured he and Clare would take off and travel around the world in style. That was his dream.

"I don't care about a bigger house," said Clare, "I like this house. It's perfect for us."

"You say that now," said Eddie. "Wait until the baby's born. This house is going to feel pretty small with all the extra stuff."

"We'll be fine."

"You knew this job was going to be intense and you agreed to it," said Eddie getting a little annoyed.

"You announced you were taking the job. I wasn't consulted. There's a big difference."

"Babe, listen," said Eddie looking into her eyes, "trust me. Everything is going to be great. I'm going to be one of the youngest publishers in the business and in no time, we'll have it all. We'll get our lives back. I promise, everything will be fantastic."

She had seen her husband caught up like that before. He'd get himself worked up into a warp-speed mode and there was no stopping him. She knew that, so she didn't try. She liked nice things but she didn't need them to make her feel whole, not the way he did.

A low-maintenance girl born and raised in New Jersey, Clare was worried about the direction Eddie was going. "It's like I'm watching a car crash happen in slow motion," she had complained to her sister. "He lives only for the moment and never looks at what's coming tomorrow. Did I ever tell you he won't watch the end of movies or TV shows?"

"What are you talking about?" said her sister.

"He always makes up some excuse to walk out of the room before the end of a movie. I think he doesn't want to know how it ends. It drives me crazy."

"That's really weird," said her sister. "Who does that?"

Eddie was now driven, but he hadn't always been like that. When she met him in junior year of college, he was laid back, and she found his "live in the moment" mantra exhilarating and fun. He earned a degree in marketing; she was an English major with a minor in journalism. Right after their graduation, he approached her with a big idea.

"Come on, Clare, we can do this," he had said with an encouraging grin, "We'll get a couple of backpacks, jump in my car and go. We'll hike the Appalachian Trail, go white-water rafting and ski in Colorado. We'll spend the whole winter in Aspen. What do you say?"

"I can't do that. I've got student loans to pay off and besides, I don't have any money," said Clare, stunned that he would even suggest it. "What would we live on?"

"We'll get jobs as we go. It'll be great. Free spirits roaming the globe."

"I don't even have enough money to buy a backpack. I have responsibilities," said Clare softly. "I can't just bail."

Eddie didn't hear her because he launched into this long fantasy about traveling around the United States and then going off to Australia and Asia. Part of Claire would have loved to do what he suggested but the timing wasn't right. She had family and financial obligations. He didn't.

The week after graduation, Clare and Eddie went out for dinner at a Chinese restaurant near campus. They'd both be leaving to go home for good in another few days. He would go to Long Island and she to New Jersey. Then, they'd be an hour and a half apart.

"Can you believe it's all over," said Eddie reaching for an egg roll. "When we were freshmen, it felt like we had all the time in the world, like it was never going to end and here we are."

"I'm going to miss everyone," said Clare. "You think life is ever going to be as much fun as college?"

"You know what I'm going to miss the most?" said Eddie earnestly looking into her soft brown eyes. "You. Seeing your beautiful face every day and looking into your big eyes and finding the answers I'm looking for that only you seem to know."

"We can see each other on weekends," said Clare taking his hand. "We'll make it work."

"I love you, Clare. I've never met a better girl than you and I never will. You ground me."

"I hope that's a compliment," she said smiling.

"It's a very good thing," said Eddie squeezing her hand. "Don't say no to the traveling yet, think about it. It doesn't have to be tomorrow. We both could get some crappy job, save up a little money and then go."

"Maybe."

"I know one day we'll get married," said Eddie. "But for now, let's have fun. Let's be citizens of the world, push the limits, go for the gold."

Clare had smiled back at him that night as if she was considering the adventure. She loved him but it wasn't in her nature to "take off to parts unknown". She was a planner. Eddie was the dreamer who operated by the seat of his pants. Several months later after the dome of their college Camelot had been lifted, Eddie and Clare broke up.

Accepted into the NYU graduate journalism program, Clare wanted to work in publishing or pen the next great novel. Eddie wanted to see the world and ski down double black diamond slopes. They swore to each other that the break-up was only temporary and they'd pick up where they left off when he returned. On a warm day in early October, Eddie packed up his car to begin his solo drive cross country to the Rocky Mountains. Kissing each other goodbye, they both promised to call and write.

"You'll be back in six months, right?" said a teary Clare wondering if she had made a mistake by not going with him.

"Give or take. I don't want to be on a timeline," he said as he squeezed the last of his bags into the trunk, "the whole point of doing this is having total freedom." He checked the skis strapped to the roof of his nine-year-old Dodge Dart, a hand-me-down from an uncle. "Maybe six months, maybe nine. Remember this adventure is about not being bound by time parameters. I want to be a tumbleweed blowing in the wind."

"I understand," said Clare softly.

Holding her chin with his fingers, he looked deeply into her eyes. "Remember, I love you. That will never change," he said as he kissed her one final time and got into his car. Rolling down his window, he grinned, dimples deepening. "Here goes nothing. Take care of yourself, Clare Bear."

As his car pulled away from the curb, Clare waved as several tears rolled down her cheeks.

Six days later he arrived in Aspen and landed a job working in the ski lodge for the season. While filling out his employment papers, he met some other seasonal workers who needed a roommate. Within hours of arriving in Aspen, Eddie Gamble had a job, a place to live and a posse of new friends. Over the next few weeks, calls between Clare and Eddie diminished and by the middle of the ski season they had stopped.

Between the vacationing women in Aspen and all the women working on the mountain, Eddie had no shortage of female companionship. When the ski season ended in May, he opted out of returning to the east coast. Instead, he traveled down to Costa Rica to work at a surf school for the summer. Within a few weeks he moved in with a British girl who worked at the school. For the next three years, Eddie bounced from ski-lift operator to surfing instructor, moving from Colorado to Costa Rica and back again. In the meantime, Clare completed her graduate program, got her own apartment in Brooklyn and started dating a corporate attorney.

After three years of being a "citizen of the world", Eddie finally returned to New York. One of the first things he did was to call Clare. She hadn't heard from him in nearly two years and was surprised when she heard his voice. He said he was back in town and wanted to see her and she agreed—for old time's sake.

She took the subway into Manhattan and checked her makeup in a hand mirror before she got off at her stop. They had planned to meet at their favorite New York City burger place on the Upper Westside. Now twenty-six, Clare had recently landed a job as an editorial assistant at a well-known food magazine. Things were going well with her boyfriend, and she wondered why she had agreed to meet Eddie. *Curiosity, I guess,* she had told herself.

When she walked into the burger joint, a tanned and healthy-looking Eddie was waiting for her at a table. He stood, smiled and waved when he saw her. She smiled back and was surprised that her heart was pounding. When she got to the table he embraced her. His touch felt so familiar. He smelled just as she remembered. As she sat, he handed her a small bouquet of flowers he had hidden next to his chair.

"God, I've missed you so much," said Eddie, his twinkling blue eyes looking deeply into hers. "You're even more beautiful than I remembered." For three hours he regaled her with stories of his travels and all the crazy people he had met along the way —leaving out the women. Laughing until she cried, she took a seat on his rollercoaster, and loved every minute of it. It was like they had never been separated.

After their reunion, Clare ended it with the lawyer and from then on, she and Eddie were always together. Soon, their relationship was back to where they had left off. Neither asked questions about the years they were apart, only caring about where they were headed together.

Clare leaned over at her daughter still sitting at the kitchen table happily coloring outside the lines in her book. "Sarah, why don't you try and color inside the lines," said Clare picking up a green crayon and demonstrating the *proper* way to do it. "See how pretty it looks when you stay inside the lines." Clare filled in a green leaf on the page and stood back to admire her handiwork. "It's better, isn't it?"

"Why?" said Sarah.

"Because it looks nicer, don't you think?" said her mother moving to the counter to cut up an apple for her daughter.

"Why does it look nicer?"

"Cause it just does," said an exasperated Clare, her back to her daughter. "It's neater. Don't you like things to be nice and neat?"

"I like my colors to go all over," the little girl said emphatically, indicating her style of coloring was not up for discussion. Clare rolled her eyes and shrugged as she put some dirty dishes into the dishwasher. She had *always* colored inside the lines and did what she was supposed to do.

"If you color outside of the lines, you can't see the princess in the picture. She looks all mixed up and messy."

"She's not mixed up, Mommy. She's free."

Ugh. She's definitely Eddie's daughter, thought Clare as she let out a sigh and started to prepare dinner. Minutes later the phone rang. It was Eddie.

"Guess what? I'm making your favorite, lemon chicken," said Clare in a playful sing-song voice.

"Nothing in the world better than your lemon chicken," said Eddie.

"What time will you be home?"

There was a long pause. "Something's come up. Mr. Andover asked several of the APs to attend a corporate dinner with the Ralph Lauren people tonight. Julia was supposed to go but she had to fly to an emergency meeting in Detroit with GM. Thomas Andover called me personally and asked me to go in her place. Also, Jonathan Barker, the jerk I've been telling you about, is hosting the dinner and I need to get on his good side since he's probably a psychopath."

"We've hardly seen you in weeks," said Clare. "Sarah doesn't even know what you look like anymore."

"You're exaggerating but I don't really have a choice. Andover called me himself. You don't say no to Thomas Andover. You think I really *want* to go?"

"Truthfully? Yes."

"Let's not do this now," said Eddie, irritation creeping into his voice. "I promise when the baby comes, I'll be around a lot more. Okay? Love you."

Clare murmured a half-hearted, "I love you, too," as she hung up the phone. *Things are so different now,* she thought shaking her head. When they met in college he was handsome in a way only a twenty-one-year-old could be with sparkly blue eyes and a disorganized mop of beachy blond hair. Though his beard hadn't completely filled in yet, it didn't stop half the girls in the junior class from having a crush on him. He wasn't the biggest, smartest or handsomest guy on campus but he was probably the most charming.

She had seen him around campus, he always seemed to be everywhere. They officially met for the first time on the College Hill. "The Hill" was literally a giant grassy mound situated across from the main student center on campus. Between classes, when the weather was good, The Hill was the go-to place for the entire student body—a giant outdoor lounge. Students smoked, did homework, read books, played guitars, threw frisbees, made out. It was the place to meet people.

It was a Friday morning and Clare had been sitting on the grass with a few girlfriends from her American Lit class. Lying on the lawn looking up at the sky, smoking cigarettes and drinking coffee, they debated which were the best parties to go to that coming weekend. With her eyes closed, Clare felt a shadow across her face. When she opened her eyes Eddie stood over her blocking the sun.

"You got a match?" he said.

Clare nodded and handed him her lighter. He pulled out a joint, lit it, inhaled and asked Clare and her friends if they wanted some. The young women declined saying they had classes to attend and pointed out that it was only 9:30am.

Eddie smiled with his infectious grin. "It's only 9:30? What the hell am I doing here? I'm going back to bed. Catch you at a party this weekend," he had said winking directly at Clare. As he walked away, he was pretty sure she was still watching him. She was.

"Mommy, do you know how to get to Princess World?" said Sarah looking up from her coloring book.

"What's Princess World?"

"It's where all the princesses live," said the little girl with disbelief that her mother did not know that. "That's where all princesses come from. You need a special key to get in. I have one." She smiled and held up an imaginary key. "They wear pretty dresses and crowns and that's where they stay until their prince finds them."

"Where did you learn that?"

"Mommy, everyone knows that. A princess can't do anything until the prince comes and rescues her. That's how it works."

"Sometimes a princess has to save herself," said Clare.

"Why?"

"Because sometimes, the prince is too busy to save the princess. The prince has too many of his own things and doesn't see that the princess is in trouble," said Clare drifting off into her own thoughts. "Keep coloring, Sarah, and try and stay inside the lines."

4

Standing in front of his bathroom mirror, his face covered in shaving cream, Eddie stared into his own eyes. He examined the strange white-bearded man he met there every morning—a familiar stranger. Soon the all too frequent emptiness began to surround him. That was the feeling that made him chase the better job, house, girl, life. As he stared at himself, he wondered if everyone had the same feelings. Then, he shook it off, like he always did .and continued his shaving ritual while reminding himself of all the recent positive changes in his life.

He was doing well at *Vacation*. He had a new son they named Joseph, or Joey as he would be called, who was the spitting image of him. After the baby was born, Eddie's wings were no longer clipped and he was free to travel and put work on the front burner. Things were going well.

He guided his razor down his left jawline and then rinsed it off in the warm soapy water collected in the sink. He brought the razor to his face again and gently stroked the blade downward. Looking back at his reflection, he was keenly aware of his anxiety. Instead of joy about his new job and new son, he felt terrified and he didn't know why. The dark feelings happened often and without warning. He tried to make sense out of them but some days he felt like a fraud. He was certain one day everyone would figure out he didn't deserve any of it and realize he didn't know what the hell he was doing. When he felt like this he was convinced everything good would vanish if he didn't reach higher.

He took another pass with the razor and was suddenly filled with overwhelming regret but for what he didn't know. So, he did what he always did. He shrugged his feelings off and tried to distract himself. Sometimes it worked, sometimes it didn't.

While dressing, he contemplated everything on his plate. He was responsible for a global sales organization; eleven salespeople in New York, one in Chicago, Detroit, San Francisco, LA and two in Miami. Julia had just added rep firms in Hawaii, Canada, Mexico, Europe and Asia to his plate. The entire magazine and website's sales, marketing and promotion departments all fell on him. Every single day, more than sixty-seven people looked to Eddie for answers to solve their problems. Answers he didn't always have. Those same sixty-seven people generated over $50 million in advertising revenue. That was his nut to crack for the year. *Fifty million. Shit.*

"How the hell are you gonna bring in fifty million?" he said out loud to his newly shaved face as he straightened his tie. His main competitor, *American Traveler* had done nearly forty-eight million the previous year and Julia wanted to beat that. That was her personal goal and it was shared by Andover's chairman. *Vacation* had to surpass *American Traveler* in revenue —a tall order and it was all on Eddie.

"You're going to have to work your ass off, Gamble," he said to the stranger in the mirror.

Everyone in the media business aspired to work at Andover. Some people spent their whole lives trying to get in the door and here was Eddie, practically running one of their biggest books and only thirty-seven years old.

The perks for all Andover employees were plentiful and sometimes outrageous. A fleet of town cars was always at the ready in front of the building to take even the lowliest assistant to a meeting. Many employees were given clothing allowances and even got discounts at some of the high-end stores and salons in New York. Thomas Andover was all about image and he wanted his people to look the part. Their brands were luxurious, chic, affluent and aspirational and his employees had to reflect that lifestyle in everything they did or said. He expected his senior managers like Eddie to live, walk and talk the part.

Because of the cachet of the company, many of the senior players at Andover were themselves larger-than-life characters. Thomas Andover would often pit one publisher against another. He firmly believed friendly yet fierce competition between his senior people resulted in more revenue for him. He routinely rewarded flamboyance and moxie with money, power and a promotion.

The annual publisher meetings were notorious for being thick with intrigue as each publisher vied for the seats closest to their chairman. Seating arrangements for those events were prepared in advance and the plan kept top secret until the program started. Where one was seated made it evident to all who was favored and who was not. Those sitting furthest from the chairman pretty much knew they should be out looking for a new job as the axe would soon fall on the back of their necks. The lucky ones seated closest to Thomas Andover could count on a good bonus, a better title with more money, and maybe even a new Audi or BMW that year.

One publisher, a pugnacious Aussie named Jonathan Barker, who was unilaterally loathed by his peers and underlings, was usually smugly seated directly to the right of Mr. Andover on the first night of the publisher dinner. Barker had been at Andover for six years and like Eddie, started out as an associate publisher at *Vacation*. After showing Andover what he was made of—ruthless with unbridled ambition—he was moved to publisher at *House & Home* and later became group publisher for three fashion titles. Cocky and arrogant, even his bosses didn't like him but they put up with his overstated bravado because he always brought in the money.

No matter what awful thing he did or said, just when everyone had counted the Aussie out, he'd rise like a phoenix from the ashes. In Miami to go on sales calls with two of his Florida saleswomen, Barker took the two women out to dinner at one of the poshest restaurants in South Beach. After having quite a bit to drink, he suggested they go back to the hotel bar for a nightcap. Sitting at the bar, the three joked around when Barker blurted out that he would love to see the two women kiss. Simultaneously grimacing and nervously grinning, the women looked at each other, unsure of the politically appropriate way to respond to their boss.

"Come on ladies, you know you want to," said Barker in his thick Australian accent slurring his words and continuing to press them. The women held their ground, looked at their boss, politely declined and tried to change the subject.

"Just a little smooch. Come on, it would be so hot," said Barker again, leering.

Without any warning, he reached a hand behind each woman's head and slammed their faces together ostensibly hoping for a scene out of some softcore porn film. What he got instead was lots of blood, a concussion, a broken nose and a double lawsuit. When Jonathan Barker pushed the women together, one woman's forehead slammed into the other one's nose, breaking it and severely bruising her forehead and eye socket. Both ended up in the emergency room and the next day filed lawsuits seeking damages.

According to the media rumor mill, the woman with the broken nose left the company and settled out of court for an undisclosed large sum. The other woman also settled and was given a promotion, a large monetary bonus and a lifetime guarantee of employment with Andover Media. With that agreement in place, that woman could come to work, read a book or take a nap for the next fifty years and they'd still cut her a paycheck.

Nothing happened to Barker because he kept bringing in the money. Bad behavior at Andover was tolerated and even revered. Playing dirty was perfectly fine. If you delivered the goods, you could do whatever you wanted. At least that was Eddie's takeaway from all the antics he witnessed in the halls and conference rooms.

Jonathan Barker was rewarded over and over despite his outlandish and inappropriate behavior. Rumors about the married Barker included sex with female clients in his office and an affair with one of his own PR people (also married) which made it highly uncomfortable for the rest of the team. Despite his extra-curricular activities, he managed to bring in the money and at the end of that year, Andover gave Barker the "Chairman's Award" and promoted him to executive vice president.

From the sidelines, Eddie observed, cataloged and processed it all. He understood exactly what was expected of him. Like Barker, he was fully committed to doing whatever it took to hit his number. If he brought in the money and the balance sheets added up, the sky was the limit. If cutting corners or taking shortcuts were a means to his end, then that's what he'd do. This was his time and his turn and he had to take it. With a natural instinct for the art of the schmooze, he planned to blow the doors off Andover Media and leave Jonathan Barker spinning in his wake.

"Eddie, your car is waiting in the driveway," yelled Clare from downstairs in the kitchen.

He grabbed his bag, ran down the stairs, kissed his wife and kids goodbye and climbed into the town car idling in front of his house. Settling into the back seat he thought having a car and driver each day was probably his favorite Andover perk. Thomas Andover didn't want to see his management on public transportation like every other poor slob in New York. His associate publishers like Eddie, commuted in style. As the black sedan pulled out of the driveway, Sarah waved frantically to her father from the front window of the house. Eddie rolled down his window and waved back.

"Stop the car," said Eddie tapping his driver on the shoulder. Jumping out of the vehicle he ran back up the front steps and opened the door. "Sarah," he called out as she came running and catapulted herself into her father's arms. He wrapped them around his daughter. "I can't believe I forgot to give you our special Daddy-Sari hug before I left."

"You did forget, Daddy, and I was so sad," said Sarah making a forlorn face.

He squeezed her tight and gave three growls making her giggle. "Love you, Sari," he said, looking back at her as he walked out the front door.

"Love you too, Daddy," she replied, waving as her father climbed back into the black town car and headed towards the Lincoln Tunnel.

Vacation's sales team was comprised mainly of women and that suited Eddie just fine. "Women," he often said, "are inherently better salespeople than men. They are more credible and honest, sticklers for details and make the art of multitasking look easy." In general, he had inherited a solid sales team who performed well with two exceptions. From day one, Lucy James, who covered fashion clients in New York, was a thorn in Eddie's side. She was great at bringing in business but difficult to manage and questioned every order he gave. The other weak link was Audrey Fineo, his west coast rep who handled the entertainment and automotive accounts in LA. She was underperforming in a territory that should have been booming. He knew at some point, his issues with both women would have to be addressed.

From the very beginning, Eddie instructed the sales team to book him for breakfasts, lunches, dinners and evenings out with clients.

"I never want to see the inside of my own office, clear?" he said during one of his first weekly morning sales meetings. When Eddie was out in the field, he made magic happen and had also pledged to Julia that he'd spend one week every month traveling to one of the outside offices.

"I want to always be client-facing," he told the salespeople. "That's what Julia hired me to do. I expect you all to fill up my calendar."

For a long time, Julia Bowman had been the *Vacation* road warrior and she was more than ready to pass the reins to Eddie. Relieved to finally hand over daily client sales calls to her new eager associate publisher, she now devoted her time to big-picture branding, setting herself up for a move into corporate. She observed Eddie's style and saw the way he deftly handled each member of the sales team without breaking a sweat. He walked the halls bouncing from one salesperson to the next offering advice, guidance or telling a joke. The staff liked having him around and the clients had the same reaction. It came as no surprise to Julia when Eddie turned out to be very popular with their customers. People were drawn to him and he knew exactly what to say to make the sale happen. Eddie made it all look so easy.

Eddie's mother often told the story of an eight-year-old Eddie walking through the school with his third-grade class. When the children passed the school principal, Mrs. Grove, she smiled and waved at them. Eddie stepped out of the class line, walked directly over to Mrs. Grove and told her that she was doing a very good job as principal. Tickled, Mrs. Grove shared that story with Marian Gamble during a parent—teacher visit.

"Your son," said Mrs. Grove shaking her head while laughing, "could sell ice to Eskimos."

By the end of his third week at *Vacation*, Eddie and Julia had decided the LA market needed his immediate attention and he should travel out there every six weeks and personally work with their LA rep, Audrey. Eddie was totally on board. He loved LA and the whole Hollywood glamour vibe. He'd whip Audrey into shape and get her selling smarter.

Soon the new associate publisher's tenacity started to pay off and the sales team began breaking new business from accounts that had never run in *Vacation* before. Fashion and beauty accounts ran most of their advertising in places like in *Vogue* or *Cosmopolitan*. When Eddie lured some of those elusive advertisers right into the pages of *Vacation*, that enormous feat didn't go unnoticed. The chairman of Andover Media was well aware of Eddie's accomplishments and Eddie was all but guaranteed a great seat at the next executive luncheon.

Coming out of the Lincoln Tunnel, Eddie's town car pulled up in front of the Hyatt Hotel on 42nd Street for his breakfast meeting. He looked down at the Franck Muller watch he had bought for himself the day he got the offer from Andover Media. He scowled, remembering the conversation he had with his wife when he showed her his new treasure.

"You spent $11,000 on a freakin' watch?" Clare had said. "Are you kidding me?"

"You only live once. I landed my dream job. It's a little gift to myself to celebrate. It's a classic. I represent luxury brands now. I can't wear a goddamn Timex."

Clare shook her head wondering why her husband needed to spend so much money on superficial things. Annoyed that she didn't appreciate his amazing new watch or his newly purchased custom suits, he never mentioned those things again. *I'm the associate publisher of one of the biggest travel magazines in the world,* he thought. *Why shouldn't I have an expensive watch? I can afford it.* He looked down at his $11,000 timepiece. It was 8:15am. *Right on time,* he thought. *Worth every penny.*

"I'll be out in forty-five minutes," said Eddie as he got out of the town car. "Pick me up in the same spot."

While he waited for his breakfast appointment to arrive, Eddie thought back to his first *Vacation* business trip. He had gone to LA and met Audrey for the first time. Until then his only contact with her had been by phone. She had organized three full days of meetings to introduce Eddie to all the big shots in the entertainment ad community. They had appointments scheduled at Disney, Sony and Miramax and dinners and lunches with HBO and most of the networks. *Vacation* had only received a small share of the ad dollars in this market and Julia wanted Eddie to turn things around—fast.

"Either you get Audrey to work that territory for every penny or get rid of her," Julia had said the night before he left on his trip.

He didn't want to start firing people a month into his new job but he would if he had to. On that first trip, he wanted to learn what was holding Audrey back, find out what mattered to her and empower her. Once he knew what made her tick, he'd devise an incentive that went beyond her regular commission.

He had arrived in LA on a Tuesday morning. They had appointments scheduled that same afternoon and a dinner later with the Sony people. He had picked up a blue convertible rental car at the airport and drove directly from LAX to the Andover Media offices in Santa Monica.

Walking down the hall headed towards Audrey's office, Eddie noticed all the salespeople and their assistants were women—blonde, leggy, and extremely thin with big boobs. He approved. Passing several offices, he stopped when he saw a little plaque on the wall next to a doorway that said "Audrey Fineo". He heard a familiar female voice and peeked around the open door of her office. Inside on the phone with a client, her back to the door, Audrey, trying to make a sale was unaware of his presence. Not wanting to disturb her pitch, Eddie quietly stepped into the room. As she continued talking, he listened and evaluated. *She's good on the phone*, he thought, *charming yet persuasive and direct*. When the call concluded, Audrey spun around in her chair and was startled to see him standing there.

When he saw her, Eddie's eyes nearly popped out of his head. *No one told me Audrey was gorgeous.* Her beautiful girl-next-door looks blew him away. She was the kind of woman that appealed to almost every guy—beautiful but attainable. She had a head of thick cascading golden––red hair and like everyone else in the LA office, she was slim, sinewy and busty. Unlike the others, Audrey's breasts were real.

I won't mind spending a few days with her, he thought while reminding himself it would remain a totally professional relationship. He assessed Audrey's figure and well-toned arms visible in her sleeveless navy dress. Her athletic body only reminded him that his wife still hadn't taken off the baby weight from her first pregnancy.

After a brief meeting to discuss their upcoming presentations, Audrey drove them to their first appointment at

Toyota. During the trip, she chattered nervously about how much she loved representing *Vacation*, how great Julia was and how much the staff hated the previous associate publisher. "Everyone was so glad when we heard you were the new AP," said Audrey laying it on thick.

As they went from one meeting to the next, Audrey overshared details of her personal life. Eddie was drawn to and amused by her cheerful candor. *She's like a machine,* he thought. *Methodical and practical, devoid of inhibitions.* He appreciated her string of gentle self-deprecating statements, each one making him laugh. His assessment—Audrey Fineo was possibly the least needy person he had ever met and he liked her—a lot. Independent and fierce, he decided Audrey was spectacular.

Turning the wheel of their rented Toyota Camry into the entrance of the Toyota compound, she pulled into a spot near the front door. She had rented the car from Avis just for this visit. During one of her trip prep phone calls the week before, Eddie had asked if she rented a Toyota for their meeting.

"Duh," Audrey had groaned over the phone, admiring Eddie's attention to detail. "I should have thought of that. Of course, drive a Toyota to the Toyota meeting."

After several phone conversations with her new boss, Audrey figured she could learn a lot from him and maybe even win the Toyota business for the first time. If that happened, it would translate into a big fat commission check and that's all she cared about.

"I heard you're having a new baby," said Audrey making small talk as she turned off the ignition.

"Just found out it's a boy. Going to name him Joe after my wife's father."

"That's a salt of the earth name. I like it."

Walking through the glass doors, they checked in at the security desk and got on the elevator.

"You want to start the presentation, or should I?" asked Eddie as they rode up.

"I could do it, but I'd love to see the world-famous Eddie Gamble in action," said Audrey with a wink.

"World famous? said Eddie flashing the Gamble grin.

"Everyone in New York said you were awesome," she said as they got off the elevator. "The staff is *really* glad you're here."

"Thank you, that's nice to know," said Eddie puffing up on hearing the NY team thought he was "nothing short of awesome".

"The last AP, Richard, was a total disaster," said Audrey. "Nice guy, but kind of a milquetoast and completely clueless. He tried to flirt with every woman on the staff and I use the word "tried" because he sucked at it. Lucy told me he used to go into her office, and put one foot up on the empty chair next to her desk so his groin was at her eye level."

"No way," said Eddie laughing.

"He told all the women in the office that he and his wife had a weekend house in the woods where they played nude volleyball and lawn darts. If you met him, you'd understand why that was revolting imagery. After a while, every woman in the office complained to HR. That's why they got rid of him. Rumor was, they got him for sexual harassment. On top of all that, he was a terrible sales manager. Clients hated him. Everyone thought he was kind of a loser."

"I heard a little about him while I was interviewing," said Eddie as they settled into the Toyota waiting room and looked over their presentation. "All right, let's focus for a minute. You'll introduce me as the new AP and give them an overview of the growth in the travel market as it relates to automotive. Then I'll swoop in for the kill and the close, sound good?" he said with a confident smile that engaged his dimples.

"Sounds perfect," said Audrey smiling back and touching his

hand lightly. She liked that her new boss was dynamic and self-assured as opposed to the previous one who had no sales game whatsoever. When Richard was the AP, nobody made money. Working with Eddie would put some extra cash in her pocket and having a good-looking boss wasn't so terrible either.

5

E ddie's first year at *Vacation* had gone by fast and ended successfully. He and his team fought for every dollar and in the end, they had prevailed.

"I want you to wine, dine and mani/pedi the hell out of those ad agency vultures so we win the lion's share of the ad buys," Eddie had told his team early in his first year.

When he hit his annual goals, Andover senior management turned around and increased *Vacation*'s target revenue number by another thirty percent for the next year. "Be careful what you wish for," Eddie had said to Julia when he found out about the increased budget.

Sprawled out in the back seat of his town car one morning, Eddie checked the latest sports scores while on his way into the city for another breakfast meeting. He looked out his back seat window at all the other commuters in cars as his driver turned off onto an exit ramp. *I'm the only one on the road with a freaking chauffeur. Hey Frank and Marian, your baby boy is flying high.*

A little groggy that morning after another late night out with clients, Eddie sipped on his second coffee to wake himself up. He and his team had taken a large group of advertisers out to dinner and then to see a new Broadway musical. At the restaurant the night before, all the clients were having a good time and a lot of important business relationships had been started or cemented. Properly nurtured, those new connections would become real business and help him get to his new number.

He remembered the smile on Julia's face when she reviewed the client guest list for the outing. "Impressive," she had said. "Good job. You've pulled together a very high-profile group for the evening." She was especially excited to see that a very senior media person on the L'Beau cosmetics and skin care account was attending. "How did you ever get Trish Gordon to accept? She never goes to anything. I can't even get her on the phone."

Vacation hadn't been getting any L'Beau business and breaking that account had become an obsession with Julia. Their competitor, *American Traveler,* on the other hand, had been carrying L'Beau for years. Thomas Andover had been very clear, he wanted Julia to break L'Beau that year. Bringing in the cosmetics and skincare company soon became Eddie's problem. "Looks like your 2004 is off to a great start getting Trish Gordon to attend our event," Julia had said.

As his driver maneuvered the town car through the dense Lower Manhattan traffic, Eddie assessed his job performance thus far. He'd been at *Vacation* for thirteen months. Weeks after he joined, he had cleaned house and rid the department of any deadwood. Some of the existing salespeople weren't performing to the level needed. He had felt bad about cutting them loose, but business was business. He couldn't afford to keep anyone on his team who didn't give one hundred and fifty percent. After a few fires and hires he had finally assembled a crackerjack team and over time developed a personal relationship with each salesperson. He didn't subscribe to the leadership by intimidation philosophy that Jonathan Barker employed. Eddie wanted his people to be happy and he wanted them to like him.

One thing he was sure of, no two salespeople had the same motivation. Once he figured out what was important to someone and what made them tick, he would play them like a fine violin. Eddie's instincts were usually spot on, and when the big deals started coming in, every member of the team thanked him for his masterclass in sales.

"You make it look so easy," said Pamela, one of the travel category salespeople.

"It's because I love what I do and I want to put more money in your pocket," said Eddie. "If you make money, I make money. It's that simple."

Each salesperson had different strengths. Colleen covered the beauty accounts and was very well connected to her clients. She had the Chanel, Neutrogena and Estée Lauder people wrapped around her well-manicured finger. As Eddie got to know Colleen, a petite blonde, he learned she was all business and strictly motivated by money. Knowing that, he created a special incentive plan for her above and beyond her regular compensation. It was to be a private agreement between him, Julia and Colleen. If Colleen broke L'Beau in 2004, in addition to her standard commission, Eddie would give her a one-time payment of $10,000. Julia had some discretionary money in a slush fund and approved it. Almost immediately he could see a change in Colleen: she could taste that $10,000 and she wanted it.

Kristen, a tall, attractive platinum blonde with sparkling white teeth that spread from ear to ear handled direct response. Her clients weren't glamorous, mostly back of the book players who sold music CDs or collectibles, but they provided a steady stream of reliable income for *Vacation* and were important to Eddie's bottom line. Kristen did a reasonably thorough job, was cheerful and easy on the eyes. Eddie had often wondered what it would be like to be in bed with her. *You don't crap where you eat, Gamble* he had told himself repeatedly. There was no chance that would happen anyway. The most important thing to Kristen was planning her upcoming wedding.

Needing the bride-to-be to grow her revenue by twenty percent in order to hit his overall number, Eddie got an idea. With Julia's approval, he offered Kristen something special. If she exceeded her monthly number for the six months leading up to her wedding, in addition to her regular commission, Eddie would grant Kristen three additional weeks of paid vacation. If she did what Eddie needed her to do, Kristen would be able to take five weeks off with pay before and after her wedding. His secret deal hit exactly the right chord and Kristen worked harder than ever before.

Eddie created a special deal for everyone. Cara, who had a two-year-old son, was allowed to work from home on Mondays and Fridays. Jennifer's husband was being transferred to Atlanta and Eddie agreed to let Jennifer work remotely from her new home in Georgia.

Veronica and Pamela, who both covered the travel category, had the biggest load to carry. They were already getting a huge percentage of the business but Eddie wanted an even bigger piece of the pie. The key to doing that was to chip away at *American Traveler's* business by persuading their clients to spend more of their dollars with *Vacation*. Since Veronica loved to travel whenever she could, Eddie offered her an all-expense paid luxury cruise for two if she hit her number. Pamela, who happened to be pregnant, would likely want more time with her new baby. He offered to give her an extra fully paid six weeks of maternity time to tack onto her regular maternity leave *and* to outfit her entire nursery.

"I'll pick out the crib myself," Eddie said with a wink.

"That's really kind of you," said Pamela as she rubbed her belly. "I'm all in."

Dan and Lucy, the sales fashionistas, would each receive a one-time $7,000 clothing allowance. Nothing mattered more to those two than having the latest Birkin bag or Gucci suit and they were pumped.

Then there was Audrey. With Eddie's regular coaching his west coast rep soon made serious inroads and broke several previously unattainable entertainment accounts.

With all the time he spent on the west coast, Eddie had gotten to know Audrey very well. They both loved to ski but neither ever got to go, because their spouses didn't ski. Clare used to, when Eddie first met her and they had even gone on a couple of ski trips in the early days. After she got pregnant with Sarah, she never wanted to go anymore. Audrey's husband had never learned to ski and had no interest. That's how Eddie came up with Audrey's motivator. He told her he'd personally take her skiing for a four-day weekend in Aspen, all expenses paid, if she broke five of her target accounts.

"Better wax your skis," said Audrey with a sly smile.

He had figured out how to bring out the best in each salesperson, except for Lucy. An inherent contrarian, she argued against his strategy and direction both privately and publicly. He tried to give her room to vent when she needed it but he couldn't charm her and that drove him crazy.

"You'd better be careful. You're driving Eddie nuts," said Pamela to Lucy one day over lunch. "He's a good guy. My business is up. Give him a break. You're always busting his balls."

"You're all so enamored with him. I don't trust him," said Lucy. "Not a single bit. Eddie is looking out for Eddie."

6

With the exception of the week her husband took off from work when Joey was born, Eddie was rarely home. His busy travel and entertaining schedule kept him from spending any meaningful time with his wife or kids. Out most weeknights, he often traveled on the weekends attending trade shows or conferences. When he did get home, it was usually late at night when the kids were asleep and Clare was already in bed. He hadn't been home for a family dinner in weeks and often stayed overnight in the city when he had a late client night and an early breakfast meeting in the morning. He started keeping a couple of extra suits, shirts, underwear and socks in the closet in his office for those nights.

If Clare complained, he reminded her that the first eighteen months in a new job were critical. "I have to make it happen now or it never will," he had said.

"Not everyone building their career abandons their family," said Clare.

"We discussed this before I accepted the job. You can't have buyer's remorse now."

She gave up telling him he was spewing revisionist history,

that she had never agreed to any of it. She remembered their conversation about his job offer quite clearly. He had been in one of his "I'm about to conquer the world" modes and had already accepted the job and informed her afterwards.

To keep herself from losing it completely, Clare kept busy with her kids, her house and the freelance work she did for her old company writing food articles for *Sugar & Spice Magazine*, a baking publication and website. She didn't make a ton of money with the writing but she could do the work at night when the kids were asleep. It kept her fresh, made her feel relevant and still kept her foot in the professional game.

After Eddie's first year at *Vacation* where he surpassed expectations, Julia gave herself a pat on the back for making such a good hire. He had done exactly what she had hoped he would. Out in the field every day, an energized sales department and the most important thing—he brought in the money. While running *Vacation*, Julia had engendered loyalty with the staff and there had been almost no turnover. She managed with empathy, believing that was important when creating and sustaining a successful team. Eddie understood that ethos but in addition, he brought a sense of play and fun, traits that were not in Julia's toolbox. She was an expert administrator, not a hand-holder or a jokester. She knew that about herself and that's why she hired Eddie—the yin to her yang.

"We're the perfect team, you and I," Julia had said to him after he brought in another big sale. "I run a very tight ship. I'm the captain but you're the cruise director keeping all the crew and customers happy. Together we get everyone safely to their destination."

And he was like a cruise director. If someone had a death in the family, Eddie told them to take as much time as they needed. When a woman in marketing was going through a nasty divorce, Eddie covered some of her accounts and told her to take time off. Whatever it was, he wanted his team to know that he was there for them, he had their backs. The *Vacation* team never worked harder or smarter than that first year when Eddie Gamble came on board.

Then something tragic happened. Pamela's baby died during delivery. The entire staff had been looking forward to the birth and when the baby died, the staff felt a deep sense of loss, too. The day Pamela came back to the office after taking a few weeks off, no one knew what to say. That first day, she stayed in her office, kept her head down and tried unsuccessfully to reacquaint herself with all her business. No matter how hard she tried, every few minutes tears welled up in her eyes and she had to fight hard to keep the rainstorm from starting.

Just before noon, Eddie's assistant had called her and asked her to come down to meet with him for a few minutes. Pamela walked down the long hall to her boss's office. It was the first time she had seen him since she had been back. When Eddie looked up and saw Pamela standing in his doorway, he gave her a warm smile, stood up and gestured for her to take a seat. Then, he closed his office door. No one ever closed a door at *Vacation* unless something bad was happening. Confused, Pamela looked at him.

"How are you doing?" he said softly. Pamela's eyes filled with tears again. "I can't possibly know how you feel, but I wanted you to know everyone's heart was broken when they heard what happened. We're a family here and we all felt this very deeply and personally." Tears ran down Pamela's cheeks. Eddie handed her a box of tissues.

"Thank you," she said sniffling, looking down at her lap so he wouldn't see her cry.

"I just wanted you to know that you should do whatever you need to do to feel better. If you want to leave early or come in late or take more time off, do it. Whatever it is, anything," said Eddie gently.

Pamela nodded and forced a half-smile. "Right now, I'm better off here at work. If I'm sitting at home, I'll only dwell on what happened. At least here I'm busy and can distract myself." Eddie nodded. "He was a boy. They let me hold him in the hospital but he wasn't breathing." Tears ran down her cheeks again. "The thing I keep thinking is, it's February and they buried him outside and I know it's stupid but I keep thinking he must be so cold."

Tears welled up in Eddie's eyes and he flicked his fingers into the corners of both to prevent his own onslaught. Getting up from his desk, he walked around to the other side and put his arms around her and let her cry while he patted her gently on the back.

"Pamela, would you let me do something for you?" he said softly. "My favorite French restaurant in New York is La Côte Basque. It's my happy place. The food is amazing, the room is beautiful and the service is incredible. To me, it's one of the most special places in New York City. Sadly, they're closing their doors soon, forever. Would you let me take you there for lunch tomorrow? It won't change what happened, but maybe for an hour or two you can be in the happy place too."

Eddie's kind and thoughtful gesture made Pamela cry harder. She didn't know him that well but she knew he was trying, in his own way, to help. She nodded and smiled. Everyone else had been treating her like glass, afraid she would break if they said the wrong thing. Eddie treated her like a flesh-and-blood person and it felt good to feel normal for a few minutes.

At 12:15pm the following day, Eddie stopped by Pamela's office and they headed off to La Côte Basque. She had never been to the famous eatery before and her face lit up when she entered the restaurant. It was beautiful inside, just as he had described: painted murals covered the walls. Everyone from the hostess to the waiters knew Eddie and all came over to greet him. He proudly introduced Pamela to everyone telling them she was one of his "top salespeople". She knew she wasn't, but it made her feel good hearing him say it.

The lunch was amazing and Eddie pulled out all the stops. He told her funny stories and turned the Gamble charm meter on high. He talked about his childhood and his family. "My parents, Frank and Marian, they're nice people, but they take everything way too seriously. I've always been more about laughter and adventure. Live for today, for tomorrow you could get hit by a bus," he said with a chuckle.

Entertaining Pamela throughout their lunch, his plan of distraction had worked. For two solid hours, she had not thought about her dead child. It was the first time she had gone for more than a few minutes without getting teary and she was grateful to laugh again after so many weeks of crying. After that lunch, Pamela remained one of Eddie's most loyal supporters. He had touched her in a deep way at a critical moment. She never forgot his kindness.

Not all of the salespeople were Eddie's cheerleaders. Lucy James, who had a knack for getting under his skin, was older than Pamela, far less pliable and always poised for an argument. Over time, the barrage of complaints from Lucy grated on her boss. He worried that her constant interrogation undermined his authority and he didn't like it. The worst part was that sometimes, Lucy was right.

If Eddie announced they were taking clients to see a Broadway show, Lucy would blurt out that taking clients to Cirque du Soleil would be a better idea. If Eddie said they were going to do a client dinner at a certain restaurant, Lucy would say the food there wasn't very good and would suggest a different one. When Eddie asked for certain reports to be done, Lucy wanted to know what they were for and why he needed them. She was a massive pain in the ass and he wished more than anything that she would resign.

He couldn't fire her because she brought in boatloads of revenue. Lucy was smart, relentless, tenacious and detail oriented. A feral dog with a bone, Lucy wouldn't let go until she got the signed order. But if her numbers started to slip, even a little, Eddie promised himself he'd seize the moment and get rid of her.

7

On another flight to LA, Eddie fantasized about spending the next few days alone with Audrey. They were going on a two-day business trip to San Diego to meet with clients and then do a big dinner with a bunch of agency folks. After spending time with her on the west coast month after month he was aware that his feelings for the beautiful woman had grown. So far, he had never crossed the line with her but he felt his resolve weakening.

The client dinner that first night was a success. Eddie had told jokes and flattered each person at the table. Audrey watched him, awed by his intuitive social skills. It was obvious every woman at the table wanted to sleep with him and every man wanted to be his best friend. That was Eddie's inherent talent. After dinner and many bottles of wine, the party dispersed, and Eddie and Audrey grabbed a cab back to their hotel.

On some level, they both knew it was going to happen and didn't try to stop it—their affair began that night. Eddie suggested they go to the hotel bar for one more drink. That nightcap became two and then three. By the third drink, the sexual tension between them was obvious.

Eddie took Audrey's hand. "You have the most beautiful eyes," he said softly.

"Where are we going with this?" Audrey said, slightly slurring her words. "I've got a husband. You've got a wife and two kids."

"There's an incredible connection between us. I know you feel it too."

"That doesn't mean we have to act on it," she said, praying he'd disagree.

"You're right, it doesn't. If you don't want to act on it, we don't have to. We'll never bring this up again."

"I didn't say that."

"That's good because in three seconds, I'm going to lean over and kiss you," whispered Eddie. A moment later he made good on that promise. Five minutes after that, they were in her hotel room.

From that night on, Audrey always scheduled overnight trips when Eddie was in LA. They always reserved two rooms but only used one.

From Eddie's perspective, having Audrey in LA was the perfect relationship. He only got out to the west coast about six times a year for three or four days at a time. She was beautiful and attentive and never whined or wanted anything from him. The fact that their rendezvous were so intermittent kept everything fresh and titillating. He'd spend a few fun-filled days with her in California, and then leave and not be bothered with the typical mundane aspects of a relationship. *It's like dating someone in prison,* he thought on one of his flights back home to New York. *I only see them when I want to.*

His long-distance set-up with Audrey also gave him some

wiggle room on the east coast with people like senior ad exec Trish Gordon. Audrey was his west coast side-chick; Trish had become his New York City hook-up and his beautiful Clare held down the family fort in New Jersey. *A perfect mix,* he thought with satisfaction.

Life was good for Eddie then. He gave his all to his job and it was paying off. Each morning when he was in town, he'd drop off a bagel and coffee with three sugars to the homeless man who now waited for him in front of the building. Then, he'd greet each lobby security guard by name and flirt with Hedwig, the old German woman who ran the building's newsstand concession. When he got off the elevator on his floor, he'd greet the elderly female receptionist and ask her how she was doing.

"How's your husband, Jane? Over that cold yet?" he'd say. "That scarf looks nice on you. The blue brings out your eyes." He made that receptionist feel special and as far as she was concerned, Eddie Gamble was aces and she told that to anyone who would listen.

As he walked through the office halls in the morning he'd make mental notes of who the early birds were. The best performers were always the first ones in. He'd stop to chat and make a few supportive inquiries about a particular piece of business or a presentation they were working on. He concluded each interaction with some positive reinforcement so that person felt validated. He didn't even know he did it, it came naturally.

After many months of hard work, things at *Vacation* gelled. Julia had complete confidence in Eddie's sales instincts and had willingly let him run the show, giving him more responsibility each month. The support people loved him because he paid attention to them instead of only focusing on the salespeople like the previous associate publisher had. Everyone really liked Eddie. Mostly everyone.

One morning walking through the Andover lobby, Eddie

bumped into Jonathan Barker as they both headed towards the front doors of the building. They exchanged greetings and discovered they were both going to meetings on the west side and decided to walk together as far as they could.

"I've been hearing good things about you, Gamble," hissed Barker with his thick Queensland accent. "Maybe too good. You get any better and I'm going to have to start watching my back."

"You don't have to worry about me, Jonathan," said Eddie grinning. "You're already five levels above my pay grade. But, nice to hear there's a good buzz circulating about me in the building. I'm trying my best but I'm still light years behind you."

"That's where you're going wrong, mate," said Barker. "Trying your best doesn't always translate into success. In this business you need to be ruthless, don't give anyone a break. I do whatever it takes to make the deal happen. I bend the rules and if need be, I break them. Sometimes I blow the fuckers up. Always remember, there's someone right behind you wanting to take your place."

"Thanks for the advice. I do bend the rules a little and I am willing to do whatever it takes, as long as it's ethical," said Eddie as they turned a corner.

"Ethics are highly overrated," snapped Barker, "Scruples are for suckers. If you think I got to the top of this organization by always doing the right thing, guess again. I got there by climbing on the shoulders of people who I eventually stabbed in the back while they let me walk all over them."

With his mouth half open, Eddie stared at Jonathan Barker. *Did he just admit that he stabs his colleagues in the back?* thought Eddie. *Jonathan Barker is a psychopath.*

"Like I said, you've got to do whatever it takes to win, Gamble," said Barker. "Take this big Andover event I'm running. We're launching it over at Madison Square Garden. I've got twenty-three A-list celebrities signed on to perform in that fucking thing. Twenty-three. A-list."

"That's impressive."

"You bet it's fucking impressive," said Barker. "You know how I did it? I lied my fucking ass off. I told Bono that Mick Jagger was in and I told Jagger that Beyoncé was in and so on and so forth. Eventually, it all comes together and who wins? I do. When in doubt, Gamble, make it up but make it good. People pick apart little lies. But, if you tell a fucking whopper, like 'I got Madonna to agree to do a special advertising section and perform at the Garden,' people just think you're awesome."

"You got Madonna to do an ad?"

"No, you fucking wanker, by the time the top brass finds out I didn't get Madonna, I've already been promoted and I'm on to another project or a new company," said Barker as he turned and abruptly walked away, leaving Eddie in a doorway of a small brick building.

As Eddie walked inside for his meeting, Barker's words echoed in his head. *"Ethics are highly overrated." Barker is one of the most successful people in the media business. Maybe I need to break a few rules when the stakes are high.* From that day forward, Eddie thought about his business from a whole new perspective, one where rules were meant to be broken if they got in the way of his endgame.

Year two at *Vacation* was as successful as his year one. Eddie and his team closed tons of new business and Andover management couldn't have been happier. Eddie Gamble was their secret weapon, a regular revenue machine.

Morning—pitch for the Absolut account, give dynamic presentation, pass out gift bags, serve up cream cheese and bagels for the greedy media planners, close the deal.

Lunch—out with the media team from Visa. They like sushi, so they get sushi. Order sake, charm the hell out of the all-female team. Flash the Gamble grin. Give them some leather luggage tags imprinted with the *Vacation* logo. Pay the bill, making sure to use a Visa card and then, close the deal.

Afternoon—meeting with executive team on L'Beau, which included the fabulous Trish Gordon, aka Eddie's New York sidechick. Pitch special section using young celebrities to showcase L'Beau skincare line. Hand out *Vacation* T-shirts. Close the deal. Give all the women a kiss goodbye and tell his salesperson he'll see them back at the office because he wants to pitch something privately to Trish Gordon.

Night—take Trish to dinner, and then back to her place. Have sex and then home to New Jersey by midnight. Kiss the kids and the next day do it over again.

As frenetic as his life was, from a business perspective, it was working. He closed the deals and his department was on target to once again exceed their revenue number. Word came down that Thomas Andover was extremely pleased.

Eddie was everywhere. He met with the marketing department on how to spin the data in the automotive and pharmaceutical categories. He stopped by the events group to discuss an idea he had about an experiential client event.

"We're a travel magazine, right?" said Eddie to the merchandising and events group. "Let's take a select group of high-level clients on a thoroughly edited and handpicked, once in a lifetime, escorted tour to Europe. I'm talking about only the most senior people, the ones who hold all the purse strings. Maybe we fly the group to Italy and we all go on a luxury trip on the Venice Simplon-Orient-Express. We could have an Agatha Christie's *Murder on the Orient Express* theme. We could take the train from Venice to London and then spend a few days touring pubs."

"That's going to cost a fortune," said the director in charge of all client events looking at her budget numbers.

"Use our barter dollars," said Eddie. "A couple of free pages of advertising in the magazine for the Venice Simplon company and our luxury trip is paid for. Make it happen."

Whatever he touched that first year and a half turned to gold. Almost nothing went wrong and the money came rolling in. Julia also couldn't believe how much better her life had become since Eddie joined the team. *This year, I'll be getting the Most Innovative Publisher Award,* she thought, *and it'll be me seated next to Thomas Andover, not the arrogant asshole from Down Under.*

Everything was going smoothly for Eddie at work, but it wasn't so great at home. Clare's feelings of isolation and neglect grew. The way she saw it, her husband dropped by for a peck on the cheek, grabbed some clean clothes and spent a few minutes with his kids before he was out the door again. She couldn't remember the last time all four of them had dinner together. *It isn't fair to the kids,* she thought on more than one occasion, *and it isn't fair to me.*

8

Walking up Fifth Avenue towards the Andover offices with Pamela and Veronica after a successful pitch to a major car rental company, Eddie praised both women. He had done the presentation but the two women had put a lot of work into the prep and that contributed to everything going smoothly.

"All your preparation paid off," he said to the two of them with a proud smile. "That meeting went as well as it could have. Trust me, we're going to get that business and you're both going to make a nice commission."

The women accepted his praise knowing full well that he was their secret weapon; their very own velvet hammer to bring in for the final kill.

"You did the whole presentation," said Pamela. "You're the one who closed the deal."

"How do you always know the answers to all their questions?" said Veronica.

Eddie stopped walking and faced them. "I do my homework and then I listen. That's the key to the kingdom, ladies. You've got to really listen."

Sitting at his desk later that day, Eddie glanced down at his prized Franck Muller watch. It had become a symbol of his own success and made him smile whenever he checked the time. In five minutes he had to leave to meet the Chandler Hotels' clients for lunch. The previous month he had convinced them to dramatically increase their ad spending with *Vacation*, a huge win for Eddie and his team. That's why he bristled when Julia announced she would be joining him that day and that she would officially host the luncheon.

"Hate to pull rank, Eddie," said Julia, "but the Chandler Hotels people expect the publisher to be there. I'm going."

He nodded but fumed inside. *You think I can't handle lunch with Chandler? I broke the goddamn business, not you. I'll be a publisher soon enough. I can wait.*

Looking out of his office window across the Manhattan skyline, he let out a satisfied sigh. While the demands of his career had forced him to back-burner most of his friendships and being on the road so much cut into time with his family, it would all be worth it. Clare had been giving him a hard time about being gone so much, complaining the kids never saw him. Those conversations often ended with raised voices as Eddie left for the office, a dinner or the airport. *She agreed to this when I took the damn job,* Eddie thought, *and it's starting to pay off. She doesn't get it, I'm the new golden boy of New York media.*

With just enough time to check his voicemail before leaving for the Chandler Hotels lunch, Eddie punched in his code. There were five messages. He listened to the beginning of each one, deleting them in rapid succession before they finished. He blew through the first four and then played the last.

"Hi Eddie. This is Andrea Marchetti, I'm in HR over at FGM, Fleming Global Media. I wondered if you might have some time today or tomorrow to give me a call back. There's something I wanted to discuss with you that could be mutually beneficial."

That's strange, he thought, *Fleming Global calling me?* FGM was his main competitor and he spent most of his waking hours pitching business *against* one of their top brands, *American Traveler*. Not a day went by when Eddie and his team didn't trash and bash *American Traveler's* editorial, advertising health and circulation methods and his tactics had been working. He had moved the needle. *Vacation* had always been the number two travel book and *American Traveler* number one. Since Eddie joined *Vacation,* things changed and now the two battling brands were neck and neck. When that shift had happened, Julia sent new numbers to corporate, projecting that they would surpass *AT* by the end of the year. Soon the new numbers would go public in the trades and everyone in the business would know what Eddie had accomplished.

He listened to Andrea Marchetti's message a second time. *Did one of our mutual clients tell FGM about all the smack talk we've been using against AT?* he wondered. *Well, too bad, that's my job.*

He jotted down Andrea's phone number on a piece of paper and slipped it into his wallet just as Julia appeared in his doorway in fresh lipstick and waved. "Time for our lunch with Chandler," she said with a smile, "let's reel them in, partner."

Lunch was at Felidia, one of Eddie's favorite Italian restaurants. Created with love by famous author and chef, Lidia Bastianich, the charming Italian bistro was situated in a townhouse on East 58th Street and served up some of the most delicious northern Italian cuisine in Manhattan. Reservations were hard to come by and Eddie took only his most important clients there. Felidia was the perfect setting for a big yet intimate schmooze. Aware that his career depended on him landing key accounts like Chandler Hotels, Eddie gave a spectacular performance at lunch and had the Chandler folks eating out of his hand.

Until this year, *American Traveler* had always gotten the lion's share of the hotel chain's ad budget. Since Eddie had taken over

Vacation's sales team, they had slowly eaten away at their competitor's lead by developing custom advertising sections, and global travel events that wowed Chandler's marketing team. Thanks to Eddie, the tables had completely turned. In the coming year, Chandler Hotels had promised *Vacation* would get the larger part of their budget.

I'll bet that's why Fleming Global called me, Eddie thought. *They're probably pissed off I'm eating their lunch and why shouldn't they be? Next year, I'll chip away another ten percent from them.*

Looking over the Felidia wine list while the waiter handed out menus, Eddie hunted for the perfect bottle to mark the important occasion. He wanted to impress. Andover's client entertaining policy and expense budget was practically unlimited. The price of the wine was irrelevant so he ordered several of their most expensive bottles. He liked buying $200 bottles of wine and not thinking twice about it. What no one else at the table knew was that the Chandler deal only happened because of Eddie's extremely close relationship with their agency's head of media, Trish Gordon. In addition to Chandler Hotels, Trish also conveniently oversaw the L'Beau beauty account. When Eddie and Trish's relationship became intimate, the advertising revenue going into *Vacation's* coffers grew substantially.

Eddie had been given five key accounts by Julia. Those were his targets and his bonuses were tied to breaking them. They were all accounts Julia had previously been unable to crack. In less than two years, Eddie had broken and then increased business with four of the five including Chandler Hotels—with a little help from Trish Gordon.

Securing the Chandler business had required extra private time with Trish but it had all been fun and worth it from Eddie's perspective. Trish was thirty-four and divorced with a well-toned body. His interactions with her were never a chore. Their "sleepover parties" hadn't felt like work at all. Trish was easy and didn't want anything from him other than a good time. She never complained or had that look of disappointment on her face like his wife. He had made sure he was seated next to Trish at the Felidia lunch and rubbed her knee with his hand underneath the table while he watched her blush and smile.

The five-course meal was superb. The expensive bottles of wine did what they were supposed to do as Julia discussed the initiatives *Vacation* had designed for the hotel chain. Promises were made and Chandler Hotels officially agreed to increase their advertising spend over the coming year. This one deal would make *Vacation* the number-one travel brand.

When they emerged from the restaurant, black town cars waited to take each person back to their respective offices. They all shook hands and hugged talking about the exciting partnership ahead. Julia had a meeting downtown and jumped in a car giving Eddie a thumbs up as her limo pulled away from the curb. Eddie saluted to her and smiled as he watched her car turn the corner at the end of 58th Street.

It was a sunny day and Eddie elected to walk back to his office. Birds chirped from the city's trees and the sun streamed down from a cloudless blue sky. It was the kind of day that made even people who loathed New York City reconsider their opinion. As he walked, he replayed moments from the lunch and Julia winking at him when the Chandler EVP finally gave the green light on their commitment to *Vacation*. It was an incredible sale. He had pulled it off—again.

Stopping to lean against a brick wall to check his messages, he let out a satisfied sigh. Buzzing through his email on his phone, he was about to continue on to his office when he remembered the message earlier from the woman at Fleming Global Media. He pulled the piece of paper out of his wallet and punched her number into his phone. It rang twice.

"Andrea Marchetti," answered a female voice.

"It's Eddie Gamble from Andover returning your call."

"Thank you so much for calling me back," the woman replied, her voice turning syrupy. He could hear her smile over the phone and was intrigued. *Guess I'm not going to get yelled at for stealing their business.*

"You're probably wondering why in the world I'd be calling given the competition between our two companies," said Andrea. "I'll get right to the point. We've heard good things about you. Very soon, we'll have an open position here at FGM and we'd like to talk to you about that role."

"Which title?" said a surprised Eddie.

"We're looking for a new publisher for *American Traveler*. The senior executives in my company have been following the outstanding job you've been doing at *Vacation*. We know Julia Bowman isn't going anywhere which means you'll be second fiddle for the foreseeable future. The open publisher role at *American Traveler* is a natural and obvious next step for your career. We think you're ready to be a publisher and were hoping you'll come in and talk to us."

"I'm flattered," said Eddie, "but I've still got a lot left to do where I am. The fact is, I'm just getting started. Also, it would be awkward and maybe even professional suicide for me to go to my direct competitor."

"It's just a conversation, thirty minutes. Don't you owe it to yourself to hear us out? If we don't say anything that interests you, you walk away."

Eddie thought for a long moment as Andrea waited patiently not saying another word. She knew the game. He who speaks first loses.

The next morning Eddie told his assistant he had a dentist appointment. He walked out the front doors of Andover Media and moved briskly downtown towards the Union League Club. *I shouldn't be doing this,* he thought nervously. *It's a total backstab thing to do. I like my job at Andover. Julia loves me and I have an amazing sales team. At the last AP lunch, Thomas Andover told me I had a bright future with the company. Why am I going to this meeting?* Pushing the negative thoughts out of his mind, he took a deep breath and continued to walk downtown. *It's only a conversation.*

The interview with FGM was being held at the Union League Club to avoid anyone seeing Eddie in the FGM building. Arriving in front of the club, he looked up and down the street to make sure he didn't see anyone he knew. Fraternizing with FGM would be extremely hard to explain to his boss. The media business in New York was small and it would only be a matter of minutes before news got back to his senior management.

He braced himself and walked through the door of the club. Two minutes later, he was escorted through the lounge and introduced to Andrea Marchetti, executive director of FGM Human Resources. Two other female HR managers were seated with her.

Flashing the Gamble grin at the diminutive brunette, the three women stood to shake his hand. For the next hour, Eddie had all three smiling, laughing and nodding. Charmed, Andrea was convinced before the meeting was over that FGM needed Eddie Gamble on their team. If the other hiring managers felt the same way, she would make him an offer he couldn't refuse.

9

Sitting in her office on the phone, Pamela rolled her eyes. Another complaining media planner from a large ad agency was unhappy with his client's ad position in the current issue of *Vacation*.

"We thought the ad was going to be closer to the front of the magazine in a more premium spot. My client is furious," said the pissed-off planner, "what are you going to do about it?"

As Pamela tried to calm the overly outraged man, her assistant poked her head in and mouthed, "Eddie wants to see you, ASAP." Pamela nodded and raised her open hand, five fingers stretched out.

After wrapping up her unpleasant call, she grabbed a notebook and pen and walked quickly down the hall to Eddie's office wondering why he wanted to see her. Pamela's year had been rough and a lot of her business had fallen through. She hadn't been hitting her monthly nut and was struggling to bring in new business and save the old. No matter how many extra hours she put in, she was unable to turn the tide. A couple of her biggest accounts had lost their entire ad budget. A new hotel had construction delays and wasn't opening until the following year, so there would be no advertising. Then there was the plane crash and her airline client had pulled all their advertising everywhere, indefinitely. Most of the things that went wrong had been no fault of hers.

Pamela knocked on the half-open door to her boss's office wondering if she was being put on official warning.

Eddie looked up at her and waved her in. "Come on in. Close the door."

He wants the door closed, thought Pamela. *Is he going to fire me?*

"Sit down, we need to talk," said Eddie.

Pamela held her breath as she sat.

"You've been having a rough time this year," said Eddie. "Both Julia and I recognize that some of the things were out of your control like the plane crash. That said, you've consistently been way below your number for the first seven months of the fiscal year. We need to figure out what to do about that. We're concerned you won't be able to pull out of this death spiral."

Tears filled Pamela's eyes and she blinked to prevent the waterworks from starting. *Please don't let me cry,* she thought. "I've been trying so hard and I keep getting submarined. All these whacky things keep coming out of left field. That new gigantic Caribbean resort got damaged by the hurricane so they're not opening until next year. They won't do any advertising until they're ready to open."

"Some of the things, nothing could have been done," said Eddie gently. "Unfortunately, in sales we don't get an A for effort. You know the game, it's about how you deliver. We've got to turn your account list around." That's when the floodgates opened and tears streamed down Pamela's face. Eddie handed her the box of tissues on his desk.

"Please don't cry," said Eddie, "What did I just say? I said, *we* have to turn this around. That means you and me. Together."

"You're not firing me?" said Pamela wiping her eyes.

"Absolutely not. What gave you that idea?" said Eddie. "Would you like me to?"

Pamela shook her head and blew her nose.

"I brought you in here to help you. We're a team," said Eddie. "This conversation is between you and me. Nobody else knows about it and no one will. I want you to do a full forensic dive into all your business. You need to do a complete account report for me. People, contact info, history, ad budgets, initiatives, and overviews of the competitive landscape. I want to know where each account ran last year and where they're running this year and their plans for next. If your clients like dark chocolate and wine tastings or going out for mani/pedis and haircuts, you need to tell me that. I want to know who had a baby and who's getting married—phone numbers, email addresses, client birthdays, the works. Together, we'll get a clear snapshot of your business, Pamela, and then we're going to turn this ship around."

Pamela dabbed her eyes again and smiled. "Thanks Eddie. It's a huge project but I'll do it."

"I want the report on my desk a week from Thursday. Make it your priority. Remember, this is totally confidential, just between you and me. None of the other salespeople need to know anything about this. Deal?"

Pamela nodded. "Just between us."

"Let's see if we can get your business going in the right direction."

Pamela smiled, thanked him and left his office much relieved. She wasn't out of the woods yet but at least this was a temporary reprieve. Management clearly had concerns about her but the axe wasn't falling yet.

On any other subject, Pamela shared almost everything with her two best friends at *Vacation*, Colleen and Lucy. But this time she kept her promise and kept her conversation with Eddie to herself. Besides, she didn't want her friends to know her head was on the chopping block. Desperate to keep her job at Andover, she intended to stay, no matter what. Going anywhere else would be a downward step and she had worked too hard to get there.

That same afternoon, Pamela got busy with her account review project. A huge undertaking but if Eddie thought this would help them turn things around—she was all for it. For the next week, she spent every waking minute, including most of her weekend, working on the big project. She arrived at work early each day and left late each night. Ten days later, on a Thursday morning, she had compiled a comprehensive, detailed account overview on every piece of business on her list. If one of her clients had recently sneezed, details were in the report. She carried the full printed version of her enormous account review masterpiece to Eddie's office. When Pamela approached his door, he was on the phone so she laid the thick folder quietly on his desk. He looked up mid-conversation, smiled, and gave her a thumbs up and a wink.

10

The next day, alone in his bedroom on Friday morning, Eddie smiled and closed the zipper on his dark-brown leather Hermès weekend bag. He had purchased the bag for practically nothing at an Hermès sample sale set up exclusively for Andover employees. Having access to and owning expensive things for a fraction of the list price was one of the many perks of being an associate publisher at his company. Over the past two years, he had developed a bigger appetite for nice things, and found he began to crave them. Owning expensive clothes and accessories, or eating in the top restaurants and flying in business class somehow validated him.

The following Monday morning he would most likely formally accept the publisher job at *American Traveler*, and would have even more perks. Until then, for the next three days, he had to keep his head in his job at *Vacation*. The timing of the *American Traveler* job offer could not have been worse. Every year on the second weekend in October, which was typically warm and sunny, Julia held a management planning summit at her beach house in Montauk, Long Island. Eddie had gone the year before and knew the weekend-long meeting would be a mixture of hardcore business planning combined with beach, massages, barbecue excursions and martinis.

At last year's powwow, Eddie had been relatively new and kept a low profile, preferring to sit back and observe rather than lead.

This summit would be different. After his second year of proven success, Julia had asked him to run the whole meeting. It wasn't his fault that he would spend three days learning every detail of *Vacation's* sales and marketing strategy for the coming year and then resign the following day to go to the competition.

Bad timing, he kept telling himself. He could still hear Jonathan Barker's words in his head. *"Ethics are highly overrated,"* Barker had told him, *"Scruples are for suckers. I got there by climbing on the shoulders of people who I eventually stabbed in the back while they let me walk all over them."*

The alarm clock on his nightstand said 7am. He had to get moving if he was going to make it from New Jersey to Montauk in time for the meeting's 11am kickoff. Traffic on Montauk Highway was often horrendous, especially on a Friday. Grabbing his bag, he headed down the stairs to the kitchen.

Clare was standing by the stove making scrambled eggs with her left hand while balancing two-year-old Joey on her right hip. Eddie put his bag on the floor by the back door and then took Joey from her.

"You're getting to be a big boy, amigo," Eddie said, straining while lifting the little boy up in the air. "What are they feeding you around here?"

"I know, he's huge," said Clare laughing and rubbing her hip. "He weighs a ton but he's always hungry. He screams if I don't keep the food coming. It's never enough. Just wait until he's a teenager, he'll probably eat us out of house and home. What time will you be back on Sunday?'

"Late," said Eddie sitting down at the table and bouncing his son on his leg. The toddler squealed and laughed with each bump.

"How late?"

"I don't know. I'll be home when the meeting is over," said Eddie, a tinge of annoyance in his voice at being interrogated. He saw a look flash across his wife's face. There was a long pause in the conversation and then Eddie spoke to her more gently. "If I tell you a time and then I'm late, you'll be disappointed, honey. It's at least a three-and-a-half-hour drive and you know on Sunday nights traffic from the Hamptons can be terrible. I'm running this whole meeting, so I just don't know. I've got to stay until everyone leaves."

"If you're going to accept the job at *American Traveler* on Monday, why would you spend the weekend in Montauk when you're about to resign? Just tell Julia. You could call her right now. Then we could spend the weekend together as a family."

"I can't back out now. I'm running the entire meeting. I know what I'm doing," said Eddie. "Let me handle this my own way. And for your information, I haven't made my final decision about the other job yet." That wasn't the first time he had lied to his wife. "Besides, if I am going to become publisher of *Vacation*'s main competitor, it wouldn't hurt to know everything Julia's planning for the coming year."

"That doesn't sound very ethical. You know what happens to moths when they get too close to the flame?"

"It's business, Clare, ethical lines occasionally get blurred. It's the way things are done now. As of today, I'm still an Andover employee so I have to go to the meeting. I don't have a choice."

"Why does Julia have to keep you all so late on a Sunday night?" said Clare bitterly. "It's probably because she's divorced with no kids and doesn't have anyone to go home to."

"Why don't you call her and ask that question?" said Eddie handing her his phone.

"You're going to start a new job and it's only going to get worse."

Eddie handed Joey back to his wife and picked up his bag. "I gotta go," he said, finished with the conversation.

"What about your eggs?"

"No time," he said, grabbing a piece of toast and stuffing it in his mouth. "See you Sunday night. Don't wait up. Give Sarah a kiss for me."

Holy shit, he thought as he walked to his car. *It's not even seven thirty and Clare's already tried to pick a fight. I'll be home when I get home, so get off my back. I don't hear her complain when my big fat paycheck rolls into our joint account.*

He got into his shiny new black BMW and pulled out of the driveway. *And, I'm going to stop at Trish Gordon's on my way home Sunday night so I'll be really late. I still have to keep Trish happy, wherever I end up working.* Once he got to *American Traveler* he'd convince Trish to pull most of her business out of *Vacation* and move it back into *AT. That would be a major win right from the start,* he thought smiling as he turned onto the main highway. Over the next two and a half days he'd put on a poker face so no one would suspect his imminent departure.

If all went as planned, on Monday morning he'd call Julia and resign. He had already cleaned out his desk the day before in anticipation of what was to come. Once news of him going to Fleming Global broke, he wouldn't be allowed in the Andover building. He let out a satisfied sigh. His career was about to take off like a rocket but at the same time, he knew the shit would hit the fan. *Julia's going to freak out, but business is business. It's not for the faint of heart. She'd do the same thing if she were in my shoes.*

Two hours later, he topped off his gas tank at the large gas station right off the Long Island Expressway, the one everyone stopped at just before they got onto Montauk Highway. The single lane road went from West Hampton all the way to the eastern tip of Long Island—Montauk. At peak times, cars could be backed up to a dead stop for ten miles.

As he drove east he contemplated the enormous change he was about to make. No one but his wife knew about the job offer. *Who knows what might happen at Julia's? Maybe I'll change my mind.* With this unlikely thought, he again felt justified in attending the weekend planning session. As his BMW wound its way through one quaint little Hampton hamlet after the next, he passed wineries and small farms with vegetable stands, once the mainstay of the east end of Long Island. When he was a kid there were loads of farms in the Hamptons. Now, most of them were gone, having been sold to real-estate developers and builders. No one wanted to grow potatoes and tomatoes when they could make a bundle selling their land for multimillion dollar beach homes. *Business is business.*

As he drove on Montauk Highway with his windows cranked open, the air smelled of sweet freshly cut grass mixed with the faint salty scent of the nearby ocean. He glanced up through the open sunroof. The sky was about as blue as it could be, the sun was shining and the jazz station on his satellite radio played John Coltrane. Passing Bridgehampton, then East Hampton, then Amagansett he saw the last sign—Montauk, The End. After Montauk, the next thing you hit was the Atlantic Ocean. He looked at his GPS to find Julia's address, only another 3.2 miles.

When he pulled his car in front of Julia's beach home the driveway was already filled. Ten years earlier, Julia had bought a tiny old distressed lake cottage. Over time, she had gutted and dramatically expanded the house into a modern showpiece. All glass and right angles, the house had even been photographed by *Home in the Hamptons Magazine* a year or two before. On her property down the hill towards the shore of Lake Montauk, was a separate bar/party room with a fireplace. Next to that was a large outdoor enclosed shower lined with natural stone and filled with hanging plants. Julia's place was charming and only a half mile from the beach. Eddie thought one day soon, he would get a little beach house in the Hamptons, too.

Shimmying his car into the only parking spot left, he took a deep breath to prepare for what lay ahead. He grabbed his bag from the back seat and stepped out of the car feeling the cool ocean breeze gently caress his skin. Only three hours east of Manhattan, Montauk felt like the opposite side of the world. Walking towards the backyard of the house, he saw his co-workers scattered around the manicured yard chatting and laughing. The blue-green water of the lake shimmered in the sun as Eddie walked into the lion's den for the last time.

Standing on the dock nestled on a small sandy beach, Eddie saw Abbie and Nan, *Vacation*'s marketing and promotions directors out on the lake trying to maneuver in Julia's rowboat. When Abbie spotted Eddie walking towards the water, she smiled and waved, simultaneously dropping one of the oars into the water. Both women screamed when they lost the oar.

"Hey Abbie," shouted Eddie with a grin while waving to them, "I hear you won't get too far in life with only one paddle."

He walked over to a small group of colleagues sitting on white wooden Adirondack chairs drinking coffee. Two uniformed waitresses were preparing omelets on an outdoor grill. A buffet table covered with spectacular beachy navy-and-cream linens was set with bagels, coffee cakes, muffins and other baked goods, some that Julia had shipped out from the Balthazar bakery in the city. As usual, Julia had forgotten nothing and spared no expense—five types of juice, bottles of mineral and sparkling water along with a huge cooler filled with every kind of soda imaginable—diet, no caffeine, lots of caffeine, all caffeine. A cream-colored tent that covered a long wooden farmer's table had been set up down by the water. That's where they would hold their meeting. Several large bowls filled with various types of candy were placed strategically down the center of the table. Soft music floated through the air from hidden speakers placed throughout the picturesque property. Julia's two Labs, Mickey and Minnie, pranced around the lawn enjoying the attention and extra ball tosses from the guests. John, head of the art department, threw a large stick into the water for the dogs but soon learned they would never tire of fetching it.

"That's about the hundredth time I've thrown that stick," John yelled as he waved to Eddie.

"Hate to tell ya, but those dogs don't look the least bit tired," Eddie shouted back as one of dogs ran over to him with a ball in his mouth. Eddie scratched the dog behind his ears, took the ball and threw it across the lawn. The dog shot after it like a rocket. *I'm going to miss these people*, Eddie thought. *It is what it is.*

Julia had a full itinerary planned for her management team of seven. Her assistant, Tracy, was also on hand to make sure everything ran smoothly and on time. The annual management off-site in Montauk had a dual purpose. First was to finalize a business plan for the upcoming fiscal year but also the gathering was a crucial team-building exercise for her senior people. During a typical work week, things moved so fast with problems constantly erupting and needing to be addressed. There was little time for her people to exchange pleasantries let alone share anything personal. Julia had said on more than one occasion that every minute spent on non-work-related chit-chat could mean losing a piece of business, so they didn't do it. Opening her home for this weekend summit once a year was also Julia's way of saying thank you and validating her team's contributions.

After Julia formally welcomed the team, Eddie took over and kicked off the Friday morning meeting at precisely eleven o'clock. One by one, each department head presented an overview of their group, current projects, return on investment of programs from the previous year and an annual budget and forecast. After everyone presented, the team did their first of several brainstorming sessions. They kicked around ideas for new revenue-producing strategies to take dollars away from the competition, in particular *American Traveler*. Eddie presented his most significant sales challenges and outlined some of the initiatives he thought would bring in additional advertising revenue. Nan and Abbie were on fire as they presented a slew of creative solutions for events, client outings and promotional programs to help bring in big sales.

"That was brilliant," said Eddie to the two women. "I love the wallet idea and the partnership with the airlines could be tremendous. Well done."

"Let's see *American Traveler* top those," said Julia with a smile. "They won't know what hit them. We're going to eat their lunch next year."

John brought everyone up to date on workflow and the marketing materials that were in development. Rebecca, who headed up custom advertising sections presented a half dozen new sellable concepts to take out to the market.

"Those are all incredible," said Julia. "What do you think, Eddie? Can your salespeople sell those little gems?"

"Are you kidding?" said Eddie making some notes. "Love the one with celebrity travel, that's a winner."

When the presentations were over, the group brainstorming session commenced. This was where they would run everything they had discussed through a sieve and fine-tune each program, banging on it hard to get out the kinks. At the previous year's Montauk summit, amazing initiatives had been developed resulting in millions in revenue and broke all kinds of sales records. This meeting was the single most important event of their year and Eddie was very glad to be there.

At four o'clock that Friday, Julia closed out the working portion of the meeting. They had twenty minutes to go to their rooms and get changed for the boat ride, cocktails and dinner at the restaurant.

Before Eddie went to his room, Julia signaled for to him to follow her down to the water. When they were out of earshot, she turned to him. "How do you think the meeting went today?"

"Everyone was great, totally on point. Ideas were flowing. You're going to have another killer year next year."

"What do you mean *I'm* going have a killer year. *We're* going to have a killer year, partner."

"Of course, I meant *we*," said Eddie blushing and quickly changing the subject. "Before we go to dinner, there's something I wanted to talk to you about without the others around. It's about Lucy."

"I know she's a pain in your ass, but she's consistently over her number."

"That's why I've wrestled with this. She's also constantly insubordinate and undermines my authority on a daily basis. I know she brings in the money but at what cost? I can find another salesperson as good as Lucy, maybe better. Someone who'll be a better fit for the entire team. I wanted you to know that yesterday, I filed a report with HR regarding Lucy's behavior. It's not enough to fire her but it lays the groundwork if she continues to be a detriment."

"I wish you'd discussed it with me before you did that," said Julia. "What's done is done, we'll have to live with it. At the end of the day, it's your sales team."

While Julia changed for dinner, her conversation with Eddie repeated in her head. She didn't like that he took it upon himself to file an official complaint about a member of *her* staff without discussing it first. It put her in an awkward position. She had hired Lucy. *What if HR had called me and asked about the complaint?* she thought. *I wouldn't have known what they were talking about. Eddie overstepped. It wasn't solely his decision to make.*

When Julia had been the associate publisher, Lucy drove her nuts, too—always questioning everything. But Julia had managed to deal with her and counted on Lucy to pull out a great sale at the last minute, usually when Julia needed it most. *Eddie shouldn't have gone behind my back on that.* Looking in the mirror, she took a deep breath, applied a coat of red lipstick, shook her annoyance off and headed outside to meet her team in the waiting limo.

After a sunset boat cruise and many glasses of champagne, the team went for a grand dinner at the iconic Montauk Yacht Club. Seated at a large table overlooking the water, they dined on fresh fish from the Montauk pier caught that same day. As usual, Eddie was the life of the party, telling jokes and amusing anecdotes and kept everyone laughing. He teased and cajoled, moving around the table for a few moments of private time with each person. Instinctually, he knew how to make every single one of them feel special, like they were the only person there. That was his talent and Julia watched with admiration as her number two ran the table.

The next morning was a repeat of the previous one. A buffet of fresh pastries from Balthazar and waitresses serving up eggs. The two dogs had gotten Nan to throw the stick that day while Rebecca rocked in a hammock that had been strung between two large trees. Eddie walked over to her and gave her a push making the hammock sway.

"Fun night last night," said Eddie. "Nice getting to know you better. Never seems to be enough time to get personal in the office. I didn't know you were so funny."

"Surprise," said Rebecca with a smile. "This is my first *Vacation* management meeting. We didn't do this in my previous company. I love it. It's been incredibly productive."

"Your ideas were so clever. You being here will be a game changer for us next year."

"Thanks, for the vote of confidence. Now, I've got to execute all these great ideas."

When the Saturday meetings concluded at three, everyone changed into shorts and sneakers and put on their light-blue "*Vacation ReCreation*" T-shirts Julia had custom-made for the occasion. "Hard work over and now your rewards," she had said when she announced the rest of the day's schedule.

After a few rounds of volleyball they all headed into one of the four tents that had been set up on the lawn. One was for tarot card readings, one for massages, one for facials and one for foot and hand reflexology. A few of the women headed directly for the facials and massages leaving Eddie and John with the tarot card reader. Eddie waited outside the tent while John had his cards read.

John emerged smiling. "Apparently, next year is going to be *my* year." he said. "Supposed to make a lot of money and find my true love. So, I've got that going for me. Your turn."

Eddie was about to go into the tarot card tent when Julia sidled up next to him and put her arm through his. "C'mon, Gamble, let's see what those cards say about the two of us. I want to see how far over your number you're going to be next year."

Julia and Eddie sat down with a woman dressed all in purple, covered with gold stars and glitter. The tarot reader shuffled the cards and asked Eddie to cut the deck. Carefully, she laid out a pattern of cards on the little table between them. Eddie looked down at the medieval characters but they made no sense to him.

"Just so we're clear, I don't believe in this stuff," whispered Eddie to Julia.

"Let's hear what she has to say. Are you a chicken, Gamble?" said Julia giggling.

"Bring it," said Eddie rolling up his sleeves and laughing.

"This card says you have been given many gifts in your life," said the fortune teller with an unidentifiable accent. "You have been very successful. People admire you, they want to follow you. You are a leader."

"Did I say I didn't believe in this stuff?" said Eddie laughing and winking at Julia, "This seems pretty accurate to me."

"This next card says you have a great many loves in your life. Children and a wife who is devoted," continued the tarot reader as she flipped over another card. "Hmm. It's showing there's something dark hanging over you. Something dramatic is about to happen. You're going to make a choice that will alter the rest of your life. It's warning that you need to be mindful of choosing that path." She stopped and looked up from the cards into Eddie's blue eyes. He stared back at her for a moment, then looked at Julia.

"That was depressing," said Julia laughing and pulling Eddie's arm. "C'mon. Good thing we don't believe in this stuff. Let's get you a massage." As Eddie got up from the table he looked back at the tarot reader who only stared at him blankly.

The rest of the management weekend went off without a hitch. Eddie remained in top form and continued to impress Julia with his creativity and clear vision on how they would move business forward in the coming year. Part of being a great publisher was knowing who to hire underneath you and Eddie was one of Julia's best hires. With him supporting her, she fully expected her boss, Thomas Andover, to move her into a corporate role within the next six months.

At three o'clock on Sunday afternoon, the management team

packed up their cars. The weekend had been a huge success. In addition to nailing down an airtight twelve-month strategy for the coming year, Julia was thrilled to see her team work so well together.

After giving Julia a goodbye hug, knowing it would probably be for the last time, Eddie drove west along Montauk Highway towards New York City thinking about the past three days and what lay ahead. For the first time since he had gotten the offer from FGM, he felt a little melancholy. *I'm going to miss those people. Maybe I can hire them away to American Traveler after a few months.*

He drove along the Long Island Expressway in heavy Sunday evening Hamptons traffic. Crossing the bridge into Manhattan, he drove downtown to Bleecker Street. Trish had said she'd make dinner for the two of them. He was looking forward to a relaxing evening without stress and that's what Trish always provided. She didn't want to marry him, she didn't want him to leave Clare. They got each other. No strings. She had a handsome paramour and he had the Chandler Hotels and L'Beau business—a perfect arrangement.

At ten o'clock Eddie climbed out of Trish's bed and started to dress.

"Do you have to leave so soon? You just got here."

"I've got over an hour's drive and tomorrow's going to be a big day."

"You do know that Julia's going to lose her mind when you tell her. You're her golden boy," said Trish. "She's not going to take it well. Love to be a fly on the wall when she gets your phone call."

"She's going to be upset," said Eddie ruefully.

"Upset? She's going to be bat-shit crazy. You just sat in on her management summit meeting. You know every move *Vacation's* going to make. And now, you're going to be the publisher of her arch-nemesis, *American Traveler*? She's gonna go nuts, don't kid yourself. Be ready for a tsunami of poison arrows."

Trish's words resonated. He had briefly considered Julia's reaction to his resignation when he was going through the interview process but pushed those unpleasant thoughts out of his mind. Now the day of reckoning was upon him and he'd have to face the chain reaction his departure would undoubtedly trigger. One thing he knew for sure, when he accepted the job as *American Traveler*'s new publisher, the shit was going to hit the fan. The *Vacation* sales team and all of his co-workers at Andover were probably going to feel betrayed. *I have a right to advance my career. Julia wasn't about to step out of my way. She would have done the same thing if she were me.*

The traffic out of Manhattan was light and Eddie made it home to New Jersey faster than he had expected. It was 11:15 when he pulled into his driveway. The bedroom window upstairs was dark. That meant Clare was asleep and he was grateful because he didn't want to deal with her questions that night. He just wanted to go to sleep.

Quietly, he went up the stairs stopping to look in on his sleeping children. Staring at each of them for a moment, he gave both of them a kiss on their head. *Love you, Sarah. Love you, Joe. Tomorrow your daddy will become publisher of American Traveler and then you two can have anything you want.* He smiled at the thought of spoiling his kids rotten.

The next morning, Eddie called in to *Vacation* and told his assistant he'd be out of the office that day. He also left a message for Julia, who was in a meeting until noon and asked her to give him a call. That's when he'd officially resign. While he waited to hear from Julia, he called his father to tell him the good news.

"You've got another job already?" said his father. "You just started at *Vacation*."

"I've been here almost two years, Dad. It was too good an

opportunity to pass up. They're going to pay me almost twice what I'm making at Andover. I'm going to be the publisher now. It's a big step up."

"You're moving too fast, jumping around like that," said his father. "You're going to piss people off."

"It's business, this is how it's done now. Eat or get eaten. You gotta step on a few backs if you want to get to the top."

"Careful, Eddie. People you step on today will be lining up to knock you off your throne tomorrow."

"I know what I'm doing, " said Eddie. "I've got this."

11

Eddie had been "out of the office" on Monday and on Tuesday morning at eight thirty, over fifty *Vacation* staffers were seated around the twenty-foot-long wooden table in their large conference room for their weekly meeting. The management team had just returned from their off-site summit in Montauk and there would be lots of initiatives and ideas to unpack and implement.

"They go away for a weekend in the Hamptons, have massages and lattes and come back to New York and dump it all on us before they dash out to a client lunch," whispered one assistant promotion manager to anyone within earshot.

By 8:38am, none of the senior management had appeared and the crowd had gotten restless. By 8:45, one of the assistants volunteered to walk upstairs to Julia's office to see what was going on. Just as she was about to leave, the conference room door flew open and the entire management team except for Eddie walked in. They looked ashen as they silently took their seats. Only Julia remained standing. Pale and stone-faced she looked around the room. Sensing something was wrong, the staff remained quiet as they waited for Julia to speak.

The publisher cleared her throat. "I have an announcement to make," she said. "Eddie Gamble has resigned effective immediately."

The room erupted in spontaneous conversation. "What happened? Where's he going? Why is he leaving? Are you kidding? Eddie left?"

Julia cleared her throat again while she waited for the group to quiet down. "It's actually a very good thing for Eddie," she said with an obviously forced smile. "He got an offer he couldn't refuse. It turns out... he's going to be the new publisher at... *American Traveler*."

The room turned into pandemonium with everyone talking at once.

"Everyone, please quiet down," said Julia raising her arms. "I know you all liked Eddie. We all did and he did a great job while he was here, but we will survive. We've got great momentum going into next year and I'm counting on each one of you to keep it going. The other managers and I will pick up the slack until a new associate publisher can be named. I hope you'll join me in wishing Eddie every success. This was too good an opportunity for him to pass up. Publisher jobs at major media companies don't come along every day."

A murmur went through the room.

"While the timing on this couldn't have been worse," said Julia gritting her teeth, "since Eddie just spent the weekend with our management team while we planned our year-long strategy, I fully understand he was not in control of the timing of the offer."

One of the marketing people raised their hand. "Julia, are you saying Eddie spent the whole weekend going over the sales and marketing strategy for *Vacation* the day before he resigned to become publisher of our biggest competitor?"

Julia paused for a moment as she looked out on a sea of wide eyes. "That's what I'm saying. He explained that *American Traveler* approached him and it wasn't until yesterday, Monday, that he got the offer. It was bad timing for us. We'll be just fine and we all wish Eddie well. Any questions?"

"I have a question," said Pamela. "A few weeks ago Eddie asked me to work on a project. He wanted me to do a full account review. Every contact. Names, phone numbers, budgets. Strategies. Creative concepts, the works."

"I wasn't aware of that," said Julia eyes now wide, jaw clenched.

"He said he wanted to review how I was handling my business," Pamela continued. "He told me the project was to be my priority and gave me a few weeks to finish it. If he's going to our competition then he's got the key to every piece of business I have. I'm screwed."

"He asked me to do the same thing," shouted another salesperson.

"Me too," said another.

"I did one, too," said a third.

The entire room began to talk at once. After Julia quieted everyone down, she took a poll of the entire sales team. Every salesperson, including the ones in the remote offices, had been asked to do a full comprehensive written account review only weeks before Eddie resigned. All the account reviews had been turned in to him the previous Thursday, right before the management meeting. Julia turned towards Eddie's former assistant seated at the table.

"Do you know anything about this? Where are all those reports? Do you have them?"

"No," said the assistant looking bewildered, "I don't know anything about it. A lot of the salespeople stopped by Eddie's office to drop off folders and files last week. They each handed it to him personally. I never saw what it was. There's nothing left in his office now. All his drawers and cabinets are empty."

"Outside offices," shouted Julia into the big black conference call pod in the middle of the table, "how did you send Eddie your documents?"

"Email," they all chorused.

"I don't think Eddie did it on purpose," said Pamela, "it was probably just a rotten coincidence. He's not like that. He always had my back."

"I never trusted him," shouted Lucy James. "Didn't I always say that?"

"That son of a bitch played all of us," said Julia getting red in the face. "He was already interviewing for the other job when he asked for all the account reviews. He knew the *American Traveler* offer was coming and he collected every last bit of information. Then he spent the weekend as a Fleming Global Media spy at our management planning meeting."

Water pooled in Julia's eyes. "I promise all of you," she said, "he's not going to get away with this." Taking a deep breath, she walked out of the room and marched directly to the twenty-third floor—the chairman's office. She knew Thomas Andover would lose his mind and do something.

When she approached the grand foyer outside Andover's office, his executive assistant and bodyguard, Sheila, who had been with him for thirty years, looked up and smiled. "Julia, what brings you here? Did he call for you?" she asked with a puzzled glance at her boss's calendar. "I don't have you on his schedule."

"He didn't call me and I don't have an appointment. I have an emergency. It's serious. I need to see him right now."

Seeing the strain on Julia's face and hearing the shrill in her voice, Sheila got up immediately, straightened her dress and went into Andover's office. A minute later she returned. "You can go in, Julia," she said softly. "He's got a little wiggle room on his schedule this morning."

Julia took another deep breath, threw her shoulders back and walked into Andover's office. Seated behind his desk in a huge room with cream-colored marble floors and twenty-foot high ceilings with walls of glass and views of the Hudson River, Andover was on the phone and waved for Julia to take a seat. While she waited, she examined the pictures of Andover standing next to various luminaries from the world of politics and entertainment. Previous visits to his office were usually to report sales and circulation numbers or some new promotional program her team had dreamed up. Occasionally, she had been summoned to the twenty-third floor when her numbers were off and given a gentle dressing down. This day was different.

Well known for a bad temper and an even longer memory, she knew Andover was not going to take the news about Eddie well. He would consider Eddie's actions a personal violation, as if Eddie had picked Andover's pocket. Andover Media was a seventy-five-year-old family business. Thomas Andover's father had built it from the ground up and there were dozens of Andover heirs, cousins, nephews and nieces employed all through the company.

Don't kill the messenger, Julia thought while she waited for him to finish his call.

The media magnate wrapped up his conversation, put the phone down and looked at Julia. "Sheila said you had an emergency. Does this have something to do with Gamble leaving? Tough break for you, he was a rising star. He'll be hard to replace. Maybe we'll hire him back from Fleming in a few years. So, what's the problem?"

Slowly and carefully, Julia laid out the events of the past few weeks. Her story culminated with the epiphany that morning that Eddie had demanded detailed account reports from every salesperson and then attended the *Vacation* management planning weekend the day before he resigned.

Thomas Andover's face remained unchanged as Julia spoke. He listened without interrupting but as she progressed, she could see her boss was trying to keep from exploding. When she finished, Andover asked her a few questions and clarified some of the details.

When she answered everything to his satisfaction, Andover spun his chair around and stared out the window at the Hudson. Julia remained seated with her hands clasped in her lap and neither spoke for nearly a minute.

Finally, the chairman turned around and stood up. "Thank you, Julia. There was nothing you could have done differently. The bottom line is Gamble is a scoundrel. He lied and deceived you. Stealing from you means he also stole from me. I don't like people stealing from me, Julia. I don't like it at all. I take it very personally. I'll take care of this."

What Eddie had done was sneaky, underhand and unethical. He absconded with Andover Media's intellectual property, and in doing so, he crossed the wrong man. Thomas Andover was one of the most powerful people in the media business and one of the most vindictive. He wasn't about to let Eddie Gamble get away with ripping him off.

As Julia left his office, Andover called out to his assistant. "Sheila," he bellowed, "get Bob Fleming at FGB on the phone."

Robert Fleming, Jr. was the chairman of Fleming Global Media, Andover's biggest competitor. While Fleming and Andover employees ruthlessly competed with each other out in the field, the two men at the top knew there was enough business to go around for both companies. They had a cordial relationship and had often been together at various business and social events over the years. Andover's son once had even dated a Fleming niece years ago when they all summered in

Southampton. Bob Fleming and Tom Andover were competitors, but on the Eddie Gamble situation, they became trusted partners.

"I've got Bob Fleming's assistant on the phone," said Sheila. "She can put you through whenever you're ready."

"Put it through."

In another moment the two titans of media were on the phone with each other. "Hello, Tom. This is a nice surprise. To what do I owe a call from you? I suppose you want to congratulate me on the incredible year FGM is having?" laughed Bob Fleming good-naturedly.

"You are indeed having a good year, Bob. Almost as good as Andover Media. Maybe you'll catch up to us next year," said Andover also laughing.

For several minutes the two men traded barbs like the old school chums that they were, and then Andover got to the point. He recounted the story of Eddie Gamble's crimes leaving out no detail. Bob Fleming listened without saying a word. Fleming and Andover had a huge rivalry but Eddie Gamble's behavior was way out of bounds. When FGM won business, their chairman wanted the win because they worked hard for it, not because they stole it. Fleming asked his assistant to call the head of his HR department and find out exactly when Eddie's official employment offer was extended. Within minutes Bob Fleming was told that Eddie Gamble had been offered the publisher job at *American Traveler* four weeks earlier and had accepted the position more than three weeks before.

When Andover learned that Eddie Gamble had accepted the job before he asked the *Vacation* salespeople for their account reviews and long before the Montauk management meeting, he thought his head was going to explode. Bob Fleming was equally incredulous. Eddie's actions had been one hundred percent premeditated.

"Sounds like Mr. Gamble meticulously planned this whole caper," said Andover. "Guess he wanted to look like a big man when he walked through the doors of FGM."

"It's very disappointing, Tom. I had heard such good things about him. I liked him when I met him," said Bob Fleming as he looked over Eddie's employment contract. "He made things happen at *Vacation*. We considered his hire as a real coup, snagging a superstar from our main competitor and at the same time, causing you to lose one. But like you, Tom, I don't want someone working for me who cheats. If he lied and stole from you, he'll lie and steal from me. I've got his employment contract in my hand right now and one of my lawyers sitting across from me as we speak. According to him, we've got a one-year iron-clad commitment with this joker."

"I understand. How do you want to handle this, Bob?"

Fleming thought for a moment and smiled. "Here's what I propose. You and I agree we can't have people like Gamble working for us or even working in our industry. The media business is hard enough without having our people stealing from each other. I'll have to honor his one-year contract but I'll make him sweat, I promise you that. However, one year from today, regardless of what kind of job he does, good or bad, even if he blows the doors off this place, he'll be terminated. He'll never be employed by a Fleming Global Media company ever again."

"I think that makes sense. I too, will pledge that Mr. Gamble will never work for an Andover company at any time in the future. So, we're in agreement, Bob?" said Andover.

"You can take it to the bank."

"I think we need to get all the media company chairmen to join us in this arrangement," said Andover. "Can't have thieves ruining our gentleman's business. When we're done, no media company in the world will ever hire Eddie Gamble again."

"You think they'll all sign on?" said Bob Fleming.

"Absolutely, except for Diamond International," said Andover. "They're such lowlife scumbags they'd probably applaud Gamble's actions."

"Don't waste your time on Diamond," said Fleming. "If Gamble ends up there working for Leach, he's hit bottom. Nobody's career comes back from Diamond. It's a media graveyard."

A week later, twelve men and women met for a drink in a dark, wooden private room at the Harvard Club on West 45th Street. Thomas Andover hosted, the chairman of the top twelve global media companies in the United States. Usually, this illustrious group got together once a year for a friendly drink around the holidays. This meeting at the end of the summer was unexpected and piqued everyone's curiosity when Andover and Fleming jointly invited them. After half an hour of gentle joking, roasting and complaining about the challenges of the media business, Thomas Andover got to the point and shared the transgressions of one Eddie Gamble with the room.

When he finished, there was unilateral outrage. Each powerful CEO there would have enjoyed decimating their competitors but only if they did it fair and square. They all had an unbreakable code and Eddie had violated it. Within minutes, all twelve pledged that none of their companies or subsidiaries in the United States or internationally would ever employ Eddie Gamble again.

Eddie didn't know it, but he had just become professional toast.

Two days later, unaware that he would be unemployed in one year's time, Eddie started his new job as the publisher of *American Traveler*. Full of ideas and enthusiasm right out of the gate, the *American Traveler* sales and marketing team was thrilled to have someone with Eddie's great reputation, contacts and genial disposition as their new boss. The salespeople welcomed him in all sincerity, figuring Eddie's smarts and contacts would help them line their pockets with added commissions over the coming years.

It came as a surprise that Eddie's first week on the job was overshadowed by some particularly bad press. An article in one of the New York newspapers reported some media gossip on what had happened with Eddie and Andover Media. The headline was, "Don't Gamble with your Vacation". Someone at Andover had leaked the story to the press. The article gave Eddie a new nickname, "Eddie Shambles". While the negative publicity put a slight damper on things, Eddie addressed it head-on at his first *American Traveler* sales meeting the following week. He characterized the stories as overblown, inaccurate and vindictive.

"Plain and simple, the Andover people are doing a hit job on me. They were angry that I left and are trying to tarnish my reputation. Think about it," said Eddie to his new team, "why would I have asked for or taken account information from them when you would obviously already have the same information? This is clearly an attempt to ruin the great year we're all going to have here. They're trying to get into our heads and we're not going to let that happen."

The room applauded.

"You know what I say?" said Eddie. "I say we're going to eat *Vacation*'s lunch. They won't know what's hit them when we're done." The room broke into more applause and cheers. Eddie effortlessly pumped them up and solidly convinced his new team that the articles and rumors were all a bunch of bull.

Back at *Vacation*, things were anything but quiet. Julia was still reeling from her number two's duplicitous behavior. Not only had Eddie lied and behaved in a treacherous way from a business perspective, but she was also personally hurt. She had really liked him. She thought of him as the smart little brother she never had. Now she was kicking herself for completely misjudging him and being taken in by his charm. She never did find out what Andover had planned as payback for Eddie's transgressions but hoped that the punishment fit the crime and then some.

It did.

12

It had been a fast-paced nine months since Eddie had taken over the helm of *American Traveler*. From day one, he hit the ground running working sometimes seven days a week. In less than a year, he and his team had broken twenty-seven pieces of new business and increased *AT*'s market share by six percent. A few of the new accounts had previously been *Vacation* exclusives too. He was certain Julia couldn't have been too pleased about that.

He continued his rigorous entertaining and travel schedule and it was all paying off. The business was pouring in at *AT*, better than he had ever dreamed. He hardly ever saw his family but easily justified his absenteeism every time Clare acted disappointed that he'd be gone another weekend.

"After I prove myself this first year at *AT*, I'll be home all the time," said Eddie to his wife on a rare night that he was home for dinner.

"I thought it would be nice to take the kids for a long weekend to see my parents," said Clare. "They haven't seen their grandparents in months."

"I want to go to Grandma's," said Sarah perking up.

"Take them," said Eddie. "I can't take time off right now. It's crucial that I'm involved on every piece of business."

"Daddy, you have to come," said Sarah touching her father's arm. Eddie leaned over and gave his daughter a kiss on the top of her head.

Clare pursed her lips as she lifted Joey down from his chair at the kitchen table.

"Sarah, why don't you take Joey inside and show him that new video I got for you," said Clare. When the children had left the room, she sat down at the table next to her husband. "What are we doing? The kids miss you. I miss you."

"I promise, next year, we'll have loads of family time. You've got to trust me on this," said Eddie. "I'm building our nest egg for the future. With the money I've made over the past few years we can start looking for that new house we talked about."

Clare backed off because she wanted to believe him and agreed to take the kids to her parents by herself. She also promised to call the real-estate broker so they could look at some houses.

With his move to *American Traveler*, Eddie had increased his compensation by nearly sixty percent, and they had socked it all away for a down payment on a new house. He had big plans. He wanted a large piece of property in an affluent town befitting his new station in life. He finally had the money to live in style. The business was going so well at *American Traveler* that the buzz on him within the FGM building was fantastic. People speculated that Eddie was on the fast track to become the next chief revenue officer for the entire company. His career was going according to plan as each piece of the puzzle fell neatly into place.

Eddie's move to *American Traveler* had not dampened his affection for Audrey. He loved his wife but he had fallen for Audrey—hard. While at *Vacation,* he had used every excuse to make trips to the west coast to see her. When he moved over to *AT* he continued to travel west and told his underlings that he personally would handle all of the big LA accounts.

With the money rolling into *American Traveler*, the media press took notice and Eddie was featured in *Media Minute Magazine*'s "40 Under 40" annual roundup. This list featured young up-and-comers in the media business. Eddie, who had just turned thirty-nine, made the list. When Julia Bowman got wind of it, she was livid. The article reported on all the innovative promotion programs Eddie had instituted at *American Traveler*—many that were the same programs he had stolen from Julia's management summit in Montauk. *I gave him his big break, and he repaid me by lying, cheating and stealing my ideas,* she thought bitterly.

Eddie had taken every program Julia and her team had come up with, put an *American Traveler* wrapper on it and peddled it as his own. When Julia called the Airline Traffic Association (ATA) board to discuss *Vacation*'s sponsorship of the ATA Ball, a program they had sponsored for twenty-six years, she was informed that ATA had already signed off on the sponsorship with *American Traveler*. She threw her phone against the wall and headed straight for Thomas Andover's office.

"I understand your frustration, Julia," said Andover with no emotion. "Gamble is all about shortcuts and greased palms. Take it from me, he walks on dead man's legs. Run your own race and stay in your own lane. People like him don't last long, I can promise you that."

"He's killing it at *American Traveler* and he's broken all kinds of new business using our ideas," said Julia.

"You know the story of Icarus, Julia. He flew too close to the sun. Right now, Gamble is flying dangerously close to the sun. And when that happens, no one will touch him. That's all I'm going to say. Trust me, he's got a one-year shelf life."

Andover's words stuck in Julia's head and she wondered if Eddie had plans to leave *American Traveler*. Her chairman had sounded pretty sure about Eddie's fate. *One can only hope,* she thought.

Given that Julia and Eddie were both in the travel business, it was inevitable they would periodically attend some of the same industry events. A few months later, both she and Eddie would be at the same black-tie travel banquet.

In the back of a black town car driven by his regular driver on the evening of the ATA Ball, Eddie was anxious. Representatives from travel companies and their ad agencies, scores of media and business vendors would descend in their finery onto the Waldorf Astoria Hotel ballroom. As publisher of *American Traveler,* the main sponsor of the event, Eddie would be seated at the dais table with this year's award winners. As his car moved slowly through traffic, Eddie had a flicker of irritation that his wife wasn't there with him to see him shine.

"Like my new tux," Eddie had said smiling a month before as he took his custom-tailored suit out of the zippered bag. "It's Armani. Fits like a second skin. Feel the fabric. Cost a fortune, but hey, you only live once, right?"

"It's very nice," said Clare sitting at the kitchen table working on an article for *Sugar & Spice*.

"I'm giving the opening speech at the ATA Ball next month," said Eddie. "I know you don't usually go to business events but since we're the main sponsor, why don't you come and be my date? I'm going to get a hotel room in the city. We could make a night of it."

"You know I hate those things. I wouldn't know anyone and you'd be off chatting people up and I'd be all alone. And, I have nothing to wear," said Clare, "Plus, I'd have to find an overnight sitter."

"Buy a new dress," said Eddie with a smile. "Get a sitter."

Clare made a face. "I don't think so. I'm not good at those things."

"I'm not going to twist your arm," he said, putting his suit back in the bag. "I just thought you'd like to come and watch me in action."

"If you want to take me out to dinner one night in the city for fun, I'd love to do that."

"Sure," said Eddie as he walked out of the room, "after I close the December issue."

She's always so negative, he thought as his driver pulled up to the front of the Waldorf Astoria. *Glad I made other arrangements.* In a couple of hours he had to give a speech to 500 people. He pushed his wife and her less than supportive attitude out of his mind. Taking a deep breath, he put a smile on his face, turned the Eddie Gamble charm up to high and strutted into the lobby.

Dozens of people milled around the large room. Ever the politician, Eddie smiled, shook hands and hugged various delegates that he knew. If there had been a baby there, he would have kissed it, whatever it took. He complimented each woman on her formal attire, knowing she had likely spent hours selecting it. He also praised each man he greeted on the cut of their tuxedo. He meant all of it, everyone did look nice. He had long ago learned that sincere flattery cost him nothing and bought him everything. Moving on to the cocktail reception, he worked the room like a concert violinist playing a fiddle, never missing a note, pitch always perfect.

Smiling and cajoling, he made sure he connected with the most important people in attendance. From the other side of the vast hall, he spotted Audrey chatting with the director of Mexico tourism. Her toned body was encased in a skintight green beaded gown few women could pull off. He caught her eye and smiled and they exchanged a knowing glance—she would be with him at the hotel later that night. Jolted out of his daydream by a media director from a large ad agency, Eddie immediately went into full "sell" mode. As he pitched, he was startled by a glimpse of Julia Bowman in his periphery.

Her presence sent adrenaline coursing through his veins causing his hands and feet to tingle. He hadn't seen or spoken to her since the day he left Andover but he had anticipated seeing her that night.

He watched his old boss work the room like a pro as she warmly greeted various clients and officials. From the corner of his eye, he saw her making her way through the crowd directly towards him. Instead of waiting for her to pounce, he headed her off and walked straight to her.

"Julia," he said with a smile, dimples fully engaged. "You look beautiful, as always. Love your dress. Blue is your color: no one else should wear it."

Julia smiled at him with her mouth but not with her eyes, a deception not lost on Eddie. "Save it, Eddie," she hissed, "Been a while."

"It has," said Eddie still smiling, "I'm coming up on my one-year anniversary at *American Traveler*. Been a crazy year."

"So I've heard. Nice stunt landing the sponsorship on this event tonight," said Julia through clenched teeth. "Who would have guessed you'd be hosting this ball considering it's been my signature event for years."

"Like the saying goes," continued Eddie not dropping his smile, "all's fair in love and war."

"I have a quote for you too," cooed Julia. "It's from *Hamlet*. Word on the street is that Eddie Gamble may find himself 'hoist with his own petard'."

"What the hell does that mean?" said Eddie, mainly irritated because he really had no idea what it meant.

"'...for whom the bell tolls; it tolls for thee,'" she whispered as she smiled and walked away.

13

Her back aching after standing over the table for hours making party decorations for her daughter's sixth birthday, Clare finally sat down in the dining room of their new home. This was the first party she had thrown since the family had moved into the bigger and grander house in a more exclusive part of the town. They had paid cash and the sale had been quick. She would have been happy to stay in their old small and cozy house, but Eddie had insisted.

"I'm the publisher of *American Traveler*, a global brand," he had said when his wife had suggested they stay where they were. "I have to keep a certain image. How would it look for me to live in such a tiny little house? People who work for me have bigger houses than we do. We can afford a bigger place. Shouldn't our kids have the best? Why do you want to live below our means?"

In less than twenty-four hours, ten little girls would be seated in her dining room for Sarah's birthday lunch. After the meal, they'd all go out for manicures at the nail salon in town. Sarah had wanted a beauty-themed party. Clare had suggested other ideas like Sleeping Beauty or Barbie but Sarah was adamant. *When I was her age, Clare thought, I was still playing with dolls and messing around in the dirt. The last thing I thought about was beauty. Things are different now, I guess.*

Tiny lipsticks hung from white lights strung through the spokes of the chandelier over the table. Strategically placed pink powder puffs were tied together with pink-and-white ribbons and there was a white-and-pink polka-dot runner down the center of the table. Each place setting had an open mirrored compact next to the plate. A pink or white hairbrush was placed where you would normally put a fork and mini-makeup kits in hot pink zippered cases filled with glosses and lotions sat behind each plate. Clare had ordered a beauty-themed birthday cake that had little lip glosses, eyeshadows and makeup brushes made of sugary fondant all sitting on the top of pale-pink icing.

In Detroit on business while all the party preparations were happening, Eddie had promised to be home on Friday afternoon to help Clare with the last-minute details. Thursday night she got a call from him saying there had been an unfortunate change of plans. A last-minute dinner had been scheduled with some automotive clients for Friday night. He promised he would be on the flight home first thing Saturday morning in time for the party. While Sarah was at school and Joey at his afternoon preschool, Clare got everything finished. She closed her eyes for a moment when the house phone rang.

"Hello, Mrs. Gamble?"

"Yes."

"It's Olivia from the front desk at the Bellmore Hotel in Charleston. How are you?"

"Okay?"

"I'm calling because housekeeping just cleaned the room you and Mr. Gamble were in this week. It seems you left your beautiful new coat that you got at our gift shop in the closet in the room. I called the phone number we had on file but the voicemail was full. You were so nice to all the staff while you were staying with us and my manager wanted to make sure you got your coat back. We called Visa and got your home phone number."

"Who is this again?"

"Olivia, from the Bellmore Hotel in Charleston. You told me you liked my green shoes the other day, remember?"

"Oh, yes, of course," said Clare slowly. "Olivia... from the Bellmore in Charleston. I remember, thank you for tracking me down. It was very kind of you."

"Just doing my job, Mrs. Gamble. You were so sweet to all the staff. I'm glad I found you. Where should I send your coat? Your husband didn't leave a forwarding address. I've admired that coat in our boutique window for weeks. It's gorgeous, not that I could ever afford it. I'll bet it looks great on you. The color is perfect with your golden-red hair." Clare glanced at her dark-brown hair in the mirror on the wall.

The rest of the conversation was a blur. Robotically, Clare gave Olivia her New Jersey address and the young woman promised to overnight the coat—the one that looked great with golden-red hair. Eddie had told her he was in Detroit. He had even called several times that week and talked about all the great automotive presentations he was "blowing out of the water".

He lied to me.

Sitting in the party-pink dining room, Clare was numb. At first, she tried to convince herself that she had misunderstood his travel plans. *Maybe he said he was going to an automotive show that was being held in Charleston. I've been so busy with the kids, maybe I wasn't listening. No, he definitely said he was going to Detroit. Just the other night on the phone he complained about how bleak Detroit was and how much he hated going there. How much he wished he was home with me and the kids. I actually felt sorry for him missing all the home time with the family.*

Dizzy and nauseous, she pushed herself up, grabbing the back of a dining-room chair for support, and walked to the kitchen sink to get a glass of water. *Who was the golden-red-headed woman the hotel staff thought was me? A colleague of Eddie's? But that woman from the hotel said the owner of the coat was "Mrs. Gamble".*

Clare stared at the wall clock. By the time Eddie got home the next day, she would be in the middle of a pack of little girls. The discussion about the coat would have to wait until tomorrow night after she put the kids to bed. Emotionally shattered, she was resigned to the wait and prayed that Eddie had a legitimate reason for all of it. Deep down she knew he probably didn't. *Will he lie to me? Of course he will. He lies all the time. Why stop now?* She took inventory of all the days Eddie was missing in action, the late nights, the missed dinners. *Was everything a lie? Is he having an affair with a golden-red-headed woman who he tells people is his wife? Does he have another wife?*

That night Clare barely slept as she moved from bouts of tears to waves of sadness and re-evaluated her entire marriage. All those odd moments that had been glossed over in the past took on new meaning. *I was so willing to accept and swallow his stories without question. I've been complicit in this.* Whenever Eddie strung together some outlandish excuse, she had gratefully accepted it rather than learning the truth. After all the years of lies, she couldn't tell what was fiction and what wasn't. She had willingly believed everything he told her with almost no pushback and her acquiescence had only emboldened him. *I didn't want to know. He knew that.*

Sitting up, she turned on the lamp next to her bed, her face still wet from the steady stream of tears. It was 3:30am. She let out a frustrated breath and laid back down. Turning onto her side, she curled up into a fetal position, arms crossed tightly across her chest hoping if she could make herself small enough she might not feel the searing pain. Eventually, she drifted off to sleep.

The alarm rang at 8:15am and Clare wearily opened her eyes. For the first ten seconds, she forgot about everything she had learned the day before. For those ten seconds she lay there in blissful peace. Then, all the new knowledge, realizations, and undeniable truths barreled in along with anxiety, fear, and the pain of betrayal. *This is my new normal and it sucks.* She got out of bed and went downstairs to the kitchen, put on the coffee maker and rummaged through the refrigerator to make breakfast for her kids.

By 8:30 she was surprised neither Sarah nor Joey were up. Her daughter had recently started sleeping later which had given Clare a little break in the mornings but Joey was always up by 7:15. Oddly, this Saturday morning the house was quiet. After all the emotional upheaval from the night before, she was glad to have a few minutes to herself.

Soon, the birthday activities would commence. She had to get Sarah dressed for her party, pick up the balloons, host lunch, go to the nail salon, and finish the day at The Scoop Shoppe for ice cream. Eddie was supposed to be flying back from Detroit and getting home in time to meet them at the ice-cream shop to catch the tail end of Sarah's party.

By 8:45am both Sarah and Joe meandered down the stairs for breakfast.

"Happy birthday, Sarah," said Clare forcing a cheerful smile when the last thing in the world she felt was cheerful.

Excited, Sarah chattered about her upcoming party while her brother Joe watched cartoons in the adjacent family room. To someone watching the scene, it looked like Clare was listening and conversing with both children but she was on autopilot. Her mind was sifting and parsing memories of her marriage—the lies, the red-head, the bullshit.

She drew a bath for Sarah and busied herself with last-minute party details. At 10:45am the front doorbell rang. It was FedEx with a package for "Mrs. Edward Gamble". *It must be the slut's coat. The entire staff of the Bellmore Hotel thought she was a really nice person.*

"Sarah, watch Joey for a minute," said Clare grabbing the package. "I have to do something upstairs."

She took the box up to her bedroom and opened it. Inside was a three-quarter length muted green leather coat with a belt. She touched it. To call it buttery was an understatement. The leather was the softest she had ever felt. She held it up. *Yes,* she thought, remembering the comment from Olivia at the Bellmore Hotel, *this color must look great with golden-red hair.* Clare, a size eight, looked at the label on the coat—size two. *Bitch,* she thought as she put the coat on. *Isn't that just great, my husband's girlfriend is three sizes thinner than me. She's probably younger too.*

She looked at her reflection in the mirror. It was a little snug but it was a loose cut and fit well enough. She wondered how the other Mrs. Gamble looked in the coat. Staring at herself she moved closer to the mirror. Something on the collar caught her eye. It was a single golden-red hair. She plucked it off, laid it on an open page of the novel on her nightstand and stared at it. Walking into the second-floor office, she got an envelope and put the single long strand of hair inside and sealed it. On the outside she wrote "SLUT" and put it into her top dresser drawer buried underneath her socks.

Despite all the emotional upheaval, Sarah's beauty birthday party went off without a hitch. The girls spent several hours playing with and applying their new makeup. By the time they left to get their manicures they all looked quite colorful as only six-year-olds with unrestricted makeup could.

"Everyone go outside and wait by the minivan. I'll be right out," said Clare as the girls headed out the front door. She went up to her room and lifted the green leather coat out of the box and put it on. Wearing the leather coat, Clare loaded the group into the car and pulled out of the driveway. It was nearly 2pm and Eddie was supposed to meet them all at the ice-cream place at 3:15. The party descended on the nail salon and the girls scattered. Within an hour, beauty services complete, Clare drove the group to The Scoop Shoppe.

Glancing in the rearview mirror, she saw her daughter's happy laughing face and for a second forgot about Eddie and his lies. Before she turned off the car engine, the girls already had the van doors open and jumped out of the car racing into the ice-cream store. Inside, Eddie waited by the counter.

"Daddy!" shouted Sarah as she ran over to her father to show him her newly painted pink nails topped with tiny encrusted diamonds. "Look at my nails. I picked a color called Flamingo Pink. Isn't that funny, Daddy, like a pink flamingo from one my jungle books. Casey got Passion Purple. Show my Dad your nails, Casey."

Soon the rest of the girls came over to show Eddie their manicures. Eddie gave each girl an equal amount of compliments and they all seemed very satisfied with his positive reaction. The girls took little Joey by the hand and got in line at the counter to decide what kind of ice-cream concoction they all wanted.

When the girls moved away, Eddie looked at his wife for the first time. Clare was standing in the corner staring icily at him. *What's with that face,* thought Eddie looking down at his Franck Muller watch. *I told her I'd be here at three. I'm here.* He smiled at her. Clare's icy stare only got more intense. *Something's not right,* he thought. *Something's out of place.* Confused, his brain shifted images around and after a minute, he realized what was different—Clare's coat. It was like the one he had bought for Audrey in Charleston. *How does Clare have the same coat as*

Audrey? I've never seen her wear it before. When did she get it? The more he looked at the coat, the more certain he was that it was exactly like Audrey's. Clare's stare was somehow connected to the coat. *Did Audrey send her coat here by accident? No, why would she do that? That's Audrey's coat. How the hell did Clare get Audrey's coat? Shit. Clare has Audrey's freaking coat. Clare knows about Audrey. Fuck.*

14

———

Looking anywhere but at each other, Clare and Eddie stewed while sitting on opposite ends of the couch in marriage counselor, Ilene Kostikian's waiting room. A friend of Clare's had gone to Ilene when her marriage hit a rough patch. She had encouraged Clare to make an appointment after she heard what had happened. Thumbing through an old issue of *Outside* magazine that was on the waiting room coffee table, Eddie was drawn to a story about the best ski areas in North America.

I wish I was on the top of a snow-covered mountain right now instead of here, he thought. *I can feel Clare staring at me, but I'm not going to look up.* Continuing to read, another minute passed. With discipline in short supply, he finally turned his head. "What?" he asked, irritation in his voice.

Clare stared at him blankly.

"What?" he repeated, more annoyed.

"How can you read a story about skiing when our marriage is falling apart?"

"What else am I supposed to do? We're in a waiting room. I

didn't know there were waiting-room rules. It was your idea to come here."

"You could talk to me," said Clare.

"I thought the reason we're here is because all of our conversations devolve into arguments. Isn't that what you told me, that we needed a mediator so we could talk to each other?"

"Maybe if you were home more often..."

"Here we go," said Eddie dramatically putting his hands over his eyes.

The door to the back office partially opened and the silver-haired therapist appeared. Ilene Kostikian's generous frame navigated around the half-open door as she stepped into the waiting room. Sticking out a beefy hand for each of them to shake, she invited them back into her private space. The simple room was what one would expect of a therapist's office; white walls, a desk and chair, a small, black leather love seat that faced a matching full-sized sofa. A smattering of framed black-and-white cityscape photographs along with several of Ilene's psychology diplomas adorned the walls. *She went to Cornell,* thought Eddie, as he examined her credentials. *Must mean she's reasonably intelligent and probably expensive.*

Ilene sank into the love seat filling up most of the space and gestured for Clare and Eddie to sit on the facing sofa. They chose opposite ends, as far from each other as possible.

"Eddie, as I'm sure you know, I met with Clare alone yesterday and we determined that it would be helpful for the two of you to come in together," said Ilene. "Clare filled me in on what's been going on over the past couple of years and specifically, what happened last week."

"Thanks for squeezing us into your schedule, Ilene," said Eddie rolling out his charm carpet. "Clare tells me you come highly recommended. I notice you went to Cornell, great school.

Who took all these amazing city shots hanging on your walls? They're excellent."

"I did," said Ilene looking over at the pictures and smiling. "Photography is a little hobby of mine."

"You've got a great eye for light," said Eddie getting up and walking over to a few of the images on the wall. "These are really good. Are they all taken in New York?"

"Stop it," said Clare, loudly jumping into the conversation. "This is what he always does, Ilene. He's trying to win you over. Don't you see? That's the way he operates. Trust me, my husband could teach a master class in charm."

Ilene let out a breath. "Let's focus on why we're all here," she said gently. "Eddie, why don't you tell me what's on your mind."

"I'll own this, Ilene. I royally screwed up," he said, sitting down and looking forlorn. "I was totally in the wrong. No excuses. I didn't appreciate Clare and got too big for my britches, started believing my own press. I don't know why I did what I did, but I regret it with all my heart and it's over. I love my wife and I'll do whatever it takes to build back her trust in me. I know it won't be easy but she's worth it."

"That's a good start," said Ilene with an encouraging smile. "Clare, what do you think about what your husband just said?"

Clare looked over at her husband with tears in her eyes and slowly turned back to Ilene. "It's bullshit."

Squirming on his end of the couch, Eddie looked to Ilene for some help.

"Why do you think it's bullshit?" said Ilene.

"That's his MO. Typical Eddie," said Clare as she narrowed her eyes. "I'm sure he had that nice little speech all prepared so you'd think he was a contrite, dutiful, loving husband who just made a teensy-weensy little mistake. He'd say all the right things so you'd think that I was the one with the problem, that I was some kind of nagging bitch. Then, we'd spend all our time in counseling trying to figure why my behavior drove him to that slut."

"She's not a slut," said Eddie softly.

"Don't you defend her," said Clare loudly.

"Okay, okay," said Ilene raising her hands, "let's all calm down and leave the name-calling at the door. It's unproductive, only fans the flames and will keep us from getting to the important stuff."

Clare and Eddie each released an audible breath.

"Let's go back to Eddie's first statement when he admitted he screwed up and that he regrets his behavior," said Ilene.

"Fine," said Clare.

"That was a great first step," said Ilene, "but my understanding from your wife is that this problem goes much further back than last week. Clare, when did you first feel like there was a distance developing between you two?"

"That's easy," said Clare, "it was when Eddie's career started to take off. That's when I became an afterthought. His job and the people at work were his first priority and I was moved to the back of the line."

"That's not true," said Eddie.

"Let Clare speak," said Ilene.

"He began to treat me like a hired hand. I kept his home clean, popped out a baby or two, had food in the fridge and made sure his shirts went to the laundry. In exchange, he put money in the checking account and I was able to pay all of our bills, just like a caretaker."

"Eddie, what do you think about what Clare just shared?" said Ilene.

Eddie looked down at his lap for ten seconds. When he lifted his head and looked at Ilene there were tears in his eyes. "I didn't know she felt that way," he said softly.

"Tell her, not me," said Ilene.

Eddie cleared his throat and faced his wife. "I didn't know you felt like that. I didn't mean to make you feel that way. I love you with all my heart."

Ilene smiled at him. "That was very good, Eddie. Clare, what do you think about his admission?"

"I don't know. How do I know he really means it?"

"I meant it," Eddie blurted out.

"How do I know it's not just another Eddie Gamble performance?" said Clare.

For the next forty-five minutes, Ilene helped the couple dig deep to where the problems had begun and discussed what Eddie needed to do to rebuild their relationship and regain Clare's trust.

For the next few months, Clare and Eddie attended weekly appointments with Ilene. The sessions unearthed a lot of previously unspoken issues.

"Sometimes, I'd get home exhausted from a business trip or a hellish day at work and you'd be waiting for me armed with a complaint the minute I walked through the door," said Eddie to his wife in one of their sessions. "No matter what I did, it was never enough."

Clare acknowledged that she, too, had played a role in their marriage problems and admitted that she sometimes could be needy and demanding. She said she often turned her anger inward and worked herself up into a snit before Eddie arrived home.

In the weeks that followed, Clare made a conscious effort to handle things better and not meet Eddie at the door with negativity. He in turn took responsibility for being too wrapped up in his work life and not making enough time for his family. Both agreed to work on their own behaviors.

Twelve weeks later, their relationship had seemingly moved to a better place. The changes each of them made started to pay off and things were much better. Eddie made sure he was home several nights a week for dinner, traveled half as much as he had before and spent more time with his kids. He also promised Clare that the affair with Audrey was absolutely over.

The truth was, Eddie hadn't curtailed his relationship with Audrey at all. He just got more creative about where and when he met her. As long as he didn't go to LA, Clare assumed Audrey was out of the picture. Though Audrey and Eddie no longer worked for the same company, Audrey's territory included the entire western portion of the US, western Canada and Mexico. Eddie had clients in those same areas. He and Audrey would meet clients in places like Colorado and go skiing or for a beach weekend in Mexico. Throughout it all, Eddie was torn. He loved his wife and kids but he also loved Audrey and couldn't or wouldn't make a choice. He was so dialed into his own public superstar image that he didn't see why he should have to give up Audrey, so he didn't—until the shit hit the fan.

Audrey and Eddie were staying for three nights at the Four Seasons Hotel in San Francisco. She had appointments during the day and so did he. Audrey had been unusually quiet that first night. They made love and when they finished, she pulled away from his embrace and sat up. "I need to talk to you about something. It's important."

"Okay, what's on your mind?" said Eddie looking at the ceiling with a satisfied post-lovemaking expression on his face.

"Eddie, look at me. This is serious."

He flipped over and faced her, resting his chin on his hand. "I'm all yours."

"Something happened. I took the test."

"What kind of test," said Eddie.

"A pregnancy test. It was positive."

"You're pregnant?"

"Seems so," said Audrey.

"Am I..."

"How can you even ask that? Yes, you're the father."

Eddie's temples started to pulse and he sat up. "How do you know for sure?"

"I know."

"What about your husband?" said Eddie.

"My husband and I almost never have sex. Trust me, it's yours."

"What do you want to do?"

"I love you. I want to marry you and have your baby. I'll divorce Phil and we can be together."

"It's not that simple," said Eddie standing up and reaching for his shirt.

"We love each other. We can make this work, I know we can," said Audrey reaching for him.

Eddie pulled his shorts on and opened a bottle of water. Sitting in a nearby chair, he stared out the window.

"Aren't you going to say anything?" said Audrey.

"I can't get divorced and upend my entire life. I love you but I don't want to leave my kids. I can't do that."

Audrey got up and put on a robe. "Then, what are you proposing?"

"It's complicated. There's my family and Clare's family to consider. Leaving my wife for my former salesperson wouldn't be good for my career, or yours for that matter," said Eddie.

Audrey started to cry. "I don't care about my husband. I love you and this is *our* child. Are you saying you don't want our baby?"

"It's not that I don't want it; these are untenable circumstances," said Eddie. "I have a wife and two children. I just can't."

Tears ran down Audrey's face.

"I'll pay for everything, and I'll even come with you," said Eddie.

"Well, thanks so much for that," said Audrey bitterly.

For hours they went around and around, neither moving from their original position. It was nearly four in the morning when they finally fell asleep. Waking at eight thirty and still angry, Eddie and Audrey dressed for their meetings. As Audrey zipped up her skirt and gathered her things she gave it one more shot. "Is that your final answer? You're not leaving your wife?"

"That's my final answer," said Eddie now annoyed that Audrey was still pushing the issue. "You knew what the parameters of our relationship were when we started. You knew I was married. I knew you were married. I never suggested it was going to be more than that."

"I didn't know I was going to fall in love with you," said Audrey. "I guess the joke's on me."

"This has nothing to do with me loving you. I do love you and I told you I'd go with you and pay for it."

"I can't do this anymore. I actually thought you were the one," said Audrey as she opened the door and walked out for the last time. She never spoke to Eddie again. He tried calling and left messages but she never picked up.

"Hey Audrey, it's me. I know this whole thing has been awful. I want to be there for you but you leaving your family and me leaving mine isn't the solution. So many people would get hurt."

After weeks of soul-searching, Audrey terminated the pregnancy and sent Eddie an email with only one sentence.

YOU'RE OFF THE HOOK.

When Eddie got Audrey's email he felt guilty in his core and promised himself he was going to mend his ways.

15

The sweet and toasty aroma of pancakes Clare had on the griddle wafted up the stairs and into the master bedroom. Standing in front of a full-length mirror, Eddie adjusted his favorite red-and-blue paisley tie. It had been carefully paired with his favorite white shirt, the one with the French cuffs. He reached for his Cartier gold-knot cufflinks and put them on. He wanted to look especially good that day. It was his one-year anniversary at *American Traveler* and the head of HR, Andrea Marchetti, had asked him to meet her for lunch. It was unilaterally acknowledged in the industry that Eddie had an extraordinary first year at Fleming Global Media. He was considered the "one to watch". Eddie took one last look in the mirror, smoothed his hair and smiled. Life was sweet.

In the last twelve months he had achieved all of his professional goals. In one year's time, advertising revenue at *AT* had grown over eight percent under his leadership. He had fired all the laggards and hired some of the best people in the business which resulted in a solid and stellar sales and marketing team who had made sales magic happen. No other magazine or website in the building had grown as much as *American Traveler* that year.

The media press had also noticed Eddie's achievements and he was regularly featured and quoted. *The New York Times* had mentioned him twice and the *Wall Street Journal* once. *Not too shabby,* he thought after the third mention. His first year at *American Traveler*, the sun shone on him so brightly it practically burned his eyes.

Everything he touched at *AT* turned to gold. He even met his lofty circulation targets for the magazine and website. A huge part of Eddie's overall success and compensation was tied to *American Traveler* revenue surpassing *Vacation* and he had done it.

There was a little spring in his step as he went down the stairs and into the kitchen that morning. Sarah and Joey were seated at the table eating their pancakes before getting dressed for school.

"I could smell those when I was in the shower," said Eddie grabbing a pancake off the plate and stuffing it into his mouth. "Delish."

"Why don't you sit down and have breakfast with the kids," said Clare removing the last pancake from the griddle.

"No time," he said with a full mouth as he reached for his work satchel.

"Daddy, it's not polite to talk with your mouth full," said Sarah emphatically.

Eddie smiled at his daughter as he swallowed the last bit of pancake. "You caught me, Sarah," he said as he tousled her hair. "You're absolutely right. Talking with your mouth full *is* disgusting. I promise, I won't do it again."

"Do it again," chirped Joey with a big grin on his face from the other side of the table.

"No, he will not," said Clare, laughing along with her husband.

"Are you going to be away this weekend, Daddy?" said Sarah. "Can you come to my soccer game?"

"I would love to come to your soccer game this weekend, Miss Sarah," said her father. "You've got a date." Sarah smiled and took another forkful of her pancakes. Joey, covered in syrup, started to get up from his chair.

"Joey, do not move. You're a massive sticky mess," said Eddie as Clare wet a paper towel to clean off her son.

"I may be late tonight," Eddie said as he reached for his phone and jacket.

"But you're home for the weekend, right," said Clare while mopping down her son.

"Absolutely, didn't you hear? Sarah and I just made a soccer date for tomorrow," he said, winking at his daughter. "I guess you forgot what today is."

"It's Friday," said Sarah. Puzzled, Clare looked at her husband.

"It's my one-year anniversary at *American Traveler*," said Eddie.

"I can't believe it's been a year already," said his wife. "The time flew."

"I'm having lunch with the head of HR and it's possible that someone may want to take me out for a drink after work to celebrate," he said. "Just wanted to give you the heads-up in an effort to be transparent like Ilene has told us to do."

"Who's Ilene?" said Sarah.

"Nobody you know," said Clare quickly. "Sarah, go upstairs and get changed for school."

"This weekend will be a family weekend," proclaimed Eddie. "How about I cook tomorrow night? I'll make my famous sausage and peppers."

Clare smiled. "If I don't have to cook, you could make peanut butter and jelly sandwiches and I'd be happy. Sausage and peppers sounds great."

Eddie returned her smile, grabbed his bag, kissed his wife and Sarah goodbye and walked out the door to the waiting town car in the driveway.

"Morning, Eddie," said his regular driver. "Happy anniversary."

Eddie grinned as he shut the car door. "How did you know it was my anniversary?"

"You told me last week."

Clare watched her husband's limousine pull out of their drive and thought how they had just had such a nice, normal breakfast. *He was old Eddie this morning*, she thought, *the man I married*. While cleaning up the breakfast dishes, her mind floated back to their college years.

They had met briefly on campus and run into each other at a party later that weekend. When she and some friends first walked into the party, Eddie was running the room doing shots of tequila with a bunch of other guys. Right away she recognized him across the very crowded and smoky room. She heard him shout "score" and everyone around the table tilted back their shot glasses, drank, cheered and then slammed their glasses on the table.

"One more time," shouted Eddie with a wicked smile holding his empty glass high in the air. Another round was poured and a second shot consumed by all. Eddie was the mayor, the center of attention, but in a good way. It wasn't because he demanded it, he was simply more fun and charismatic than anyone else and everyone wanted to be around him. Clare observed him from the sidelines, listening to his comments and watching the reaction of other people. They initially gravitated to him because he was fun, but they kept coming back because of his big heart. She wasn't sure why she knew it, she just did. The cute guy with the dimples leading the rounds of shots cared about all of them and people instinctually knew it. When the drinking game was over, Eddie looked around the large room and spotted Clare. He smiled at her, as if he expected she'd be there.

Later that night, Clare and Eddie shared a beer outside on the stoop. By the end of that first night, they were finishing each other's sentences. After that, for the remainder of college, they were never apart. Back then, Eddie at the center of the crowd fascinated and awed the quiet, understated, Clare. He was an extrovert and she was most definitely an introvert. His antics and larger-than-life personality took the spotlight off her so she could enjoy the party and bask in his glow.

Clare wiped the last bits of syrup off of the table and wondered how the hell she and her college sweetheart had grown so far apart.

Eddie's town car wound its way through the New York City streets and pulled up in front of the Fleming Global Media building just before 9am.

"Have a great anniversary day," said his driver as Eddie got out of the car.

"I intend to. You have yourself a nice weekend," said Eddie with a smile. "See ya Monday morning."

Before he walked through the revolving doors of FGM, Eddie watched his limousine pull away and took the moment to consider his incredibly wonderful life. Smiling as he crossed through the lobby headed towards the elevators, he passed Jonathan Barker, enfant terrible of media, who had recently parted ways with Andover to take a senior vice president role at FGM.

"Gamble," said Barker with his nasal Aussie twang. "Heard today's your one-year anniversary."

"That's right," said Eddie, enjoying the recognition. "Good news travels fast."

"I've heard they've got something extra special planned for you to commemorate the occasion," said Barker with a wicked smile.

"Yeah?" said Eddie raising an eyebrow. "Like what?"

"Aww, I wouldn't want to spoil your big surprise, Gamble. I'll wager to say, it'll take your breath away," said Barker as he got on his elevator. "Good luck to ya, mate."

As Eddie waited for his elevator, he wondered what kind of festivities had been planned. Walking through the halls of *American Traveler*, everything was eerily quiet. The receptionist and a few of his sales people waved to him as he passed, nothing was out of the ordinary. *Maybe it's going to be at my lunch with HR,* he thought as he sat down at his desk, opened his computer and ticked through his nearly 100 new emails.

After several meetings, the last with an events planner who was putting together a big client extravaganza for *AT,* it was lunchtime. Andrea Marchetti had asked him to meet in her office before they went to lunch. Promptly at 12:45pm, a smiling Eddie knocked on the white molding of Andrea's open doorway.

"I believe we have a lunch date," said Eddie flashing the Gamble grin.

Andrea looked up from her computer and let out a long slow breath. "Eddie, would you come in and have a seat for a moment. I need to discuss something with you."

"Sure," said Eddie still smiling while taking a seat. "What's up?"

"It's not my call. This is coming from the top," said Andrea. "I'm just going to tell you straight out. Mr. Fleming doesn't think you're the right fit for us. He wants this to be your last day at FGM."

"What? I don't understand," said Eddie leaning forward. "Is this a joke? Today's my one-year anniversary. We're supposed to be celebrating. This is a joke, right?"

"I'm afraid not," said Andrea nervously.

"I'm crushing it at *AT*. Ad revenue is up. Circulation is up. Morale is up. Everybody's making money. Especially FGM. This has to be some kind of misunderstanding."

"I'm sorry. I don't have any further explanation for you," said Andrea. "As you probably know, New York is a 'hire at will' state and Mr. Fleming simply doesn't think you are the right fit for FGM."

"This is insane. I've surpassed *all* of my target goals. You can't do this," said Eddie starting to raise his voice. "I have a signed contract."

"Yes, and your contract expired yesterday," said Andrea looking a bit pale.

Eddie was incredulous. "I've done everything that was asked of me and more. This is so messed up. You know it and I know it. I want to speak to Bob Fleming right now."

"I'm afraid that's impossible."

"You can't do this to me. I'm calling my lawyer."

"I would advise you not to do that," Andrea continued, "We have far more resources than you and frankly, anyone who's tried in the past has gone bankrupt from the legal costs alone."

"What is happening here? This makes no sense."

"Let's put it this way," said Andrea choosing her words carefully, "Mr. Fleming and Mr. Andover go way back. They were on the same rowing team at Harvard."

16

If you ended up working at Diamond International, for all intents and purposes, your career was pretty much over. "The DI" as it was referred to in the business was without question at the very bottom of the media and publishing barrel. Like the schlocky tabloids and websites they owned and operated, their employees looked like residents of the *Island of Misfit Toys*. Salaries were significantly below the industry average, and most of the management treated the staff like indentured servants. The only reason anyone worked there was because they couldn't get a job anywhere else. Eddie knew that. Everyone in the media business knew that Diamond was the proverbial "end of the line".

Over the years, Eddie and his colleagues had often joked that the employees at the DI were the personification of the inscription on the Statue of Liberty. "Give me your tired, your poor, your huddled masses yearning to breathe free, the wretched refuse of your teeming shore..." What ended up on the shores of Diamond International were essentially media refugees. People who had nowhere else to go. The place was filled with older, slower people who had essentially given up and had little to no enthusiasm for their jobs. A number of them appeared to have personality disorders and various addictions which precluded employment elsewhere. Some of them had started their careers at prestigious media companies like Andover or Fleming but through a series of unfortunate events had ended up at Diamond.

There was a strange phenomenon with the people who took their first steps into the DI. Most selectively forgot that they were walking into the belly of an incredibly mediocre beast. Once they checked in, they never checked out because there was truly no place else to go. They never left—unless they were forced out. In short, the DI was a media graveyard.

A year after being fired from Fleming Global Media, despite working every contact he had and every angle he could think of, Eddie had been unable to land another job. He secured a few small consulting projects but with the bills piling up from his big new house, two luxury cars, and expensive private schools for the kids, Eddie started to panic. In the year he had been unemployed, they had burned through a fair amount of their savings and started using one credit card to pay off another.

Relentless in his pursuit of another position, Eddie had knocked on every door in New York, but found them all tightly shut. Given the circumstances of his departure from Andover, he understood why they didn't want to talk to him, but his abrupt firing from Fleming Global Media was still a mystery. What he couldn't figure out was why every other media company in the city wasn't interested in talking to him. What precipitated his fall from grace eluded him and no matter how many people he asked, no one had any answers. If they did, they weren't talking. He'd even gone after lower-level jobs and senior sales positions but none of them ever gelled.

Reluctantly, he pushed through the revolving doors of the

DI. *It's only temporary,* he told himself. *Need to get back in the game. Six months at Diamond and I'm out of here.*

He'd never been inside the Diamond International building before. This was the last place someone like him wanted to be seen. Still, there he was walking down the hallway to meet the in-house recruiter. He noticed a markedly different vibe there than at *American Traveler* or *Vacation.* Those companies had an optimistic buzz one could feel. Phones ringing, people moving briskly from one meeting to the next. Everyone dressed to the nines, talking fast, trading quips, smiling. They were glamorous beehives. The DI building was quiet and people moved lethargically. No one talked to anyone else and if they did, it was only to pass on required business information with no sense of joy or accomplishment or any interpersonal interest. The employees of the DI methodically plodded through their day waiting for 5pm to appear on the clock. Even though it was morning, Eddie sensed the vast majority of Diamond employees were already waiting for the clock to strike five. *This place is like hell,* he thought, *but, it's only temporary.*

Seated in a small conference room half listening to an HR manager wearing an ill-fitting suit, Eddie assumed the middle-aged man had recently gained twenty or thirty pounds. The buttons down the front of his shirt strained to stay inside of the buttonholes, his yellowed undershirt was visible through the gaps. *Note to self, gain fifteen pounds—buy bigger shirts.*

The HR manager prattled in monotone about the wonderful work ethic at the DI under the leadership of CEO, Kenneth Leach. He shared info about some of their recent acquisitions and talked about the chief revenue officer role they had in mind for Eddie at *The National Spectator.* While the man wearing the shirt whose buttons were about to pop extolled the many wonders of *The National Spectator* editorial product, Eddie was puzzled and stunned. *Is he talking about The National Spectator?*

You'd think he was describing The Economist, as opposed to that slimy, politically-incorrect, conspiracy-theory supermarket D-List celebrity rag.

Everyone knew Ken Leach settled scores on the front page of the *Spectator* while he pushed his right-wing extremist agenda. It was common knowledge. *It's a job,* Eddie told himself, *it's only temporary. The National Spectator readers may be dim-witted and mentally unstable but they still buy cars, paper towels and nail polish. I can still sell advertising to Honda, P&G and Revlon.* Lost in his own inner dialogue, Eddie realized that the HR director had stopped talking and was waiting for Eddie to respond. It was showtime. For the next fifteen minutes, Eddie outlined his previous accomplishments while occasionally flashing the Gamble grin and dimples for added effect. He knew his pitch was working when the HR manager smiled and nodded at everything Eddie said. *I've still got it,* Eddie thought.

"Well," said the manager as he stood up and shook Eddie's hand, "I had heard great things about you and you didn't disappoint. You've had a remarkable career and I'm sure Ken Leach would like you. I've got Ken's calendar and I'd like to get you in to see him sometime later this week."

When Eddie's meeting was over and a second appointment with the CEO was on the books, he went directly to a newsstand and bought a copy of every tabloid in *The National Spectator's* competitive space to prep for his meeting with the notoriously dreadful Kenneth Leach. As he pawed through the various magazines and tabloids he'd occasionally be drawn in by some outlandish headline and found himself sucked into some of the articles. "Woman Gives Birth to Litter of Puppies" and "Princess Diana Still Alive Living on Secret Caribbean Island" were two that caught his eye. *Who the hell believes this crap? Idiots. But, idiots still buy and consume products.*

He had never looked at any of the DI brands before and was

surprised to see that their low-brow tabloids carried a ton of advertising. He knew most of the advertisers from his previous positions and figured he could do this job with his eyes closed. Before his meeting with Leach, Eddie spent a few days poring through their advertisers. He put together charts and ad spend within each advertising category and crafted a three-, six- and twelve-month plan for blowing the doors off *The National Spectator*'s ad budget.

On the morning of his interview with Leach, Eddie woke up extra early to give himself plenty of time to get into the city by public transportation. With no company town car waiting for him in the driveway, he'd have to bus it into New York City just like every other poor slob in the metro New York area. Still in bed, the faint sound of Clare snoring softly next to him made him turn his head and look at her. *She hasn't aged a bit since college,* he thought. *Still has that quiet beauty.* For a fleeting moment he wondered why he hadn't been more faithful to her. Why he sought out other women besides his wonderful wife. He didn't know the answer and it made him uncomfortable to think about it so he pushed it out of his head. Today was his interview with Ken Leach so he focused on that and went into the bathroom to shave.

When he emerged fifteen minutes later, Clare was no longer in bed and he heard rumbling and banging coming from the kitchen downstairs. Since the "green coat incident" things had never been the same. Working with the marriage counselor had helped for a while but once Eddie lost his job and they lost their health insurance, the cost of counseling became prohibitive. They had both crossed over a precarious relationship bridge and when they tried to go back to the other side, it seemed impossible.

Clare only spoke to him about household- or kid-related things like which bills she would pay first or what the dentist said about Sarah's teeth. All other topics of conversation between them had ceased. At first it bothered him when Clare pulled further away. He tried to engage with her but after dozens of attempts were rebuked he finally stopped. *She'll get over it,* he told himself. *After I get this CRO job at Diamond, I'll concentrate on Clare and the kids. She's still mad. I get it. I was pretty awful. I'll get this job and then I'll spend more time with my family. I'll make it up to her.*

He adjusted his tie and took one last look at himself in the bedroom mirror. *Sharp,* he thought. *You're going to blow Leach away.* He smiled in an attempt to convince himself it was true and walked down the stairs and into the kitchen. Packing school lunches, Clare looked up as Eddie reached for the coffee pot and grabbed a banana.

"I've got my big interview with Diamond this morning. I have a good feeling."

"You must have me confused with someone who gives a shit."

"It affects you, too," said Eddie.

"Whatever."

"We can't keep going on like this. Ilene told us we had to call a truce if we want to rebuild our relationship."

"Who said I wanted to rebuild?" said Clare, a look of disgust across her pretty face.

"You did. We both did."

"No, only you did," said Clare. "But what you really meant was, you wanted things to go back to the way they were before I got that slut's coat in the mail. Back to when you had me tucked in at home like a housekeeper. I took care of your kids and did your laundry while you galivanted around the world wining, dining and fucking whomever you pleased. You'd stop by the house every few weeks to get a change of clothes. For a few minutes you'd play Daddy and pat me on the head. Why would I want to rebuild that farce? Our marriage was a joke. It only worked for one of us and it wasn't me."

"I can't do this right now. I don't know what you want. I've got this interview today and..."

"You know what I want?" said Clare, her voice getting louder, "I want the man I married instead of some cheap imitation." Turning abruptly, she walked out of the room and up the stairs calling for the kids to hurry up or they'd be late for school.

What the hell just happened? Eddie thought. *She pulls this crap today when I've got my big interview?* Blood pumped through his veins and his heart beat through his chest and he started to get angry. *I need to keep my head clear.* He took a few deep breaths in through the nose and blew out through his mouth and calmed himself down.

"Shitty timing as usual, Clare," he yelled into the empty room as he walked out the back door slamming it behind him.

"I hope you bomb," shouted Clare from the top of the stairs.

"Who are you talking to, Mommy?"

Clare spun around. Joey, still in his pajamas stood behind her looking up.

"No one, honey. Just talking to myself, again."

Two hours later, Eddie was seated in a chair outside Ken Leach's office trying to psych himself up. *You can do this. You're a superstar. You were the associate publisher of* Vacation *and the publisher of* American Traveler. *You broke all kinds of records. Andover gave you the Top Grossing Newcomer Award. Diamond is a total dumpster fire compared to Andover and Fleming. They should be down on their knees thanking God I'd agree to work here. I could do this job with my eyes closed. I'll whip National Spectator into shape and bring in business Ken Leach never dreamed of.*

"Mr. Gamble," said Leach's assistant softly, "Mr. Leach is ready for you now."

Flashing the Gamble grin, causing the assistant to blush, he walked confidently into Leach's office and shook his hand. It was well known throughout the industry that Kenneth Leach was a difficult and unpleasant man. Often described as someone who "sucks the air out of a room", and a compulsive liar, Leach was a blowhard and viewed by nearly everyone to be a "massive dick".

While Leach was generally considered an awful human being, he could also give a master class in the art of laying on the charm to get what he wanted. He regularly told stories about himself that were simply untrue, like how he had gone to medical school before getting into media. He kept the "massive dick" part of his personality under wraps until someone crossed him. When he set his sights on something or someone he wanted, he was as smooth as silk. He wanted Eddie Gamble to be the next CRO of *The National Spectator* so he laid it on thick.

Leach had big plans to upgrade his senior management team by filling it with higher caliber people. He'd been tracking Eddie's meteoric career at Andover and Fleming and had followed his revenue numbers in the trades. He knew Eddie had created double digits year-over-year growth at two of the topmost competitive companies and he wanted him to do the same at Diamond International. Leach dished out the compliments like warm maple syrup dripping over a hot stack of waffles, liquid sweetness seeping into every crevice before it soaked in.

By the end of the meeting, the two men had struck a deal and an offer was extended. Each got what they thought they wanted. Eddie got a CRO title running a national sales team and Leach got his own personal velvet hammer who had extensive relationships in the ad business and a track record for growth. Eddie's Diamond International compensation package wasn't anything close to what he'd been making at his previous companies. There were no limousines, gym or golf club memberships but still, it was a senior management job even if it was at the worst company in the business.

During their meeting, Leach disclosed that morale at Diamond was at an all-time low and it had to be remedied or he was going to lose people. "You have a reputation for being an even-tempered, positive leader, not a divider. You're someone who brings people together. That's exactly the kind of leadership the *Spectator* needs right now," said Leach. The caustic CEO may have been a pathological liar and a bully but he was aware of his own strengths and weaknesses. He wasn't going to change so he simply hired cheerleaders and buffers between him and the rest of his company. He had to or he wouldn't have any employees at all. Well aware that he was a nasty piece of work and rather proud of that fact, Leach spent his career surrounding himself with nicer guys to mitigate his own demon angels. Leach had heard the rumors that were still circulating about Eddie's previous unethical behavior but it didn't concern him at all. He kind of liked it.

When Eddie got home to New Jersey late that afternoon, Clare was in the kitchen when he walked through the door. She looked at her husband, his face was slack. *He didn't get it,* she thought. Eddie stared at her for a moment and then pulled a bottle of champagne from his bag.

"You got it?"

"I got it," he said with a grin.

"Then, I'm glad for you," said Clare with little emotion.

After dinner, when the kids had settled in the family room to watch a show on TV, Eddie uncorked the champagne, poured two glasses and sat next to Clare at the kitchen table. He told her about his conversation with Leach and the lofty goals they had for him.

"It's going to be an intense first year," said Eddie building up steam. "I'll have to mine every relationship that I've ever had.

The luxury brands won't run in a supermarket tabloid, but I've still got friends at mainstream companies like Toyota and American Airlines. I can get them in. I know I can."

"You think you can get Toyota or American Airlines to run in *The National Spectator*? Why would they want their brands in that sleazy rag?" said Clare, starting to clean up the dinner plates.

Eddie sat back and peered at his wife. "Would be nice to get a little support," he said, bristling. "I came home with great news. When did you become the advertising expert?"

"I'm not, but I am a consumer," said Clare getting up from the table now that the conversation had gotten chilly.

"I can make it happen," said Eddie with bravado. "Leach said I 'bring class to the company'. People who read the *Spectator* buy cars and take trips too. It's all in the way you couch it. I'll show advertisers how the *Spectator* can help their company expand their customer base. I've got a whole idea for a marketing and promo program that will knock their socks off."

"Whatever you say," said a weary Clare.

"And what are you saying? That I work for a shit brand? That I'm a loser?" said Eddie as he stood, a scowl on his face.

"You've had a lot of jobs over the last few years," said Clare.

"It's called a career, Clare, something you know nothing about," said Eddie over his shoulder as he walked out of the room taking a swig out of the bottle of champagne.

17

While giving his inaugural speech to the advertising team in *The National Spectator* conference room, it was painfully evident to Eddie that he hadn't inherited the B-team. In his estimation, the motley crew in front of him was, at best, a D-team. Despite his concerns about the quality of the staff, the battle-scarred employees around the table warmed to his inspiring words. There had been a string of incompetent and abusive publishers prior to Eddie's arrival and their new boss was a welcome change.

"I've read all of your personnel files: you're a very impressive group," said Eddie. "I have tremendous respect for each and every one of you and the experience you bring to the party. Together, we'll take *The National Spectator* to new heights of media success."

Everyone had applauded.

"And listen up," said Eddie with a devilish smile, "we're going to have fun while we do it. No reason we can't enjoy ourselves while getting the job done, right? All I ask is that each one of you be smart about your business. Do your very best and enjoy yourselves while we take over this town."

The room full of grateful employees broke into applause and cheers. When Eddie flashed the full Gamble grin replete with dimples and a wink for emphasis, the crowd swooned. Several of the staff wondered what it would be like to sleep with him. The rest wanted to hang out with him after work and have a beer. Eddie was a hit.

As the months went by, his consistent attention to every member of the staff made each of them feel like maybe, they weren't such losers after all. They all began to stand taller and try harder—for him.

Soon Eddie's predictions came true. Ten months after he took over at the *Spectator,* revenue numbers were way up and Ken Leach congratulated himself for hiring Eddie Gamble. With an eighteen-month corporate strategy plan in place, Eddie and his team were charged with breaking a specific list of major accounts, increasing revenue by thirty percent and growing the circulation.

Under Eddie's leadership, his team hit all their goals—except for one. Leach had been very clear during the hiring process, Eddie's success and tenure was dependent upon him meeting *all* the goals. In addition to his monetary objectives, Eddie was also expected to create huge buzzworthy events around the *Spectator* to increase circulation at the newsstand and in supermarkets. It was a tall order for a publication that most considered a rag.

"I'm confident I can grow the circulation," Eddie had said to Ken Leach during his interview. "It will take some creativity and a fair amount of elbow grease, but I'll make it happen."

"I'm glad you're so confident," Leach had said with one eyebrow raised, "because boosting circulation is one of the main reasons I just made you the offer. Don't fuck it up, Gamble."

Eddie had a modicum of experience growing circulation at Andover and Fleming having worked closely with both company's circulation departments. He figured he'd recreate the steps he'd taken at his previous jobs and it should work for the *Spectator*. Still, he'd need a little luck on his side. *The National Spectator* was a completely different animal than *American Traveler* or *Vacation*. He had his work cut out for him.

As soon as his Diamond International health insurance kicked in, Clare insisted they resume counseling sessions with Ilene Kostikian. The first few meetings were somewhat productive but on their fourth session, Eddie started out making small talk and trying to charm the therapist. Rolling her eyes as each patronizing sentence dripped out of Eddie's mouth, Clare got angry.

Sensing some hostility in the room, Ilene turned to Clare. "Last time we met, you said sometimes you felt like a single mother. You mentioned Eddie wasn't home much and when he was, that he was emotionally unavailable. Do you want to talk a little more about that?"

"Not really," said Clare looking away.

"As I recall," said Ilene, "you said Eddie was more open and present when he was out of work, is that right?" Clare nodded. "But if I heard you correctly, when he started working again, the distance between you returned." Clare nodded a second time.

"Look," said Eddie with a smile, "I know I've been working crazy hours and the burden of the house and the kids falls on you. In another six months, after I hit all my goals at Diamond, I promise, everything will quiet down and I'll focus on our marriage and the kids."

"How do you feel about that, Clare?" said Ilene.

"I've seen this movie before. My life stays on hold until Eddie's next career goal is met."

"That's not fair," said Eddie. "I do it all for you and the kids."

"Give me a break," said Clare letting out an obviously phony laugh. The husband and wife traded barbs for the remaining five minutes of the session until Ilene finally stopped them.

"I know this may sound a bit cliché but it works. Start having date nights," said Ilene. "What kind of food do you like, Clare?"

"French," said Clare looking into space, still fuming.

"Perfect. Get a sitter, get dressed up and the two of you go out for a romantic dinner at some expensive French bistro," said Ilene. "Get to know each other again as Eddie and Clare, not the mom and the executive—leave those people at home. Can you try that?"

Clare and Eddie nodded with skepticism. "We don't have any plans this weekend," said Clare. "I could try to find a sitter for Saturday night.

"All right then," said the therapist, "start this weekend. I look forward to hearing all about it at our next session."

As the couple walked to their car in silence, Eddie remembered he was supposed to fly to San Francisco on Saturday. He looked over at his wife who half-smiled at him as she got into the passenger seat. *I'll change my flight and go on Sunday*, he decided.

Over the next few months Eddie paid more attention to Clare. He shortened some of his trips and made a point of bringing her little gifts each week. When he did have to travel, he made sure flowers were delivered to the house while he was gone. He also built in more time for the kids on the weekends and kept up with their "date nights". His obvious effort went a long way with Clare and soon she was a little hopeful that maybe they could get back to where they used to be.

At work, Leach was breathing hard down Eddie's neck. After increasing *The National Spectator* ad revenue by twenty percent that first year, Leach only demanded more for the second year.

Year two he expected Eddie to bring in an additional ten percent.

Required to squeeze blood from a stone, Eddie did what he did best—schmooze. He upped his entertaining and hit the road, traveling to the magazine's outside offices for a sales-call blitz. Face-to-face contact, a handshake and a hug was how Eddie Gamble closed deals. It meant time away from his family, and came at an inopportune time for him and Clare, but it couldn't be helped. Eventually, Eddie's strategy started paying off and the ad dollars started rolling in.

Growing *National Spectator*'s circulation was a different and more challenging problem. No matter how many new distribution deals Eddie and his circulation team instituted, the increase in the *Spectator*'s readership was negligible. Rumor on the street was that Leach was looking around for Eddie's replacement. With his head on the chopping block, Eddie panicked.

Growing a magazine's circulation is no simple task. You couldn't sweet-talk your way in or buy someone lunch to build a larger circulation. Each additional pair of eyeballs were directly tied to a publication's overall profitability. Eddie's employment agreement with Diamond stipulated he make *The National Spectator* the number-one tabloid in terms of circulation. At the end of his first year, the *Spectator* was still number two. When advertisers only had money for one tabloid, they'd buy the number-one book. Being number two often meant you got nothing. If the *Spectator* was in the number-one position, that would mean a dramatically stronger profit and make Leach's board members extremely happy. When the board was happy, Leach got bigger bonuses and as far as he was concerned, that's all that mattered.

Measuring circulation is a tricky business. The actual number was determined by an outside audit of both mailed subscriptions and newsstand copies. Eddie didn't have much control over subscriptions other than discounting them. Desperate to not lose another job and not given enough time for slow and steady organic growth at the newsstand, he came up with an idea on how to grow newsstand sales—fast. If he did it, he'd be able to increase and manipulate the newsstand numbers practically overnight. It wasn't ethical, but he believed he had little choice because of the impossible goals given to him by his boss. He told himself it was only temporary and as soon as the *Spectator* became the number-one tabloid, he'd take a more legitimate approach. Until then, he'd do whatever it took to keep his job.

The end justifies the means, he told himself on more than one occasion.

Reaching out to his network of contacts, he was soon connected to someone who knew someone else and put his seriously unorthodox plan into action. When everything was ready to go, he called his printer in Des Plaines, Illinois, and upped the tabloid print order by a hundred thousand copies.

"Are you kidding?" said the head of printing production. "You want us to print an extra hundred thousand copies? We haven't had that kind of increase from you guys since I started working here. That's more than twenty years ago. Where's it all coming from? Newsstand or subscription?"

"Newsstand," said Eddie without hesitation.

"How the hell did you do that? Those newsstands are all in cahoots with each other. They're locked up tighter than a gnat's ass. They're like a drug cartel. We've never been able to get them to play ball before."

"There's a new sheriff in town," said Eddie laughing. "Change the print order and take it up by a hundred thousand, partner."

The production manager's surprise at the sudden jump in

the print order wasn't out of line. Everyone in the business knew that the newsstand industry was a fixed racket. The giant global conglomerates that owned them decided how many magazines they would take and sell, not the media companies. Whatever wasn't sold was returned to the publishers and those returns were reflected in the publication's audit which authenticated the magazine's circulation. If those "unsold" magazines weren't returned, they were considered sold. Eddie figured if a hundred thousand extra copies of the *Spectator* weren't returned, but let's say, ended up in a landfill in New Jersey, who would ever know? When the audit happened, it would show those hundred thousand copies as "sold". *I'll only do it long enough to give me time to grow the circulation legitimately,* he told himself.

After locating a small mom-and-pop trucking company based in Teaneck NJ, he hired them to pick up unsold *Spectator* copies from all the New York metro newsstands and dump them in a landfill outside of Newark. With a little creative accounting using the slush fund in his T&E budget, he'd use that money to pay for the missing copies. No one in the Diamond accounting department or Ken Leach would ever be the wiser.

For the first six months, Eddie's illicit circulation scheme went flawlessly. No complaints from the newsstands and the guys with the trucks experienced no problems dumping the issues into the open garbage pit. Even the printer in Illinois was thrilled to be printing more issues, because it meant more money for his company. In a short period of time, Eddie had single-handedly made *The National Spectator* the number-one tabloid in America. The trade press took notice and started calling the *Spectator* the "Queen of the Sheets". When Leach's board congratulated the CEO on a job well done, his bonus was assured, and he put a hold on replacing Eddie.

18

With the *Spectator's* circulation humming along, Eddie focused his energy on bringing in more ad dollars. He hosted massive *Spectator* events around the country creating a higher profile for the brand. That effort required a lot of late nights and amped up his business travel.

Trish Gordon, his old client and occasional "side-chick", had switched agencies and moved off the Chandler Hotels and L'Beau business. She was now responsible for placing all the media for one of the largest mass skincare lines in America. The brand was a perfect fit with the demographics of the *Spectator* reader and Eddie happily rekindled his "friendship" with her. Spending one night a week with Trish while garnering millions in ad revenue for his company was a small price to pay—and truthfully, he really liked her. She in turn enjoyed having the charming media powerhouse with the dimples in her bed. Everyone got what they wanted—except for Clare.

Eventually, Eddie was back to his old ways, getting cocky and sloppy as people who live large often do. One night, after a meal of Mexican takeout and countless shots of tequila at Trish's place, they moved on to cocaine. Eddie had gotten a small vial from one of his vendors as a token of their appreciation. He had tried coke a few times before but as time went on, he liked it more and more. He always brought a little with him on the nights he spent with Trish considering it money well spent. If coke was what floated Trish Gordon's boat, then that's what he'd bring. As long as her ad budgets kept funneling money into his company, he'd entertain her in any way she wanted.

Soon, Eddie had several "Trishes" in different parts of the country sending their media budgets his way. There was the older single woman named Laurie in San Francisco who ran all the media for a major Japanese car company. Never married and at least ten years older than Eddie, she took good care of herself and in his estimation, still looked pretty hot. Each time he traveled to the west coast, he took Laurie out for a romantic dinner, including expensive bottles of wine. Charming the hell out of her, he'd invite her to spend the night in his hotel room as if it had just occurred to him. She'd pretend to be surprised but always accepted.

Carmen, his married female client in Miami, placed all the media for a large cruise line. In an unhappy marriage, Carmen looked forward to the evenings with the dashing publisher from New York. Eddie scheduled his trips to Miami whenever Carmen's husband would be out of town. During the days, he made sales calls with his Florida rep and at night Carmen would be waiting for him in his hotel room. They'd do a few lines of coke, go out for drinks and dinner and later tumble into bed. It suited both of them and Eddie's business was better than ever.

That second year, *The National Spectator* sponsored the first "Celebrity Charity Ball". The event was structured to raise money for twenty celebrities' pet charities. In exchange for his company hosting the event, the twenty celebrities agreed to attend the ball and participate in all the publicity surrounding it. The public could buy tickets and rub elbows with their favorite movie star and the advertisers got the rub off from the celebrities. It had all been Eddie's idea and the DI brass was impressed.

A couple of years passed and Eddie was back on stage sitting on industry panels giving his insights on the state of the media business; people wanted his opinion. He was a player again. The constant merry-go-round of work, booze, drugs, late nights and clandestine romantic rendezvous had worked well for him for over two years. He was firing on all cylinders and things had turned out better than he had dreamed.

Though he had fallen back into the pattern of rarely being home or seeing his wife and kids, he justified his absence because the money and bonuses kept pouring in. Like Ken Leach, money justified a lot of things for a lot of people.

He was out in Detroit and had just finished a presentation at GM when he got a call from Ken Leach.

"Ken," said Eddie loudly as he walked to his car in the parking lot with his Detroit rep, "we just killed it at GM. I was about to call you to tell you the good news. You must have ESP."

"I need you back to New York for a meeting tomorrow morning," said Leach. "Cut the trip short and get a flight out tonight."

"No problem," said Eddie. "The main reason I was here was for GM. The other meetings aren't as important. I'll be there tomorrow morning."

When he landed in Newark that evening he picked up some flowers to bring to Clare. He figured walking in with flowers would make his first evening at home in weeks more pleasant. *Can't hurt to grease the wheels with some petunias,* he thought.

Both Clare and the kids were surprised when Eddie opened the front door.

"Daddy," five-year-old Joey shouted as he jumped up from

the dinner table and ran to greet his father. Eddie picked up his son and gave him a bear hug.

"How you doing, amigo? Did you get bigger since I last saw you?" said Eddie with a wink. "What are they feeding you around here?"

"Hi Daddy," said Sarah, coyly standing by the stairs. Eddie walked over to his daughter while still holding Joey and put his free arm around her shoulders giving her a squeeze.

"I think you got bigger too, Sarah," said Eddie.

"You always say that, Daddy," said Sarah.

"What are you now, about thirteen or fourteen?" Eddie joked.

"She's nine," said Joey correcting his father.

"I knew that," said Eddie, winking at his daughter.

"What are you doing home?" said Clare from the kitchen doorway. "You weren't supposed to be back until Thursday."

For a second, Eddie thought he detected irritation in her voice. "I brought these for you," he said, presenting the flowers and a bottle of wine. "I thought we could have some wine with dinner tonight."

"We've already eaten," said Clare, "I didn't expect you home. I've got a sitter coming. I have my book club tonight. You should have called." She turned and walked back into the kitchen.

"Nice to see you too," said Eddie looking down at Joey and Sarah.

"Well kids, looks like it's going to be just the three of us tonight. Mommy has *her book club,*" he said in a persnickety voice. "Clare," he shouted into the air, "cancel the sitter, the kids and I can manage on our own."

That night Eddie cracked open the bottle of wine and he and his kids played board games until it was time for them to go to bed. After he read them bedtime stories and they were tucked in, Eddie went downstairs and opened a second bottle of wine and leaned back on the couch to watch the news. He couldn't remember the last time he had been alone in his house just watching TV. The truth was, he couldn't remember the last time he'd been home at all. *It's nice,* he thought, *I should do this "home thing" more often.*

It wasn't long before his thoughts drifted from home life to his work and he took a look at his calendar. In two days, he had to give a presentation at one of the big pharmaceutical companies in New Jersey. The pharma was about to launch a blockbuster diabetes medication and was looking for one mass publication as their anchor book, a common practice in the US once restrictions were lifted in the nineties. *If I can land that plane,* he thought, *I'll blow my numbers out of the stratosphere. I'll work on it after my meeting with Leach tomorrow morning. Next Tuesday, slumber party with Trish Gordon seems in order. Nice.*

Lost in thought, he didn't hear Clare come in through the back door and only realized she was home when she threw her bag with a thud onto the kitchen counter.

"How was the book club?" Eddie called out.

"Nobody read the book," said Clare from the kitchen.

"Isn't the point of a book club to read the book?"

"It's really just an excuse for us to get together every month," said Clare walking into the family room where Eddie was sitting. "If you say it's a book club then you have a purpose. I doubt people could justify getting together to gossip once a month. So, we call it a book club."

Feeling mellow, Eddie walked over to the wall unit and took out a fresh wine goblet, poured another glass and handed it to her. She took it without speaking and downed it in one big gulp.

"I've got an extremely busy week this week and next," said Eddie, "starting with tomorrow morning I've got a…"

"I'm going to bed," said Clare as she abruptly walked out of the room.

19

Awake but still in bed at dawn the next morning, Eddie's mind was flooded with a million unfinished ideas and projects he had going on at the office. Clare snored softly as he got up and quietly went into the bathroom to shower and shave. Twenty minutes later, dressed in his new gray custom-made suit and his favorite red striped tie, he drove to the bus stop to catch his ride into the city.

At 10:20am, he walked into the large empty conference room on the fourth floor. Coffee was on the sideboard so he helped himself to a cup while he waited for the others to arrive. Within minutes, the room filled up. *Wow,* thought Eddie, *all the top brass are here. I'm the only publisher invited. Nice. Me and the senior executives of DI. Very cool.*

Once everyone was seated, Ken Leach called the meeting to order and asked his assistant to bring in the boxes. The young woman left the room and returned moments later wearing plastic gloves and pushing a metal wheeled cart that held two large, water-stained cardboard crates.

"Open the boxes and remove the contents," said Leach as if proclaiming a royal decree.

The young woman opened the top of one of the boxes, and retrieved several water-damaged copies of *The National Spectator*. The room remained silent.

Leach looked directly at Eddie. "Why don't you tell us what this is," he said, looking into Eddie's eyes with a death stare. Confused, Eddie looked around the room for help from the others but none came.

"I'm not sure what you mean," said a bewildered Eddie. "Why do you have old wet boxes of the *Spectator*? Did I miss something?"

A heavyset man with thick black hair and glasses who Eddie didn't recognize pushed his chair back from the large table and stood. Sifting through papers in the open leather portfolio in front of him, he found the document he was looking for and cleared his throat.

"Good morning, Mr. Gamble. I'm Jeffrey Berkowitz. I'm a partner at the law firm of Berkowitz, Siegel & Kelly. We represent and protect most of Diamond International's interests here and abroad," said the lawyer with a strong Brooklyn accent. "According to Mr. Leach, it has recently come to his attention that you were behind a plan to illegitimately alter the circulation numbers of *The National Spectator*."

"What? That's crazy," interrupted Eddie. "I don't know what you're—"

"Let me stop ya, Mr. Gamble," said Berkowitz firmly. "We were tipped off to this a while ago and hired a private investigator to look into it. Naturally, a scandal like this is somethin' we'd have to keep a lid on. If our advertisers thought for a New York minute we were trying to defraud them it could mean a material loss in revenue for the company."

"Of course, but what does this have to do with me?" said Eddie, sweat forming on his upper lip, "I don't know anything about this."

"That's where we disagree, Mr. Gamble," said Berkowitz. "Our PI went to the newsstands and watched the boxes of the *Spectator* get loaded onto trucks. He followed those trucks to a landfill in New Jersey. He watched your hired thugs dump thousands of issues into a garbage pit."

"Why would you think they're my people?" Eddie said, starting to seriously sweat.

"Because we threatened to prosecute them, and they gave you up, you jackass," said Ken Leach, jumping in. "So, here's what you're going to do. You're going to clean out your desk in the next twenty minutes and our security guard over there," he said, nodding to a middle-aged bald man in a uniform standing in the corner, "is going to walk you out of the building. And then, I don't want to ever see your face again. You've put me and Diamond International in an extremely dangerous and vulnerable position. When I hired you, I knew you relied too much on your ability to glad-hand people but I didn't figure you for a cheater. You couldn't make your goals so you pulled a scam. Now, get out of my sight, before I have you arrested."

"You can't fire me," said Eddie, "I've got another year on my contract."

Leach looked around the room with a smirk on his face until his eyes rested on Jeffrey Berkowitz. The lawyer responded to Leach's unspoken cue.

"Actually, Mr. Gamble," said Berkowitz reading from another document. "Your contract is null and void if you commit any crimes while employed at Diamond International. Stealing issues and dumping them in a landfill in order to put out fraudulent circulation numbers would indeed qualify as criminal. Not to mention the fact that you used your T&E money to do it and lied about what the money was used for on your expense account."

Eddie looked around the room as a dozen pairs of eyes

peered back at him with a mix of disgust and pity. "Do you have any idea what I've done to elevate this rag," he said, his voice getting louder. "When I joined this company, you were hemorrhaging money and you expected me to pull rabbits out of a hat. And, I freaking did! I brought all my contacts, my relationships and major mainstream advertisers into your schlocky tabloid. I grew the ad revenue by thirty percent and put *The National Spectator* on the map. Yeah, I cut a few corners but only because your goals were unrealistic. You should be grateful."

"This is a one-time offer, Mr. Gamble," said Berkowitz. "We won't prosecute you because we'd rather not have this information go public. I'd advise you to take this gift and leave immediately. You have my word, what happened will remain in this room."

After signing several non-disclosure agreements, twenty minutes later, with no goodbyes to anyone, Eddie was escorted out of Diamond International. When he stepped outside onto the pavement he bumped into some of his Diamond colleagues going into the building who had no idea of what had just happened.

"Hey Eddie," said another publisher, tapping him on the arm. "Let's do lunch next week?"

"Sure," said Eddie forcing a smile, "sounds good, I'll call you." With his head spinning and the blood pulsing at his temples, he waved and walked away from the building. *What the hell just happened? This isn't possible. What am I going to tell Clare?* One thought bled into the next as he walked the city streets with no destination. That familiar sense of dread crept up and soon overwhelmed him. He knew the feeling well. Sometimes the depression lingered for months as if someone had pulled a dark sack over his body that let no light in. It was happening again and it scared him. He needed to get home—fast.

Somehow, he managed to get himself to the Port Authority Bus Terminal on 42nd Street but had no memory of boarding the bus. Lost in thought, he nearly missed his stop. When he walked to his car, his feet felt heavy and he wondered what to tell his wife. He'd have to tell her something but he wasn't going to tell her he had committed fraud. *I'll say that Diamond had some big layoffs and unfortunately, I was one of them. It happens in the media business all the time. She knows that.*

When Eddie walked into his house in the middle of a workday, Clare, in the kitchen making a batch of chocolate-chip cookies was startled.

"What are you doing home? Are you sick?" she asked. Disheveled, Eddie stood in the doorway but couldn't speak. From the look on her husband's face it was clear something was very wrong. She stopped stirring and put the mixing bowl and wooden spoon down on the counter. "What's wrong?"

Shaking while tears pooled in his blue eyes, Eddie started to sob. Clare walked over to her husband and put her arms around him. "Tell me, what's happened?" she said. "Whatever it is, we'll get through it."

"Diamond let me go," he said, his voice catching. "I'm out. I don't work there anymore."

Clare wanted to scream, stamp her feet and throw her arms up in the air. She wanted to shout, "again?", but she didn't. Instead, she put her arms around him and rocked him slowly.

20

For the next nine days Eddie stayed in bed getting up only to use the bathroom, which happened infrequently because he ate and drank little. Clare spent hours talking to him and rubbing his back, and tried to cheer him. Nothing she said broke through. Her husband was in a dark place and didn't seem to have the will to climb out.

Joe and Sarah tried to talk to him but he responded with only flat one-word answers.

"What's the matter with Daddy?" Sarah asked her mother.

"I told you, honey, he's got the flu," said Clare.

"But he's not sneezing or coughing like I do when I have the flu."

"It's a different kind of flu, it's more of a head cold," said her mother, relieved when her answer seemed to satisfy the curious ten-year-old. Frightened by her husband's condition, Clare called their old therapist, Ilene Kostikian. She hadn't talked to Ilene in a while but it was clear her husband needed professional help.

After much pleading, Clare convinced Eddie to meet with Ilene. The following day she drove Eddie to the therapist's office.

It was the first time he had dressed in ten days. She watched him as he slowly got out of the car appearing to be in physical pain. He had lost weight and his skin was pasty and loose. He needed a shave and his hair was matted and unkempt. He looked broken.

With his hand hovering over the doorknob of Ilene's office door he turned to walk back to the car when the door swung open.

"I thought I heard someone out here. Come on in, Eddie," said Ilene with a welcoming smile, waving to Clare still in the car. "I hear you've had a rough few weeks."

Eddie snorted softly as he followed her to her office. "That's the understatement of the century."

"Things could always be worse," she said with a reassuring smile.

"Doubtful."

"Let's break it all down," she said as she closed her office door. "If you can parse things into smaller packets it makes them easier to digest."

For the next two hours Eddie talked and Ilene listened. It was obvious the man sitting in front of her had fallen apart. He talked about his job, his childhood, his parents. He reminisced about high school and being the college golden boy and later Madison Avenue's golden man. He agonized over how everything had disintegrated in a single day until Ilene pointed out that it really hadn't.

"I don't mean this as a judgment," said Ilene softly. "From everything you've told me, what happened at Diamond International was the culmination of a lifetime of gaming the system."

Eddie had never connected all those dots before. It wasn't just the circulation stunt he had pulled. He had taken shortcuts and made controversial choices all along the way and many of them had come back to bite him. Ilene pointed out that it wasn't just the big things, it was the little ones too.

"Natural charm is a gift but if not carefully used, it can be a curse," said Ilene. "Having personal magnetism can carry you a long way and open a lot of doors. But if you're not careful, you'll find you're out of runway. Maybe what you need now is a fresh start."

After further discussion and a call later that day from Ilene to his wife, it was decided. Eddie should go away for a while, clear his head and get a fresh perspective on life. Ilene had suggested he go someplace quiet where he could do some internal work. "Somewhere you've been before where you were the happiest. Anything come to mind?"

Eddie's happy place had always been in the mountains on skis—flying down a snow-covered run with the sun on his face, knee-deep in fresh powder.

"Ilene called me," Clare said later that same day after speaking with the therapist. "She thinks you should get away. She said you talked about going to Colorado for a while."

"What do you think?" said Eddie.

"I'm exhausted and I don't know what to think anymore. Frankly, you being in Colorado won't be much different than when you were away all the time traveling on business."

"I won't go if you don't want me to."

"Since when did what I want matter?" said Clare. Eddie looked down at his feet. "I don't know what to say. You're no good the way you are right now and if going out there for a few weeks will get your head in a better place, then do it. I wouldn't mind time by myself, anyhow."

"You really think I should go?" said Eddie, not sure if he even had the energy to travel.

"I'm in favor of it, but only if you really take the time to work on yourself," she said. "It's the end of January. Go for a month.

You're clearly no good the way you are right now and I'm tired of babysitting you. I've already got two kids."

"I'll work while I'm there. I'll get a job on the mountain, work the ski lift or something," he said, "like I used to."

"Just get your act together."

A week later, Clare put her husband on a plane headed out west. When the plane started its descent into the Denver airport, Eddie felt the first flicker of excitement and anticipation and knew Ilene had been right. A month or two in Vail would surely give him the rest and perspective he needed to start over.

21

C hili Warren was one of Vail, Colorado's oldest ski bums and proud of it. Born and raised in Texas, if you asked, he'd gladly tell you that he came from a long line of trash. A high-school dropout, he started drinking and doing drugs mainly because that's what everyone in his small town did. Before he turned seventeen, he had worked his way up to gun smuggling. While running guns for a few years had its perks, free room and board at a Nebraska State Correction Facility was not one of the benefits he had planned on.

Ever an optimist, Chili spent his year in the medium security prison reflecting and figuring out what to do with his life. After much introspection and because he shared his cell with a guy who had worked several seasons at a Colorado ski resort, Chili latched onto the idea of completely changing the direction of his life. As soon as Nebraska Corrections gave him his "get out of jail card", he headed to Colorado to start over. That had been thirty-eight years earlier and he never looked back.

It was the perfect sunny and dry Colorado ski day. A fresh dusting of white powder covered the mountain, which for the locals meant all was right with the world. Chili stood on his skis mid-mountain catching his breath after a good but rigorous mogul run. He was one of those people whose age was difficult to figure out. After a lifetime of being outside, his craggy, sun-kissed face covered by a mostly gray handlebar mustache and shaggy mop of dark-brown hair laced with strands of gray, made it hard to tell where time and exposure to the elements met. His lean, wiry body was all muscle and he maneuvered the most difficult mogul runs without breaking a sweat. Everyone was surprised when they found out Chili was in his sixties.

Leaning back on his skis, he drank in the beauty of the pristine white mountains dotted with evergreens, a scene he considered his good fortune to look out on every day. Each morning, he reminded himself that he was one of the luckiest men on the planet. Looking up at the sparkling snow-covered peak behind him, he spotted another skier working his way over the same moguls he had just come down. *Not bad,* he thought, assessing the other skier's skill. *He shouldn't bend his knees so much, but he's not bad.* Minutes later, Eddie reached the mid-mountain plateau and skied up to Chili with a deliberate exaggerated stop causing a cascade of snow to spray over the older man.

"Chili," screamed Eddie with a giant grin, "Are you crazy? You went straight down that run. I mean straight down, man. You got some kind of death wish?"

Chili gave him a wry smile, pulled out a cigarette, lit it, inhaled and slowly blew out the smoke. "Ain't got no death wish. May look like I'm out of control up there but I know what I'm doing. On the slopes, safety always comes first. Remember that. Fact is, you're just plain old slow, Gamble. You ski like a fuckin' baby. You wearin' diapers inside those ski pants?"

"I would have to if I skied the way you do," said Eddie laughing.

Chili smiled again, took a long drag, flicked his cigarette into the snow and pulled down his goggles.

"C'mon, let's see what you got, baby. Two beers says I beat you to the bottom by three minutes." With that, Chili turned and pushed off down the slope. Eddie followed right behind but within moments the gap between them spread as Chili's speed accelerated.

He's a freaking lunatic, Eddie thought as he followed him, *he's gonna crash into a tree. I wonder if it hurts when you crash into a tree or if everything just goes dark like when you get anesthesia.* Trailing behind, Eddie pumped his way to the bottom of the hill. When he got there, Chili was already sitting at a table smoking a cigarette and finishing his first beer.

"I was just about to send the ski patrol out lookin' for you," said Chili letting out a puff of smoke. "You get lost or somethin'?"

"Give me a break," said Eddie kicking off his skis. "I was right behind you the whole way." Chili got up and smiled, handed Eddie a beer and nodded his head towards a group of attractive women in color-coordinated ski outfits. The two men moved to the other side of the après-ski area and leaned against a wall next to the concession to get a better look at the group of twenty-two-year-old snow bunnies.

Eddie took a swig of his beer wondering why beer always tasted better after skiing. When he was a kid, his father used to let him have the first sip from his beer can at family barbecues. His mother would almost always say "Frank, don't give Eddie so much beer, he'll become an alcoholic". He remembered his father drank Rheingold. *I don't think they even make that brand anymore, probably because no one besides Dad liked it.*

"How long you plan on stayin' in Vail?" asked Chili.

"How long are you planning?" said Eddie.

"I'm here for the duration, my friend. I've finished my journey and arrived at my destination, you know what I mean?"

Chili had somehow worked it all out. Colorado was home. He skied in the winter and guided white water rafting trips in the summer. He had plenty of snow girls to keep him warm when it was cold and tents full of nubile nature girls in the raft on the river when the snow melted. For a man who grew up in a trailer park, a hundred miles west of Nowhere, Texas, he somehow had figured it all out. Despite being incarcerated during his formative years and learning how to make weapons out of plastic combs and Popsicle sticks, from Eddie's perspective, Chili was one lucky bastard. *And, he can ski like hell,* Eddie thought with admiration.

"You've got quite the life here," said Eddie looking around at the majesty of the scenery. "I wish I could follow your lead."

"Why don't ya? I think we've got room for one more on this mountain," Chili said as he laughed and took a long drag on his cigarette.

Why don't I stay here forever? thought Eddie. *Because I have two kids, a wife and a big fat mortgage in New Jersey.* He laughed thinking about the reaction of his parents if he chucked it all and stayed in Colorado. *That would be the final nail in the coffin for old Frank and Marion Gamble.* Eddie let out a deep breath.

"What's on your mind?" asked Chili.

"Just thinking about what my family and friends would say if I told them I was going to stay here. What did your family say?"

"Well, let's see. After I got out of jail, working at a ski lift was a definite step up in the world," said Chili. "My ma was glad I had a job. My old man was drunk twenty-three hours a day so I'm not sure he even knew I was out of prison. He's dead now so it don't matter. What's important is living a clean life in the most beautiful place on earth. Don't get much prettier than

Colorado." He looked out at the glistening peaks sparkling in the sun. "Never get tired of looking at this."

Despite his difficult start, Eddie thought Chili Warren might be the happiest man he had ever known. He didn't want much, and all he wanted, he already had. *Ironic,* thought Eddie, *an ex-con from a trailer park had it all figured out. Most people spend their whole lives chasing happiness along with a fortune in therapy trying to find it. Go to a good college. Marry the right girl. Have a couple of kids. Buy a house. Take the family on vacation. Pay your bills and then, get old and die.* Eddie was a little envious of the old ski bum. Chili Warren, nicknamed because he always carried a small tin of chili powder in his pocket and sprinkled it on everything he ate, including ice cream. Chili, the man who started with nothing and had been rewarded with everything.

"Tell me something," said Eddie as he finished the last of his beer. "How come you're always so goddamned happy? What do you know that the rest of us don't?"

Chili smiled, ordered another beer and faced Eddie. "I don't know shit."

"You must know something."

"It's not about knowing somethin'. It's about somethin' I got."

"What have you got?"

"I got me a whole boatload of those endorphins. It's all about the endorphins. You either have 'em or you don't. I got 'em in spades. I got so many of 'em, I can't even cry at a funeral. I'm so freaking happy that if I had a wife and you slept with her, I'd go out for a beer with you the next day and ask you how you liked it. I can't stay mad, even if I want to, even if I should. It's just something you're born with. All those folks out there looking for that American dream can look all they want. If you don't have the right juice inside, won't matter."

"What if you don't have any endorphins?"

"You're screwed."

"Frank and Marian would just love to hear that."

"Who the hell are Frank and Marian?" said Chili.

"Some people with no endorphins."

"Then they're screwed too," said Chili with a snort.

The two men picked up their skis and headed back towards the lodge. Though they had only met the day before, Chili was going to introduce Eddie to the personnel director at Vail Mountain. He figured Eddie should be able to get a lift operator job or work in the restaurant at mid-mountain like he did. He said the company was always looking for good people and he had decided Eddie was good people. *He might not have endorphins,* thought Chili, *but I like him anyway.* He walked his new friend right into the personnel director's office, introduced him to Ben Davis, and gave Eddie a thumbs up as he left.

"Give me a minute while I look over your application," said Ben sitting down at his desk. "Chili's been with us for a long time. A recommendation from him goes a long way with me. He's kind of a legend around here."

Eddie watched as Ben read through his application and wondered if it had been smart to have four beers before his interview. *Too late now,* he thought. Considering he was applying for a job running a ski lift, alcohol on his breath was probably not a good idea. He looked at the top of Ben's head and saw the man was starting to lose his hair. Eddie ran his fingers through his own hair and when he brought his hand down, there were a few hairs in his hand. *Shit, am I losing my hair?*

"Tell me about yourself," Ben said as he looked into Eddie's blue eyes. "I see you went to Columba College, Irish Christian Brothers, right? They're a tough bunch. My high school in Ohio was run by the brothers. Rather free with the back of their hands, if you know what I mean."

"Yeah," said Eddie, "I've heard they were pretty brutal in high schools back in the day. They kind of mellowed out at the college level. Probably because most of the college guys were bigger and would hit back." Eddie thought back to Brother Harrington. A nasty, bitter son of a bitch, who acted all holy and pious but was essentially full of shit. *It was his fault I got kicked off the baseball team, just because I missed a few practices. I was their best player.*

"What brings you to Vail, Eddie?" asked Ben Davis.

"It's one of the most beautiful places in the world. I think the bigger question is, why doesn't everyone come to Vail?"

"The head of our PR department would like the way you think. I see you've spent a long time working in the media business. Making a career change or is this just a one-season deal for you?"

"That's the sixty-four-million-dollar question."

"No worries," said Ben. "A lot of our employees are at a... crossroads. It's fine with us as long as you make a commitment to stay for the season."

"You have my commitment for the rest of the season," said Eddie shaking Ben's hand.

When he walked out of Ben's office Chili was waiting for him at the end of the hallway.

"Thanks, amigo," Eddie called out. "You didn't have to wait for me."

"You had that lost dog look, Gamble. I know that look. I was lost once. Glad you got the job though. I think this calls for a beer," said Chili with a grin.

"Two beers, and I'm buying."

22

Daily snowfall provided fresh powder and extended the spring ski season several weeks longer than usual. After Eddie arrived in Vail broken and lost, the restorative powers of the mountain released its magic and within a few weeks, he started to find his footing. Concerned he'd be much older than the other workers at the resort and wouldn't fit in, it turned out he wasn't the only one over forty trying to 'find themselves'. In the ski world, it didn't matter how old you were. If you could ski, and he could, you were automatically part of the club.

Surrounded by happy skiers during the days and non-stop partiers at night, Eddie unexpectedly had the time of his life. Most of the mountain resort employees resided in a run-down apartment complex called Mountain High—affectionately called Mountain Sty or simply, "the Sty" by all who lived there. He shared a two-bedroom apartment there with two male lift operators in their twenties that only cost him $500 per month. With what he earned on the mountain, he had enough to cover his costs and plenty left over for partying. It was the camaraderie on the mountain that helped him heal. Every twenty-four hours, hundreds of new tourists descended upon Vail eager to get on the slopes—new people to party, ski and flirt with. It was like college without the tests and papers. Everything was easy, no pressure ever.

That season, Eddie and Chili became good friends often eating meals together, or having a few après-ski beers after an afternoon of skiing. Preferring to observe the festivities from afar, Chili usually parked himself on the edges of an ebullient crowd, several beers lined up on his table and a pack of Marlboro in front of him. From there he'd watch Eddie effortlessly float from table to table telling jokes, complimenting people on a great run or making some young woman giggle when he remarked that she had the prettiest brown eyes in the Rocky Mountains.

Though wrapped up in the Vail lifestyle from day one, Eddie called Clare every day and talked at length with his kids. Two weeks after his arrival in Colorado, Clare noticed a huge difference in his voice.

"Hey, Clare bear, how are you?" said Eddie cheerfully over the phone.

"You sound good," said an astonished Clare, "more like your old self."

"Being here, away from all the bullshit in New York has been mind-altering. My head is clearing. I'm starting to feel a lot better."

"I'm glad."

By mid-April, as the resort prepared to close for the season, the staff who had become a family, got ready to pull up stakes and move on to their next summer gig. Some would return in the fall for another ski season and some would move on to parts unknown never to be seen or heard from again.

Since arriving in Vail, Eddie was keenly aware that he woke every morning with a level of happiness he hadn't felt in years.

His skiing improved and he had made many friends, including Molly, a sultry, dark-haired, twenty-nine-year-old from Sydney, Australia. Molly had been on her high school and college ski teams and this was her second winter working at Vail. Between the two ski seasons, she traveled around the United States picking up odd jobs. When the resort closed that spring, she planned to head back to Sydney for the first time in almost two years. Molly and Eddie had no illusions about their relationship: it was one of mutual convenience that provided a warm body next to them in bed.

On that last week, Eddie sat on the front steps of his apartment building reading a letter from his parents wanting to know when he was coming home. They reminded him that he had two children and a wife in New Jersey. When he finished reading their condemnations, he crumpled the letter in his hand. *Good old Frank and Marion, always stating the obvious.*

Looking up, he saw Chili walking across the Sty's parking lot towards him carrying a couple of empty cardboard boxes. The ski lifts would stop running in three days and everyone in their temporary world would soon scatter. Dropping the boxes by Eddie's feet, Chili sat down next to him and pulled out his smokes.

"Looking forward to getting back on the river?" said Eddie.

"Yup, be nice to have a little change of pace," said Chili as he took a long drag. "Running those river trips is usually a good time unless you got a prima donna on board. Then it becomes the ship from hell. Fortunately, don't get too many of those. Need any boxes?"

"I don't have much stuff," said Eddie, "I'm not sure where I'm headed anyway."

"Thought you were going back to Jersey."

"That's probably where I'll end up," said Eddie looking out at the mountain.

"You're a funny one," said Chili shaking his head.

"Yeah?"

"You could sweet-talk the kernels off an ear of corn. Telling jokes, making people smile with no effort whatsoever. You know what you got?"

"No, what have I got?" said Eddie with a grin.

"Personal magnetism. You can't buy that. You can't bottle it. You may not have all those endorphins, Gamble, but you've got the magnetism gene and that's pretty damn valuable. Go back to your wife and kids. Go do what you're good at, connecting with people."

"What if I can't do it anymore?" said Eddie quietly. "Back east, everything crashed and burned. I don't know if I can go back. I'm not sure I still belong there."

"Don't be a fucking crybaby," said Chili good-naturedly giving his friend a light punch on the arm. "All these people out here, they want what you already got, a wife and kids. Get back on your horse. You'll be fine."

Chili tossed his cigarette, picked up his boxes and started to climb the stairs to his third-floor apartment. Before he was out of sight he turned back and looked down at Eddie. "I ain't kiddin', Gamble, it's time for you to go."

Eddie did go back to New Jersey at the end of May. The transition from the carefree life on the slopes to suburbia with all its responsibilities only underscored the unhealed wounds. It was obvious to Clare that her husband's "sabbatical" in Colorado had been therapeutic. He was more like the old Eddie, the one she had met and fallen in love with in college. But their time apart had created an intangible distance between them.

Each had crafted their own independent life and being together felt strange and confining.

"The summer is dead anyway," said Eddie on the phone to his parents when they questioned why he was waiting until September to look for another job. "I'll reconnect with business friends and headhunters when school starts. That way I can spend more time with the kids while they're off from school."

"The early bird catches the worm," said his father.

"Your father's right, Eddie," said his mother. "The first one in line gets the pie."

"What does that even mean, Mom?"

"It means, he who snoozes loses," said Frank Gamble with a snort.

"Clare's making good money with her freelance writing and we still have savings in the bank. I want to spend time with Sarah and Joe before I jump back into the shark tank," said Eddie before he ended the contentious call.

As he had promised, Eddie commandeered the kids' summer activities giving Clare a much-needed break—especially from their daughter. Eleven-year-old Sarah had morphed into a sullen pre-adolescent often responding angrily to anything her mother said. Only Eddie could get their daughter out of one of those moods and Clare gladly turned over the parental reins.

That summer, Eddie took his kids to the beach, amusement parks, the circus and made weekly trips to Owen's Diner for their famous grilled cheese and bacon sandwiches. The three spent a week down the Jersey Shore and did family nights out at the movies followed by visits to the local ice-cream shop. That summer his kids had a season's pass on the nonstop Daddy fun train.

After two months of entertaining his kids and enjoying it, Eddie realized that this was the first summer he had spent any quality time with them. Sarah was already on her way to teenagerhood and Joey was already seven and he hardly knew them. He had always been working and traveling. That summer he found out that he really liked his kids and more importantly, he liked being their dad.

23

When September rolled around, Eddie reached out to old contacts and colleagues for leads on jobs. All of his career transgressions and missteps had mainly been kept under wraps with the exception of "taking files" from *Vacation* which had been reported in the newspapers. What happened at Fleming Global Media and why he was dismissed after a kick-ass year was still a mystery to him and to everyone else in the business. Not wanting any bad publicity, Diamond International also hadn't leaked anything about his circulation scam.

Despite everything being kept under wraps, all the doors that had once been wide open were shut tight. He may have changed after being out in Colorado and spending the summer with his kids but the media companies who once clamored for him were not interested. Even the headhunters wouldn't take his calls.

Am I too old for media sales? he wondered. *I'm only forty-four. That's not so old.* Sometimes his mind drifted to dark places, conjuring up giant conspiracies. Time after time, he'd get close to a job offer and the door would slam shut with no explanation. *No entry for you.*

While the big media companies wouldn't give him an audience, a few small independents showed some interest. After all, he was the former luxury brand publisher of *American Traveler* and *National Spectator*. To small independent publishers, Eddie Gamble was still a big deal. They couldn't attract or afford star power like his. He had managed large national sales teams that generated millions in revenue. To them, Eddie still looked pretty good.

That's why it wasn't a total surprise when Two Rivers Publishing reached out. Two Rivers was a startup owned by sixty-year-old Roger Bermel. He had inherited millions from his family and then made even more in the 1990s' bull tech market. He had a fat wallet and a thousand ideas, most of which would never get funded unless he funded them himself. Bermel had a passion project that he had been trying to get off the ground for years. He thought Eddie might be the one to help him do it.

Single by choice, Bermel had no children of his own but was deeply involved in the lives of his nieces and nephews. They *were* his kids. He attended every school concert, every soccer game, every graduation. He was a second father to them all. Everyone's favorite uncle—Uncle Rog.

Several years earlier, after spending a weekend with his sister's kids, he had an idea that he couldn't shake. After doing some research, Bermel discovered that approximately twenty percent of American adults never married—just like him. That meant, with a US adult population of about 200 million, there were approximately 40 million single adults in the country. He figured many of those single people were also committed and involved aunts and uncles—just like him. Convinced he could tap into a huge underserved and lucrative segment of the market, his dream was to launch a new magazine and website called *Aunts & Uncles*. The new brand would reach those forty million single aunts and uncles with bank accounts, no kids of their own and no college tuitions to save for—a marketer's dream.

While Bermel was willing to bankroll the project, he was smart enough to realize he knew nothing about media. He needed to find a media pro, someone with big advertiser experience who could come in and build the business from the ground up.

Through his vast network, he reached out to a number of players in the media business. Most people he connected with were polite but no one had any interest in leaving their cushy jobs at fat-cat companies. They weren't about to take a chance on an unproven niche opportunity like *Aunts & Uncles*. A few even questioned whether anyone would buy it. After months looking for a publisher/president with no success, Bermel turned to media executive recruiter, Curtis Fried. The older recruiter, now in his seventies, wasn't getting the plum job assignments anymore and he gladly took the search and started to canvass the market. After dozens of phone calls and emails, Fried learned that Bermel had already approached many of the usual suspects on his own and been turned down.

"Someone called me about this job six months ago. I think his name was Roger Bermel," said one senior media exec Fried called. "I told him then I wasn't interested and I'm still not. Too hard a sell. I'm not convinced there's an audience for it."

Pretty soon it became clear to Fried that *Aunts & Uncles* was not going to draw a big-name executive that his client wanted so he took a different route. *Maybe,* he thought, *I can find someone with the right skills, contacts and experience who is "in-between jobs".* He dug through his database and within an hour had a shortlist of three names. One of them was Eddie Gamble.

Fried called Eddie about the new project and Eddie's initial reaction was to run in the other direction. He had been a senior executive for major national brands and now this headhunter wanted him to work for some ill-conceived niche launch that probably wasn't going to make it. He told Fried he wasn't interested. Six weeks later, with no other opportunities on the horizon, Eddie called Curtis Fried back.

"I've been giving it some thought," said Eddie. "The more I think about the concept and the untapped market for *Aunts & Uncles*, the more I like it. It's grown on me. Being at a startup could be really exciting and round out my résumé. Plus, I'd get to create all the rules and establish the corporate culture the way I want it." The truth was, there were no other offers coming and that dreaded creep was seeping into Eddie's head again.

"Absolutely," said Curtis, "*Aunts & Uncles* is a phenomenal opportunity. Roger Bermel is a genius. He's made a fortune over the years."

With nothing else on the horizon, Eddie convinced himself that *Aunts & Uncles* was going to be the most exciting opportunity of his entire career; and he needed the money. He and Clare had blown through a lot of their savings over that past year and while they could hang on a while longer, Eddie had to secure a job. *Besides,* he thought. *It's only temporary, a way for me to get back in the game. I'll launch Aunts & Uncles, blow the doors off the place and become the hottest startup of the year. Then, all the big companies will be all over me again and I'll be able to pick and choose where I go.*

Three weeks later, after several interviews with Bermel and promises of an outstanding launch, Eddie walked into his new offices on East 43rd Street. It was a relatively small office in an old building but Bermel had been told the floor above was vacant and the building's owner said they could take more space as they grew. Carpenters and painters were busy in every corner getting it ready for the new hires to move in the following week. As the new president and publisher of *Aunts & Uncles*, it was now all up to Eddie and he was confident he could make it happen.

24

Two days after he started, Eddie was running at full speed in the New York advertising game again. Old Eddie was back, rocking and rolling the way he had before. Only this time it was even sweeter. Now, *he* was the big boss; the Ken Leach or the Thomas Andover. His new company was tiny by comparison but still, it felt good to be the head honcho and he was pumped.

With the Gamble charm on full display, Eddie hired a small team of great salespeople and reconnected with many of his old advertising colleagues. He attended industry events, hosted potential client dinners, and in time resumed overnight "meetings" with clients like Trish Gordon and a few select others—some old, some new.

He galvanized his sales team into a small army of *A&U* believers and set up pitch meetings all over New York City. After their fourth agency presentation was met with a lukewarm reception, it became clear buyers were highly skeptical of both the concept and the execution.

"Sorry Eddie, you know I like you, but I don't get it," said one senior media buyer. "Aunts? Uncles? Doesn't speak to me. I can't green light a buy. I'm sorry."

"Aunts and Uncles?" said another media planner making a sour face, "Eddie, c'mon, man. You know I really want to buy from you, but this is dumb. I can't sell this to my client. I'd look like an idiot."

Undaunted, Eddie and his team kept at it. He figured they simply needed to do a better job articulating the value proposition. He and his marketing person did additional research, worked a lot of late nights and came up with a new way to present *A&U*. The next time they got pushback from disbelievers, they were locked and loaded.

"Let me ask you something, Gina," Eddie said to the thirty-something senior media buyer sitting in front of him with her arms folded and an unconvinced look on her face. Gina held the purse strings on a huge toy company advertising budget. "You and I go way back. You're single and I think you once told me you have a few nieces and nephews, right?" The woman nodded and pointed to two photos in silver frames on the table next to her desk. One was of a little boy and the other, a little girl.

"Hannah's seven and Aaron's six. They're my sister's kids. My brother's having a baby this month too," said Gina. "I guess I'll have to make room on my desk for another picture frame."

"I'll bet you're their favorite aunt," said Eddie as he flashed the Gamble grin.

"They call me Auntie Gigi," said Gina laughing.

"And, I'll bet Auntie Gigi dotes on Hannah and Aaron. You probably overbuy for Christmas and birthdays or for no reason at all. You always show up with a gift, am I right?"

"Guilty," she said as she blushed and nodded.

"Wouldn't it be great to have a monthly magazine with activity ideas for different age groups, local concerts and plays that you could take your niece and nephew to?" said Eddie. "Wouldn't you like suggestions on craft ideas for a rainy Saturday afternoon and gift ideas for the holidays? Or stories about things that other aunts and uncles do with their nieces and nephews?"

A glint of understanding appeared in Gina's eyes and she slowly nodded her head. "Now that you mention it, that would be pretty great. I never know what to do with them. I could definitely use ideas." Eddie gave a side glance to his sales person sitting next to him.

"I'll tell you what," said Gina sitting forward and unfolding her arms, "I'll do a small buy... as a test." Eddie grinned, triggering his dimples and he winked at his salesperson. *One down, ninety-nine to go.* The next night, Trish Gordon also agreed to run an ad schedule for her theme-park client in the *Aunts & Uncles* launch issue. Soon other advertisers followed but they all had one condition, the audience had to be bigger to make it worth their while.

Keeping the sales pedal pressed down to the floor, he flew around the country, meeting with all the major advertisers he'd sold to in previous jobs. He approached GM, Mattel, Arby's and dozens of others. One by one, partly because they were mildly intrigued by the pitch and partly because they liked Eddie, the big companies agreed to give *A&U* a try if he got his circulation numbers up. Eddie even flew to Oregon to meet with Nike, they said *maybe*.

"If you can guarantee a minimum of a hundred thousand," said their senior marketing manager, "Nike will do a test."

Aunts & Uncles was different and provided a fresh and unique story for marketers. Early on, it was clear that the *A&U* story resonated with single media buyers who were themselves aunts and uncles. Eddie had his sales team pull together a list of all the single media buyers in the New York metro area. They cross-tabbed that list with the appropriate accounts and came up with a master list of single buyers who were likely to be an aunt or uncle. One by one, Eddie and his small team took their show on the road and picked off each person on the list. The strategy worked, and soon they were getting more positive responses.

With the concept buy-in from media planners secured, the second and bigger obstacle was the circulation. Larger advertisers like Nike and Hasbro were clear: the only way to get them in was to guarantee a minimum of a hundred thousand pairs of eyes. Anything less was a waste of time to these companies.

Having learned his lesson from the Diamond International debacle, Eddie made no plans to hire trucks or dump anything into a landfill in New Jersey. This time, he was committed to doing everything on the up and up—no major shortcuts... maybe only a few little ones. He figured if they were small transgressions no one like Trish Gordon or Nike would ever know or care.

Over the years, Trish had stuck by him. From his glory days at *Vacation* and *American Traveler* through the dog days at the *Spectator*, she was fiercely loyal as long as he allocated a certain amount of playtime for her. They had been doing their special dance for nearly ten years, longer than some married couples.

Despite Trish's devotion, even she needed to see the *A&U* circulation at a certain level to justify the ad buy to her client. In bed one night, she reminded Eddie that he had to take some steps to ensure the numbers or she couldn't pull the trigger on the ad buy.

"What if I make you a deal?" said Eddie stroking her hair.

"What kind of deal?"

"I'll guarantee you a hundred thousand in circulation and if I don't deliver, you and your client pay nothing," said Eddie.

"You realize that deal is completely tilted in my favor, right? If you only reach ninety-nine thousand, I don't owe you any money. My client gets a freebie?"

"That's what I'm selling. If I don't make it, it's free," said Eddie. "No risk whatsoever for your client."

"You're boxing yourself into a tight corner. You sure you want to make this bargain?" said Trish.

Eddie nodded and smiled. "I'm not worried. I've got a consultant buying up lists. We're doing all sorts of subscription promotions," said Eddie. "I did this before at Andover and Fleming. It's not rocket science."

"Andover and Fleming had deep pockets and you're a startup," said Trish. "If you offer this deal to everyone and don't hit your number, you're screwed."

"If the advertisers won't sign on for anything less than a hundred thousand pairs of eyes, I'm screwed anyway. We can get the circulation to where it needs to be."

With his decision made, Eddie and his team took the hundred thousand circulation promise out to the market and within a few weeks had secured advertising commitments from twelve major companies to run in both the magazine and website. All the advertisers were given the same deal. If *Aunts & Uncles* didn't reach a hundred thousand readers, the advertiser owed them nothing. Eddie didn't share this arrangement with Roger Bermel.

A circulation consultant named Andrew Lehman was hired to build *A&U's* subscription list and get them to their target number.

"A hundred thousand subscribers for your first issue is going to be expensive," said Andrew, his eyebrows raised as he looked over Eddie's business plan. "You're looking for a very specific demographic. I'm not going to lie to you, this is going to be hard to accomplish."

"That's why I hired you," said Eddie. "In previous jobs, I've moved the circulation number easily, without tremendous cost. I think it's very doable. We have to get creative."

"Bottom line, you'll need to buy lists to find your readers. Fleming or Andover use their other magazines to seed new ones, it costs them practically nothing," said Andrew. "You don't have other magazines to pull from. You'll have to pay for every pair of eyeballs you get."

"Just do it," said Eddie. "I need a hundred thousand for this first issue. After that, the advertisers will stay and we can grow the readership more organically. Buy cheap lists, offer subscriptions for free. Do whatever you have to do to get me there."

As the launch of *A&U* neared, Roger Bermel's dream was coming to fruition. From Eddie's weekly reports, Bermel figured he was on track to make a nice profit. After all the naysayers over the years who said there was no market for his magazine, he was about to prove them all wrong.

When that first issue finally closed, Eddie reported that they had sold in over forty advertisers including ten major players at a circulation rate base of one hundred thousand. Based on Eddie's numbers, Bermel figured the first issue would bring in nearly $140,000 in revenue. As he read over the final plans for the *A&U* launch party, a small, classy affair that would include key members of the media press, Bermel let out a satisfied sigh.

When the first issue of *Aunts & Uncles* came out it got favorable coverage from the trade press. Unfortunately, *A&U* did not make their hundred thousand reader commitment. Andrew Lehman had only been able to squeeze out ninety-two thousand readers. Bermel, unaware of Eddie's promises, had expected the advertising revenue would cover a substantial portion of the company expenses. Even with a disappointing ninety-two thousand in circulation, he figured they'd still bring in enough to float the business.

"Push the circulation numbers higher," said Bermel as he sat in Eddie's office going over the reviews of the magazine a week after launch. "Take it from a hundred thousand to a hundred and fifty." Eddie nodded.

Eight weeks later, a young woman who handled the billing for *A&U* sat in Bermel's Fifth Avenue office with a large brown folder on her lap.

"Roger, there's something funny with the *A&U* accounts receivable," said the bookkeeper.

"Let me guess, advertisers are dragging their feet on paying their bills," said Bermel looking at an unrelated document on his desk. "They pay big companies right away but drag their feet with the small ones who have less cash flow and really need the money. Send them second notices."

"That's just it. I already did and I made a few phone calls too," said the bookkeeper nervously. "We may have a little problem."

The bookkeeper filled Bermel in on the circulation deal she had recently learned Eddie had made with all the advertisers. There would be no revenue coming in from the first issue, none at all.

Bermel started shouting and pounding his fist on his desk making the bookkeeper cry. Not only had Eddie kept the truth from him, but now they couldn't make payroll or pay their bills. He summoned Eddie to his office. When Eddie explained that he had no other choice but promised he could turn things around, Bermel gave him another chance. He agreed to keep *A&U* afloat for a few more months using his own cash. Though the initial group of advertisers were delighted to get a free ad in the first issue, when Eddie wouldn't give them the same guarantee for the second and third, they all pulled out.

Five months later, *Aunts & Uncles* closed its doors for good.

25

Months later and still unemployed, forty-six-year-old Eddie worked his phone renewing connections and trying to uncover job opportunities. When he wasn't in his home office, he was in the city trying to talk his way into a job—a cup of coffee here, a sleepover there.

With the kids getting older and money tight, the decision was made to pull the kids out of private school temporarily. Clare took on additional freelance editorial projects to pay their bills. The income from her writing was now enough to cover the basics but left little for the extras. After all the ups and downs, truths and lies, Clare Gamble was barely holding it together.

Nearly thirteen, Sarah hardly noticed her larger-than-life father was around the house all the time now. Her world was wrapped up in her friends, sharing secrets about which boys they liked and who they would marry one day.

Joe was the only one really glad to have his dad around. He'd never had his father all to himself and he liked it.

It was nearly noon on a Wednesday. Silently, Clare moved around the first floor of their home like a hummingbird, straightening sofa pillows and stacks of magazines on the coffee table. After dusting the last side table, she moved on to the kitchen, cleaning the counters and wiping down the food spatters on the backsplash and the grime from inside the microwave. When the kids were at school, Eddie and Clare were alone in the house from eight until four. Busy with their own endeavors, they barely spoke to each other the entire day. Eddie stayed upstairs in his office and Clare did her editing work at the kitchen table. They lived separate lives—together.

When Clare went upstairs to put the wash in the dryer, she'd occasionally overhear some of her husband's phone calls. A part of her felt sorry for him because he sounded so desperate.

"Hey Jack, how the hell are you, amigo?" Eddie said loudly into the phone with almost too much enthusiasm. "It's Eddie... Eddie Gamble." Brief pause. "It sure has been a while and we've gotta change that, my friend." Another long silence. "I totally understand, deadlines are deadlines. Call me back next week. I'll be here. Looking forward to catching up."

For the longest time, her husband had succeeded at everything without breaking a sweat. He made it look effortless. Now, the golden boy had lost his luster.

Down at the foot of the stairs, she heard him wrap up a call and she moved quickly into the kitchen. Soon, he came down the steps with his phone in his hand and placed it on the kitchen counter while he rummaged through the snack cabinet. Pulling out several bags of chips he poured some into a large bowl.

"Had a great call with a recruiter today. Don't want to jinx it but there might be something opening up at Blaine & Vicks," said Eddie with his usual bravado. "I'm meeting the recruiter in the city tonight for dinner. Might be a late one but it will be worth it. Going to take a shower now and get ready."

"Had a great call with a recruiter today, don't want to jinx it," said Clare softly mimicking her husband once he was out of earshot. *I've heard that song before,* she thought as she looked through the stack of mounting bills on the kitchen table. The shower turned on upstairs and moments later Eddie's phone that was still sitting on the kitchen counter began to vibrate. Clare ignored it and continued looking through the bills. When his phone vibrated for the sixth time in five minutes, Clare picked it up to see who needed her husband so urgently.

Six new text messages from the same unidentified number had come in. She clicked on the messages. They were from a woman.

EG, miss you to pieces. Can't wait to see you tonight. Am even cooking. Don't worry, I won't poison you. Xo

EGGY, I need me some EGs and Ham. Xox Lol T.

Forgot to ask, do you like salmon? I can't remember. Love ya. T.

What time will you get here? I've got a bottle of Cabernet already decanting. Xo

Are you staying over? Say yes.

I changed the sheets just in case. Xox

Staring at her husband's phone, Clare examined her own emotions to get a handle on exactly what she felt. After the initial shock of reading the brazen texts from "T", she waited for her emotions to catch up to the new information. To her surprise, she didn't want to cry or scream, she felt very little. Then the anger kicked in, not because her husband was obviously cheating on her but because she had been so willfully ignorant for so long. That's when she knew—she didn't love her husband anymore and probably hadn't for a long time. She simply no longer cared.

Not emotionally up for a showdown, she said nothing to Eddie that day. *He can go have salmon with "T" tonight on her clean sheets,* she thought. She picked up her own phone and scheduled a session with their marriage counselor.

Thirty minutes later, Eddie bounded down the stairs freshly shaved and smelling good. "I'm going to shove off in a few minutes," he said, gathering his things.

"It's only three o'clock. Can't you wait until the kids are at least home from school so they can see you for a few minutes?" said Clare deliberately screwing with him.

"I wish I could but I have to meet this other guy for drinks first. You know how important it is for me to network right now."

"Yes, so important."

"It is what it is," said Eddie with a resolute smile. "Don't wait up, this will probably be a late one." He leaned over and kissed his wife on the top of her head and walked towards the back door.

"Eddie," said Clare, "I've made an appointment for us to meet with Ilene Kostikian again. I'm feeling like our lines of communication are blocked. We agreed that if either of us felt that way, we'd both go back to see Ilene."

"Okay," said Eddie somewhat surprised, "if you feel that way. When?"

"Tomorrow night, six o'clock," said Clare. "Don't make any evening plans in the city."

26

S itting at opposite ends of the leather couch in Ilene Kostikian's office, they had arrived early and waited while Ilene, in an adjacent room, returned a phone call to another patient. Clare looked out the window. A little brown bird sat on a tree branch on the other side of the glass. The light-green spring leaves had started to open and the bird moved his head around, surveying its surroundings, eventually looking directly at Clare.

At the other end of the sofa, Eddie thumbed through a copy of *GQ* he had plucked out of a stack of magazines piled on the coffee table. He scanned the masthead hoping he might know someone who worked there that he could talk to about a job. The clock on the wall ticked loudly breaking the heavy silence in the room.

The door to the inner office opened and Ilene shuffled in. "Sorry," said the therapist taking a seat opposite the couple, "one of my patients was having a bad day, had to talk her through something. It's been a while since we've gotten together. Why don't you bring me up to date."

Eddie and Clare looked at each other but neither spoke.

"Eddie, why don't you start," said Ilene.

"From my perspective, things between us have been fine but apparently Clare feels like 'our lines of communication are blocked'," he said, making air quotes with his fingers. "We agreed to come back if either one of us felt that way, so here we are. A lot has happened since we last saw you. I launched a new magazine and website called *Aunts & Uncles*. Unfortunately, the investor pulled the plug after only a few issues. We were doing great, too. It was—it was a big disappointment."

"I can imagine," said Ilene.

"I've had a number of career changes that have kept me preoccupied. That may be why Clare feels the way she does. But everything that happened was beyond my control."

"Instead of telling me how you think Clare feels, tell me how you feel," said Ilene.

"I'm a little tired. The job market has changed," said Eddie. "I'm finding it challenging finding the right position. It used to be easy but not anymore. Something will turn up. I can tell you I'm working my ass off looking for a new job so I can provide a nice life for my family," said Eddie.

Clare closed her eyes and laughed under her breath causing both Eddie and Ilene to look at her.

"What's on your mind, Clare?" said Ilene. "I get the sense there's something you want to say."

"He spent a whole winter skiing in Vail," said Clare in a loud, clear voice.

"You told me to go," said Eddie looking at her and then at Ilene.

"Clare, talk to him, not me," said Ilene.

Clare turned and faced her husband. "You left us and spent three months in Colorado skiing while you got your 'head together'. I supported it at the time, because you were depressed and I thought you needed the space. I held down the fort and took care of our kids so you could 'find yourself'. All the while, you were probably out there screwing anything that moved," said Clare as she turned back to Ilene. "It's never enough for him. He's always looking for something better, something newer, someone new."

"Talk to your husband," said Ilene firmly.

"What's this all about?" said Eddie.

"Why don't you tell Ilene about the texts from 'T'?" said Clare gritting her teeth. "How was the salmon? Were the sheets as clean as she promised?"

Stunned, Eddie turned his head away to hide the tears in his eyes.

Clare stared at the back of her husband's head and then faced Ilene. "He won't tell you about the texts because he wants you to think he's a great guy," she said. "The fact is, he's a compulsive liar and cheater. Yesterday, I found texts from a bunch of women he has obviously been sleeping with."

"You were looking at my phone," Eddie said as he whipped his head around.

"You're like a cat chasing a shiny toy. You've spent your whole life running in circles grasping for the newer sparkly thing," said Clare. "Did you ever watch a cat chase a laser light, Eddie? That's you chasing after jobs, people, things. You and your $400 custom shirts, $800 loafers and that obscene $11,000 watch you bought for yourself. I hope you're still enjoying your fancy German watch, because guess what? We can't make our mortgage payments."

"It's a Franck Muller, and it's Swiss," said Eddie.

"I don't care," screamed Clare, "What are they going to write on your tombstone? Here lies Eddie Gamble and his expensive Swiss watch. He must have had a wonderful life."

"You're being ridiculous," said Eddie.

Clare closed her eyes and let out a primal scream. "I don't know what you want anymore," she said, "and I don't think you know either. Maybe it was because you were so goddamned charming and likable that doors flew open. It was all too easy. You walked through those open doors without a care, never considering that maybe you hadn't earned it. I don't know what matters to you. Certainly not me, not the kids, not your parents. The kids hardly know you. One day they'll be grown and they won't *want* to see you. I feel sorry for you. You've missed half of your life chasing things that don't matter."

"Okay," said Ilene, eyes wide, "that's a whole lot to unpack."

"Well, unpack this. I'm done. I want a divorce," said Clare looking out the window at the little bird still standing on the branch.

"Clare," said Eddie reaching for her.

She brushed his hand away and stood up. "I don't love you anymore and I'm pretty sure if you dig deep, something you rarely do, you'll see you don't love me either," said Clare with no emotion in her voice. "And the sad thing is, I wonder if you ever did."

"Okay, let's back this up a little," said Ilene looking a little panicked. "Eddie, do you want to respond to Clare?"

Eddie looked at his wife. "I think—"

"Let me stop you," said Clare holding up her flat palm as she walked across the room. "I've got nothing more to say and no patience or interest in listening to any more of your bullshit. I'm filing for divorce. I consulted with an attorney this morning and I want you out of the house by Monday." She pulled open the office door.

"Clare," said Eddie getting up to follow her.

"You used to be able to convince me of almost anything," said Clare. "I believed in you. Now, I feel nothing when I look at you. Your words bounce off me like I'm wearing a bulletproof vest."

She turned to walk out the door. Eddie got up and took a step towards her. "Don't you dare follow me," Clare hissed. "I've been crystal clear. We're over. You don't even like salmon. Isn't that ironic?"

27

E ddie moved out of the family home the Monday after that fateful therapy session, and moved into an apartment on the other side of town. The complex was essentially known as a "divorce club" for men, filled with husbands wanting to live near their kids. A few months later and still unable to land a new sales management position, the New York job market was a castle with a moat, its drawbridge always up. Every time he tried to scale the walls, he'd slide into the alligator-filled waters below. No matter how hard he tried, the doors to the castle remained unapologetically shut.

Walking down Madison Avenue after another terrible interview, he looked up when he felt a drop of water hit his face. The sky overhead was gray and the wind had picked up. If it rained, he'd duck into the New York Public Library. He'd done that before. If it remained dry, he'd camp out in Bryant Park until his two thirty meeting with Curtis Fried, the same recruiter who got him the job at *Aunts & Uncles*. People respected Curtis. If anyone could help Eddie get back in the game, Curtis could.

Wandering along 42nd Street on the outskirts of Bryant Park, he bought a hot dog from a street vendor and looked around for an empty table or bench. On the 41st Street side of the park, he spotted two people getting up from a table and he sprinted across the open space. He grabbed the empty seat, grateful for a tiny victory.

Eating his hot dog slowly, enjoying the saltiness of the meat, he watched dozens of vignettes play out around him. Business people escaping their office at lunchtime to read trashy novels. Watchful teachers herding children through the streets and praying they didn't lose any. Nannies pushing babies in strollers, and lonely broken men drinking whiskey out of not so hidden bottles in paper bags. It was classic New York.

A family of four speaking in a foreign language Eddie couldn't identify breezed past him. They reminded him of his own family; a mother and father and a girl and boy around fifteen and eleven. He watched the parents point at buildings and other structures around the park. The boy appeared interested and attentive like Joey would have been. Conversely, the teenaged girl looked bored, her eyes only on her phone, like his daughter so often was. *Looks familiar*, he thought as he took the last bite of his hot dog.

Watching the family reminded Eddie of the last weekend he spent with his kids. It hadn't gone well. From the minute she walked out of the house, it was obvious Sarah was determined to sabotage their visit. He had pulled up in front of Clare's house and Joe came bounding out the front door carrying his weekend bag. Jumping into the passenger seat of the car, he rattled off everything he had done or thought since he had last seen his father. Eddie listened while keeping one eye out for Sarah.

A full ten minutes passed when Clare came outside holding up a finger. Five minutes later, her face buried in her phone and her body language sending a clear message, Sarah walked sullenly down the sidewalk. She got into the back seat and shut the door without saying a word.

"You all set?" said Eddie to his daughter.

"Do I have a choice?" said Sarah while her brother chattered on cheerfully.

"Hold on a minute, Joe," Eddie said, holding up his hand. "What's the problem, Sarah?"

"No problem."

"She wants to hang out with her stupid friends," said Joe. "She likes some boy named Jason."

"Shut up, asshole," screamed Sarah smacking Joe on the head. "You're an idiot."

"That's enough, Sarah," said Eddie. "Why don't you go back into the house. You're not a hostage. If you don't want to come, you don't have to."

Sarah smirked, stuck her tongue out at her brother, got out of the car and ran back into the house.

I could have handled that conversation with Sarah much better. I will next time, he thought as he stood up to leave Bryant Park for his meeting. It was then that he noticed a homeless man with long gray hair sitting on the bench next to him. Something was familiar about the man. It took Eddie a minute to place him. He smiled and walked over. "Hello amigo, it's been a long time."

The homeless man stared up at him.

"Remember me?" said Eddie.

The homeless man examined Eddie more carefully. "Maybe."

"I used to work in the Andover building."

The homeless man peered at Eddie with a glint of recognition. "You used to bring me a bagel and coffee with..."

"Three sugars," said Eddie. "No butter, only cream cheese."

"You stopped coming."

"I got another job in a different part of the city."

"You've got less hair," said the man.

"I could say the same for you," said Eddie with a rueful

smile. "Wait here." Eddie walked away returning minutes later with a hot dog and a cup of coffee. "I had one of these a little while ago, they're delicious." He handed the hot dog and coffee to the man."

"Thanks," said the homeless man as he bit into the hot dog. Eddie reached into his pocket, pulled a twenty-dollar bill out of his wallet and handed it to the man. "Get yourself something to eat later. I think it's going to rain. You might want to find some shelter. It was good to see you." The homeless man nodded as Eddie waved and walked away.

At two thirty sharp, Eddie knocked on Curtis Fried's office door. It had been a while since he had seen the recruiter. When they greeted each other, both noticed the other one looked older.

"Guess it's been a couple of years since we've met in person. Maybe more than a couple of years," said Eddie.

"I presume you're here today because you're in the market for a new role," said Curtis. "Heard what happened with *Aunts & Uncles*. A real shame they shut you down. You had some good buzz going in the industry before they pulled the plug. It happens."

"One day things were buzzing along, I mean really moving and then I got the phone call that Bermel was done. Didn't have the stomach for the costs of a startup, I guess."

"Like I said, it was a shame," said Curtis. "Of course, there was that other little matter..."

"Let's not litigate that right now," said Eddie. "It wasn't what it looked like in the press. You know how the media is, they blow things out of proportion for a headline. I didn't do anything wrong, just took a few shortcuts. I mean, we were a startup, you gotta take some risks."

"Sure. I understand," said Curtis.

"It's been about a year since *A&U* and I'm still looking for that perfect role. You're so well connected. If anyone can find me the right job," said Eddie, "it's Curtis Fried."

Curtis appreciated the compliment but at the same time knew it would be nearly impossible to place Eddie Gamble in the New York media market. Rumors about him had been floating around for years and Curtis didn't have time to waste on someone he was never going to make any commission on.

"I like you," said Curtis appearing suddenly uncomfortable, "I remember when you used to kick ass in this town."

"Still can," interrupted Eddie flashing the grin.

"I'm going to be straight with you because I think you've always been straight with me," said Curtis. He paused. "You're finished in New York. No one will meet with you. No media company is going to hire you. I'm not passing judgment, I'm just telling you how it is."

"What are you talking about?"

"You've been blackballed in this town," said Curtis. "I'm forbidden to send your résumé to some companies. I tried and I was told not to do it. Every recruiter in New York knows that."

"What do you mean?" said Eddie, a look of bewilderment on his face.

"I hate to be the one to tell you, but better you know the truth," said Curtis gently. "If you want my advice, get out of New York. Go somewhere else, start fresh. Philly maybe, or Boston. You might have a shot there, because in the Big Apple, you're poison."

The rest of the meeting was a blur. Eddie didn't hear anything after the word "poison". Curtis was either unwilling or unable to elaborate on why Eddie was media's *persona non grata* but the recruiter had been emphatic.

"You're absolutely sure?" said Eddie. "Everyone?"

"If you don't believe me, ask another recruiter. It's over for you in this town."

When Eddie left Fried's office, he walked slowly along Manhattan streets with no specific destination. With thoughts swirling, he tried to make sense out of what he had just learned. *That explains why it's been impossible to get a meeting with anyone. At least I know I'm not paranoid,* he thought, *there really is a conspiracy against me.*

After aimlessly walking for an hour, Eddie waited at Port Authority for the next bus back to New Jersey. He had learned painful things he wished he didn't know. He wanted to call Clare and tell her what happened. She would know what to say, help him sort things out. But he couldn't call her. They were officially separated and she only spoke to him when absolutely necessary. New Clare had no interest in old Eddie.

When he got home to his small two-bedroom apartment, he flipped on the light. Empty takeout boxes and old magazines and newspapers were strewn about. He stepped over a large, almost full garbage bag on the floor and opened the bottle of bourbon he had purchased on his way home. He poured himself a generous glass and flipped on a baseball game, the word *poison* echoing in his head.

28

———

Eight months after his meeting with Curtis Fried, something finally popped. Someone he had worked with back at *Drake's Downbeat*, knew someone in Philly who had an advertising rep firm. They were an independent company that sold ads for a group of Philly-centric publications and websites. It was a "small potatoes" operation that paid a fraction of what he had previously earned, but it was a job and would provide health benefits for him and his family. He took it.

The terms of his divorce had been finalized and required he fully cover Sarah and Joe for medical until they turned twenty-one. If he was unemployed, he still had to pay for it out of his pocket and the past year without a job had depleted a big chunk of his savings. With the new position in Philadelphia, he could cover his child support and pay his rent without having to dip into what little was left of his nest egg. Legal fees from the divorce had eaten up a large portion of what he and Clare had left. After they sold their house and split the proceeds, Clare took her half and put a down payment on a small colonial home. It was on the less expensive side of their town and the kids could stay in the same schools. Eddie would live on his salary from the rep firm and make his child support payments using his proceeds from the house to supplement. He sold his Franck Muller watch to fix his old Jeep Cherokee.

With his new job in Philly, Eddie moved again and took a rental apartment further south in Jersey for an easier commute. On weekends, he'd drive north to spend some time with a few old friends or his kids. He hoped after spending a year with the Philly Ad Group, he could parlay it into something more lucrative, still having fantasies of getting back into the New York ad game.

Despite his career ups and downs, Eddie still had a few good friends left in the media business who occasionally invited him to parties or to their weekend homes in the Hamptons. It felt good to go out to Montauk or East Hampton and kick back the way he used to when he was on top of the world. Whenever he was in Montauk, he made sure to never cross paths with Julia Bowman. He had been warned by mutual friends that she was still furious.

He kept trying to find out why he had been tossed out of the New York media world. Some of his old friends thought Julia Bowman was behind it, but Eddie knew she didn't have that much power. He wondered if it had something to do with the whole circulation fiasco at *The National Spectator* and the "landfill incident" in New Jersey. Ken Leach had said they wanted to keep everything quiet so he doubted Leach was behind his ouster. He also didn't think Diamond International had that much influence.

For the longest time, Trish Gordon remained ever loyal, inviting Eddie to New York for dinner and a slumber party from time to time. Eventually, she moved on after she met a rich divorced banker from Connecticut and things started to get serious.

"EG, I'll always have a special place in my heart for you,"

said Trish. "We've been doing our little dance for over ten years, but I met this guy from Greenwich and I want to give him a clean shot. I can't if you're still in the picture."

Eddie had understood when Trish told him but he kind of missed her.

His separation from the media business had been so complete. No amount of digging brought him any closer to the truth. *One day I'll get my career and my life back*, he told himself over and over. In the meantime, he focused on his son, the only one who still liked spending time with him.

Sarah hadn't spent a weekend with him in months but he kept trying. The last time they were together, she had been openly snotty and rude, parroting comments that sounded as if they came directly out of her mother's mouth. Later, on a call with Clare about a medical bill, he was about to accuse his ex-wife of poisoning their daughter against him when he learned that Sarah had been giving her mother an equally hard time.

"She's like fourteen going on thirty," said an exasperated Clare. "She doesn't listen to anything I say. If I ground her, she goes out anyway. Half the time, I don't know who she's with. I need some help from you."

"When she's with me she barricades herself in the bedroom and plays with her phone the whole time," said Eddie. "She only talks to me when she wants something to eat or needs a charger."

"We've got to do something," said Clare, "we're losing her."

"Let's not overreact. We'll figure it out."

"The way you and I figured everything out," said Clare. "Look how well that turned out."

Eddie's employment at the Philly Ad Group provided a very low salary: most of his compensation would come in the form of commissions. Within a few weeks, it was evident that all of the properties he represented were an extremely hard sell, never first on the list for an advertiser. He had expected he'd make twice as much in commission. Most months he was just able to pay his rent and fixed bills. Occasionally he had to tap into his dwindling savings.

Sitting at the desk in his apartment one evening, Eddie looked out the window. It was almost dusk and he had been working the phone for the better part of the day trying to sell advertising to anyone who would listen. He hadn't made a sale in weeks and was worried his employer might cut him loose. To pre-empt this, he started looking for other job opportunities online. He reached out to a few old colleagues hoping someone would connect him to a better job. *I remember when recruiters called me daily and begged me to take an interview,* he thought. *Now, they won't even take my calls.*

Desperate to make something happen before he found himself unemployed again, he went through his old Rolodex and reached out to someone he had worked with right after college. He hadn't talked to the guy in a long time but figured it was worth a try. *Andy liked me. Of course, it's been twenty years ago but still...*

"Hello," said a woman's voice on the other end of the line.

"This is Eddie Gamble, I was trying to reach Andy Reardon. Do I have the right number?"

"He was my husband," said the woman. "Asshole took off and joined some commune in New Mexico or Nevada five years ago. Left me holding the bag, three kids, a mortgage and a car payment. I have no idea where he is. If you find him, tell him I hope he drops dead."

A week later, the Philly Ad Group let Eddie go.

29

Driving west on Route 70, his skis strapped to the roof of his Jeep Cherokee, forty-eight-year-old Eddie Gamble turned the car radio volume up as high as it would go. After three days on the road, he was close to his destination—Vail, Colorado. The place where he had always felt good, normal and happy.

That season he'd spent in Vail had revived him after a particularly difficult period in his life. It was also one of the best times he had ever had. Skiing, and the restorative friendship with Vail's mountain sage, Chili Warren had made him whole. It had been five years since he'd been out there, but he was certain he'd find everything the same. He expected Chili would be right where he left him, smoking a cigarette and drinking a beer right after a mogul run down the mountain. Chili didn't have much education, but Eddie had always thought he was one of the smartest men he had ever known and the most content. Picturing the old cowboy made Eddie smile and he pressed on the accelerator.

On that sunny and unusually warm January morning, Eddie cracked open his car window and inhaled a deep breath of fresh

Rocky Mountain air. The wide-open road in front of him was surrounded by crystal clear blue skies and snowcapped peaks on the perimeter. He told Clare he needed a reboot after being let go from the Philly Ad Group and was going to work out west for four or five months. He called Vail Mountain, talked to his old manager and got himself a job.

"Eddie Gamble, how the hell are you? Of course I remember you," said Ben Davis, the Vail HR manager. "You looking for work?"

"I might be," said Eddie. "Got anything?"

"Your timing is impeccable. How soon can you be here? I've got a sales opening at the ski shop in the main lodge during the week and a second spot on the cleanup crew at one of the mid-mountain restaurants on Sundays. You want them?"

Eddie smiled as he ended the call. *Maybe the Gamble luck has returned.*

The drive across the country had been rejuvenating. He cruised up the road to the Vail Mountain resorts to sign his employment documents. With everything in order, he got back into his car and headed over to the Sty, his old home, to see if he could find an apartment in need of a roommate. Wandering through the workers' complex for ten minutes, he asked passersby if anyone knew of an available bed. He was going door to door when the shuttle bus from the mountain pulled up and a bunch of girls in their twenties got off. Eddie ran over to them, flashed the Gamble grin and asked if they knew of anyone who needed a roommate. While they gave him some leads, a man in his thirties with long brown hair in a ponytail walked by carrying a snowboard.

"Hey Ronin," said one of the girls. "This guy's looking for an apartment."

"Perfect timing, mate," said Ronin with a Australian twang as he walked towards him. "One of my roommates broke his leg skiing and went home yesterday. We've got an open bed. You cool with weed?"

Eddie nodded and ten minutes later, he was writing a check to Ronin for his portion of the rent. His new roommate helped him move his stuff from his car to the condo and that night he shared a pizza and many beers with Ronin and his other roommate, Lars, from Denmark.

"If you don't have your free ski pass yet, I can hook you up until you get it," said Ronin as he handed Eddie another beer. "I run the lift at the base of the mountain. Just come to my lift, and I'll let you on for free. Consider it a roommates' discount."

Eddie smiled. *The Gamble luck is back.*

In the morning, Eddie got up early and dressed to ski. His shift in the ski shop was from two to nine, so he planned to squeeze in a couple of hours of skiing before work. Taking the free shuttle bus over to the mountain with Ronin, he waited for his roommate to get in position by the lift. When Ronin signaled, Eddie got on the line and within minutes, Ronin waved him through. Soon, Eddie was on the lift flying through the air heading to the top of the mountain.

It had been a while since he had been on skis. The ups and downs over the last few years hadn't left much time or money for ski trips. Happily surprised his skills were still intact, it was his lungs that were still adjusting to the physical exertion. By the third run, it felt like he'd never left. He took the lift from mid-mountain up to the top and stood over a double black diamond mogul run. Taking a deep breath, he looked down at the daunting trail in front of him and wondered if he would break his legs or his hip trying it after so much time had passed.

"What are you, a goddamn chicken?" said a vaguely familiar male voice from behind. "The only way down this mountain is on skis, unless you want me to call the ski patrol and have them take you down on a stretcher."

Eddie spun around. Chili Warren, cigarette hanging out of his mouth, head in a cloud of smoke, stood there smiling. "I heard you was back," said Chili. "Stopped in to talk to the boss last night and he told me." Eddie smiled and slid over to greet his old friend. He and Chili gave each other a warm embrace and updated one another on what had transpired over the past few years. Eddie only shared the highlights.

"What brings you back to Vail?" said Chili. "Your wife must be pretty forgiving if she let you take off again."

"We got divorced. I needed a little recalibration. So here I am."

"Sorry to hear that. As I recall she sounded like a nice lady. Maybe she wasn't so nice?"

"She was better than nice. I fucked up," said Eddie, his eyes filling up. "I had the best thing in the world but I kept looking for something better around every corner."

"Nobody's perfect. Hell, I ended up in prison. Important thing is that we learn and don't make the same mistakes again. Everyone who comes into your life leaves their mark. Some leave a big mark and others just a tiny scratch."

"I lied. Everything was about me. I cheated on her and believed my own press. I thought I was too big to fall," said Eddie. "She finally had enough."

"Now you know where you went wrong, so you'll do it different next time."

Eddie nodded.

"Sorry about the wife, but you came to the right place," said Chili as he tossed his cigarette butt into the snow. "Damn good to see you, Gamble. I thought about you many times over the years. Let's see if you still got it."

Three seconds later, Chili was gone, a rocket shooting down the mountain. Eddie watched the old ski bum effortlessly maneuver the double black diamond mogul hill. *It's now or never,* he thought as he pushed off and followed his old friend down the slope.

A few days later, the weather forecast predicted that a squall was coming and called for heavy snow for three days. With nearly blizzard conditions, most of the upper lifts were closed, and there was talk of closing down the entire mountain. Treacherous conditions persuaded many vacationers to abandon their ski plans for the day. Only the extremely hearty or stupid ventured out onto Vail Mountain that afternoon. All the remaining skiers with nothing else to do flooded the restaurants and shops. That day, Eddie did record sales in the ski shop. It got so crowded at one point that the checkout lines had a wait of nearly thirty minutes. At 4pm, with his shift over, Eddie bolted out of the ski shop to meet Chili, hoping to get one good run in before all the lifts shut down. By 4:30pm, the only skiers left on the slopes were mountain employees, ski patrol and people with a death wish.

The flurries had already started when Eddie and Chili met at the bottom of the mountain. When the chair lift came round, Chili and Eddie hopped on and started the long frigid ride up the mountain as the snowflakes came down harder and the icy wind picked up steam.

"Gonna be a big storm," said Chili as he lit a cigarette and took a drag. "Should make some fine conditions tomorrow with all that fresh powder. Ain't nothing beats that."

"I'm counting on it," said Eddie as Chili's smoke went into his face and made him cough. "You need to quit those things, they're gonna kill ya."

"I've been smoking for over fifty years. Don't guess I'll be stoppin' now."

"Seriously Chili, how many packs do you smoke every day?"

"Are you some kind of vice police? You want to know how many women I've screwed too?"

"Fifty years, you must have smoked half a million butts."

"When I get to a million, do I get a prize?" said Chili with a wry smile.

Eddie laughed and shook his head. "You should think about it, amigo."

"And you should think about getting off this lift," said Chili as the chair reached the top and he pushed off onto the slope with Eddie following right behind. For the next ninety minutes, the two friends raced each other up and down the mountain. Though Chili was nearly twenty years older, Eddie could not out-ski him. *Damn,* thought Eddie as he chased the older man, *that old bastard can move.*

By the end of March, ski jackets started coming off as the daily temperatures rose. The feeling on the mountain changed, everyone was more relaxed but at the same time a little sad. The season would soon be over and all the new friends would scatter.

Wearing his navy-blue ski boots with his skis slung over his shoulder, Eddie walked over to the lift keeping an eye out for Chili. *Be great to get a few more runs in with him before it gets dark.*

"I think he had the flu or something," said one of the lift operators when Eddie inquired if he had seen his friend. "That's what somebody told me. He must be really sick cause this is the first time he's missed a day of skiing, ever."

As Eddie took the lift up over the snowy peaks he scanned the slopes for Chili's red ski jacket. There was no sign of him. Later, when he reached the bottom of the mountain, he spotted the older man sitting on a bench near the lodge sipping a beer. Eddie smiled, kicked off his skis, tossed them over his shoulder and marched towards his friend.

"Where have you been, old man?" said Eddie putting his skis on a rack and sitting down. "I heard you had the flu."

"Flu ain't so bad, I reckon," said Chili. "I think you need a beer. I'm buying."

"Won't say no to that," said Eddie. Chili handed Eddie a bottle and sat next to him enjoying the sun on his weathered face. Nearly seventy now, he could still out-ski anyone on the mountain with the exception of the kids training for the US Olympic team.

"Doctor wanted me to have some tests," said Chili. "Cost me a small fortune."

"What kind of tests?"

"I don't know, CT this, MRI that. A bunch of 'em. They took half my blood. They filled so many vials my one arm dried out and they had to tap into the other like a goddamn maple tree."

"Everything okay?"

"You know doctors, they get their tail in a bunch about the littlest thing," said Chili as he took a drag on his cigarette. "Just a false alarm."

"Well, that's good news. You ready to head back over to the Sty?" said Eddie. "The shuttle is leaving in five minutes."

"I'm going to get a few more runs in while it's still light out. Conditions are about as good as it gets. Nice and warm and the sky is clear. Don't want to waste it. Remember that, Eddie, never waste a single day. You don't get them back."

Eddie walked over to the rack and picked up his skis. "I've had enough for today. I'm going to take a hot shower and watch a game or something. Stop by later if you feel like it. Otherwise, see you tomorrow and I'll beat you down the mogul run." Seeing the shuttle about to pull out, Eddie hoisted his skis over his shoulder and ran towards it.

30

When his alarm sounded the next morning, Eddie was groggy. He and his roommates had stayed up until two in the morning – drinking beer and watching reruns of college basketball highlights. He smelled freshly brewed coffee in the air and heard banging noises coming from the kitchen.

"Hey Eddie. You better get up. It's almost eight," shouted Ronin from another room. Eddie heard the front door open and slam shut and the apartment was silent. Jumping out of bed, Eddie wandered into the kitchen hoping his roommates had left some coffee in the pot. They had and he poured himself a cup. He started work at eight thirty that morning and raced to catch the 8:10am shuttle over to the mountain. Dressing quickly, he gulped down his coffee and bolted out the door, boots in one hand, skis over his shoulder.

Climbing onto the bus with the other workers, he sat back for the short ride. Even at that early hour skiers were already waiting for a lift and the mountain was bustling. When the shuttle pulled into the main mountain ski area, there were several police cars and an ambulance with its lights flashing. Eddie and several of the other workers walked over to the cop car and looked up. The ski patrol was halfway up the mountain bringing someone down on a stretcher.

"What's going on?" said Eddie to one of the cops. "The lifts haven't even opened yet. What happened?"

"There's been a fatality," said the policeman. "Ski patrol found someone in one of the Back Bowls. They think the person has been there since last night because no one except maintenance has been up there this morning."

"At night, it's below freezing up there," said Eddie shaking his head while watching the ski patrol maneuver their way down the slope with the stretcher. "People shouldn't ski alone in the Back Bowls. It's so dangerous. That's really sad."

Later that morning when he took his break, Eddie ran into Ben, the HR director, outside the main lodge. Ben was on his phone and Eddie waved. Ben held up one finger, asking Eddie to wait.

Seconds later, Ben ended his call and walked over to Eddie. "Look, I'm just going to say it. The person the ski patrol brought down the mountain this morning. It was Chili."

"What?" said Eddie.

"That ambulance that was here this morning?" said the director. "It was for Chili."

Tears filled Eddie's eyes. "I don't understand. What happened?"

"Looks like a ski accident," said the director shaking his head. "He was in one of the Back Bowls. Some of the lift operators remembered him going up late in the afternoon. It must have happened yesterday and no one realized he was still up there when they shut down the mountain for the night. Right after sunrise this morning, one of the maintenance workers was up top fixing a lift runner when he looked over the side of the mountain and saw a body sprawled out down below. We sent the ski patrol up right away. Didn't know it was Chili until they called down to us."

"This makes no sense," said Eddie, tears now running down his cheeks. "Chili knew this mountain better than anyone. He knew every nook and cranny, every dip, every turn. He must have had a heart attack or something."

The director shook his head. "Nope. Got a call from the medical examiner half an hour ago. Cause of death was from the fall. Chili went right over the side at Blue Goose Gulch."

"That's impossible. You know him. He was an expert skier but he was also a careful skier," said Eddie.

"Everybody on the mountain loved him. He'd been working here long before me," said the director wiping away his own tears. "This is a terrible day."

"I skied a few runs with him yesterday afternoon. He said he was going to do a few more," said Eddie now overcome with grief.

"I don't know if you knew it, but Chili wasn't well."

"He told me that he'd been for some tests but that everything was fine."

The director gave a little laugh. "That's Chili," he said. "Always a tough guy. He wasn't fine. I only knew because I had to process some of his medical documents for him and he swore me to secrecy. He had terminal cancer. Started in his lungs and it spread everywhere. There wasn't much they could do and he didn't want to put himself through any treatments. They gave him a couple of months."

Eddie let out a sob. "Chili went out his own way, doing what he loved best. He didn't take a wrong turn," said Eddie, his voice catching as he looked up at the mountain. "He was too good a skier. He had his one last great run and then took the big ride over Blue Goose Gulch. God, I'm going to miss him."

31

A mid-mountain service was held at dawn a week after Chili Warren's death. Based on the huge attendance, it was evident that the old ski bum had been loved.

"I don't know about the rest of you, but Chili had a huge impact on my life, more than I had realized," Eddie had said to the crowd of people who gathered to say goodbye to their old friend. "I met him quite a few years ago. I was at a low point in my life and somehow, he had the right words at the right time. Judging by the number of people here today, I'm guessing I'm not the only one he had that effect on. What I do know is, the world is an emptier place without him and Chili Warren will be dearly missed."

When the service was over, nearly one hundred Vail Mountain employees skied slowly down the slope in single file, each holding a can of chili powder high in the air as they descended. When the last person reached the bottom, there was a massive group hug.

The black cloud of Chili's death made the remaining weeks somber ones. At the end of May, the mountain officially closed and Eddie drove east back to New Jersey. Chili's death had hit him hard and he was committed to taking his friend's advice. He was going home to straighten out his life. No more cutting corners, no more running away. Chili's voice was now in his head. "Running away don't solve nothing, only makes things worse," the older man had said to him on more than one occasion.

Eddie had sublet his one-bedroom apartment in Weston NJ to a college student until the end of the spring semester. School had ended the second week in May and the student had already cleared out by the time Eddie returned. Pulling into the driveway of the old Tudor-style ramshackle property, he took his bags out of the car and looked around. The spring flowers were out and the air smelled good. Returning to New Jersey signaled a new beginning for him. He had made a lot of decisions and a lot of promises to himself on the long drive back from Colorado.

First, he was going to get a job, work hard and put himself in a better financial position. Second, he was going to repair his relationship with his kids. Sarah was going to be the harder of the two but he was determined. Third, he was going to apologize to his ex-wife for being a world-class dick.

The next morning he drew up a list of business contacts and researched possible job opportunities. He called Clare to let her know he was back and in a better place. She was polite but not overly congratulatory. *Fair enough,* he thought, *I put her through hell.* After their divorce was finalized, Clare had gone back to work in Manhattan as an editor for a food magazine. Sarah, now fifteen, was a sophomore in high school and Joe, in middle school, had started playing the guitar in a middle-school rock band. Chili's voice echoed in his head. 'Never waste a single day. You don't get them back.' Above all else, Eddie wanted to get to know his kids again.

After some initial inquiries it was clear the media doors were still closed to him. He'd have to look elsewhere. He applied for any sales job available—cars, computer equipment, even underground storage space for housing data in case of a nuclear holocaust.

"That's a pretty grim pitch," Eddie said grimacing when the employment agent told him about the underground storage job, "talking about Armageddon every day."

"It's not everybody's cup of tea," said the overweight fiftyish blonde recruiter with a thick Jersey accent. "We live in a nuclear age. Wake up. Shit happens. Companies have to protect their data, it's that simple. Don't read so much into it. You need a job, right?"

Eddie was hired, but after a week of training and three weeks out in the field, he found the pitch and the conversations too depressing and was soon looking for another job. He called Clare to arrange a weekend with his kids, the first one in a long time.

"How's it going to work? You have a one-bedroom apartment," said Clare. "Where will the kids sleep?"

"Joey can bunk in with me and Sarah can have the couch in the living room."

"Sarah's fifteen, she needs her privacy. She won't want to sleep on the couch."

"It's one night," said Eddie. "What if I take the kids separately? Joe this weekend and Sarah next, just to get things rolling again."

"I'll ask them," said Clare hearing the emotion in his voice. "Don't be surprised if Sarah doesn't want to do it. She's still pretty angry that you took off."

"I'll make it up to her. I promise."

"Your promises don't have much currency around here."

"I know I've screwed up but I'm going to fix things, I swear," said Eddie.

"Sure, whatever."

"There's something else. I wanted to say that I'm sorry."

"For what?" said Clare.

"For everything," said Eddie quietly. "You deserved so much better and I was awful."

"Thank you," she said quietly.

"I can't change the past but I can try to be a good father to our kids and be a good ex-husband to you," said Eddie.

"I appreciate the apology. Time will tell."

The following Saturday, Eddie picked up his son for the weekend. Clare's new house was much smaller than the one she and Eddie had shared together. It was a sweet, old white clapboard house with a small front porch and wooden steps up to the front door.

Pulling into Clare's driveway, he texted Joe to let him know he was there. He hadn't seen his son for months and was looking forward to spending the next two days with him. A curtain on an upstairs window moved slightly. Someone was looking out but not wanting to be seen. When Eddie looked up, the curtain moved back into place. He turned the radio to a country-western station and waited for his son to appear. Soon, Joe bounded down the steps with a backpack over one shoulder and a guitar case slung over the other.

Eddie smiled and waved. *He looks taller. He looks like me when I was his age. Good-looking kid.*

"Hey Dad," said Joe as he opened the back door and put his bag and guitar on the seat.

As Joe climbed into the front seat Clare walked out onto the front porch. "What time are you bringing him back tomorrow?" she shouted.

Eddie held one hand out the window with five fingers extended. Clare nodded, waved and went back into the house. The curtain on the second-floor window moved again.

"How about we go to a diner for breakfast?" Eddie said to his son. "So, where's your bedroom located in the house?"

"Mine's upstairs in the back."

"Whose bedroom is upstairs in the front?"

"Sarah's, we're both upstairs. Mom's room is downstairs in the back."

Eddie nodded and backed out of the driveway.

That night their conversation was somewhat stilted and awkward because so much time had passed. When Eddie suggested the teenager play his guitar his son perked up.

"My band is going really well, Dad. We've played at a few parties," said Joe.

"That's fantastic," said Eddie, "Your mom didn't tell me."

"Mom said you used to play guitar in college," said Joe.

"I dabbled a little," said Eddie puffing up and smiling as he reached for his son's guitar and attempted to remember the old chords for "Stairway to Heaven". He couldn't and shook his head as he handed the instrument back to his son. "I used to be able to play that song with my eyes closed."

"You just need to practice," said Joe.

"I'd like to hear you and your band play sometime. Mind if I crash one of your gigs?"

"It's mainly for kids," said Joe, a wary look on his face.

"I'll stand in the back, drop in just for a few minutes. No one will even know I'm there."

"Maybe."

The following afternoon, during their car ride back to Clare's house, Eddie brought up the notion of another visit. "How about we do this again the weekend after next?" he said as they pulled into Clare's driveway.

Joe didn't reply right away. "I think Mom's got plans for us that weekend," he finally said, visibly uncomfortable.

"Oh yeah, what's up?"

"We're going camping," said Joe.

"Your mother is going camping?" said Eddie. "Since when does she camp?"

"Mark's taking us," said Joe quietly.

"Who's Mark?"

"A friend of Mom's."

"A boyfriend?"

"I guess," said Joe. "He's an electrician. When the lights in our kitchen blew out, he came to fix them. That's how they met."

"You like him."

"He's really into camping. We've gone with him before," said Joe. "He has every kind of camping gadget you can imagine. He showed Mom how to fish and how to cook dinner over a fire."

"Sounds like fun."

"You should have seen her the first time," said Joe laughing and getting more animated than he had the entire weekend, "she freaked out about everything; the bugs, the noises, the shadows. Mark had to walk her to the bathroom with a flashlight every time. She's better now. Goes to the bathroom at night by herself and everything."

As Joe opened his door Eddie forced a smile. "I'll check with your mother about another weekend for us to get together."

"Sure."

"Love you," said Eddie.

"Love you, too," mumbled Joe as he grabbed his stuff from the back seat and closed the rear door.

The following week, a friend of a friend reached out to Eddie about a sales technology job.

"I could really get behind this product," said Eddie enthusiastically to the director of Sales Genie. "I used to run sales teams so I totally appreciate this kind of tool. I know I could sell the hell out of it."

"Let me be brutally honest, it's not an easy sell," said the director. "It's a very crowded field and two other companies have a much larger market share than we do."

"It gives us something to shoot for," said Eddie with confidence. "I thrive on tough sells."

"Naturally, one of the main reasons we'd hire you is because of your extensive list of media contacts," said the director. "We'd expect you to tap into your contacts and open some doors for us."

"I'm more than happy to do that," said Eddie. "I know everyone in the media business. I've got contacts at just about every company."

A week later while Sales Genie HR was drafting Eddie's offer letter, there were some internal misgivings over his hire.

"I'm not a hundred percent sold on Gamble," said Sales Genie's SVP of sales to the HR director. "He's got a spotty record so I'm putting him on a short leash. He's got three months to make things happen. If he doesn't perform, we cut him loose."

The Sales Genie job posting had said it paid $85,000 a year, not even close to what Eddie had earned in previous jobs. He had assumed the $85,000 was the base salary with additional commission, but when he got his offer letter it told a different story. He would receive a salary of $45,000 and had the potential to earn another forty plus in commission. That would barely cover his rent, child support, and car insurance. He had already resigned from the underground data storage company when he got the verbal offer from Sales Genie so he'd have to make it work.

The following Monday, he reported to the Sales Genie office in Hoboken, New Jersey for training. When the SVP introduced him to the rest of the sales team Eddie noticed he was much older than their other salespeople. *They're all kids,* he thought, *what am I doing here?*

"Our strategy is to identify companies that are dissatisfied with their current system and are looking for a change," said his boss as they walked through the halls. "We're counting on you and your connections to get us into some of those big media companies like Andover or Fleming Global Media. If we can flip one of those, the others will follow."

Sitting at his desk in a large bullpen, Eddie went methodically through his contacts and left messages, texts and emails for former colleagues from Andover, Fleming Global, Diamond International and anyone else he had come into contact with during his halcyon days. Most of his calls and messages went unanswered and those who did respond couldn't or wouldn't help. Determined to make a go of it, he kept at it.

Over the following weeks and months, Clare encouraged her daughter to spend some time with her father. Sarah agreed to a lunch only.

"She doesn't want to stay over?" said Eddie.

"Baby steps. She's still angry," said Clare. "If things go well with your lunch and the weather's good, take her for a walk in a park afterwards. A little bit at a time."

When Eddie pulled into Clare's driveway that Saturday, a tall man with brown hair wearing a baseball cap and a red tee shirt was mowing the lawn. The man looked up, smiled and waved. Eddie waved back. *Friendly gardener*, he thought.

A few minutes later a sullen-faced Sarah pushed open the front screen door. She was followed by her mother who stood on the porch as Sarah slowly walked down the front steps. Sarah pulled open the passenger door and got into the car without looking at her father.

"Hi kiddo," said Eddie attempting to lean over and give his daughter a kiss. She pulled back towards her side of the car, blocking his hug, looked down at her phone and began texting. *It's going to be like that, is it?* Eddie thought. *I guess I deserve it.*

Looking over at his teenaged daughter, who was almost a woman, he wondered where the little girl had gone. Sarah, who used to hang on his every word and held the keys to Princess World. What happened to her demands for "Daddy hugs" every morning and night? He pictured her at three, four, five and even six, but the years after that were fuzzy. *Because I was never around.* She turned her head slightly and that's when he noticed a small gold hoop ring sticking through her right eyebrow. *She's got an eyebrow piercing,* he thought, *why didn't Clare tell me about that? Jeez.*

They drove to a diner not far from a state park that had walking trails. It was a beautiful, warm fall morning and Eddie planned they'd go for a walk after their meal. Once they were seated in the restaurant, conversation at the table was one-sided with Eddie doing most of the talking.

"How's school?"

"Okay."

"You join any clubs? I was in a ton of clubs when I was your age. In college, your mother and I were both in the public service club and coed volleyball together."

"Clubs are for losers," said Sarah still focused on her phone.

"You got a hoop in your eyebrow. Did it hurt?"

"Are you going to lecture me?" said Sarah still looking at her phone. "Cause Mom already did."

"How about you put your phone down so we can talk," said Eddie as the waiter placed their sandwich plates in front of them.

Sarah puffed out her cheeks, placed her phone on the table and picked up her sandwich. Though her father carried the conversation through most of their meal, by the end her responses moved from one word to two. After lunch, Eddie suggested they go for a walk in the park. Much to his surprise, she agreed.

The sun was out and the warm breeze caressed their skin as they walked along the trails stopping periodically to look at strategically placed sculptures. Standing in front of a large one made of metal entitled *The Cowboy*, Eddie and Sarah both looked at it from various angles.

"I don't get the Cowboy part," said Eddie squinting and stepping back. "Looks like a bunch of black-and-red metal to me. I think I'd call it Bloody Squished Spider."

Sarah giggled for the first time that day. "Me too," she said, trying to hide her tiny smile. Eddie thought maybe, he'd found a crack in her armor. After that reaction, he made a point of poking fun of every piece of art in the park and soon Sarah joined in. By the last one, they were having a full conversation about how dumb each sculpture's title was.

"Who makes up these names?" said Sarah pointing to another one. "That one is called The Serpent."

"How is that a serpent?" said Eddie. "It's square. Have you ever seen a square serpent?"

Sarah snorted and half-smiled as Eddie gave her a wink. They had a moment before she retreated back into her shell.

Exhausted from doing so much of the talking, Eddie turned on the car radio as he drove his daughter home. Sarah played with her phone while Eddie listened to his favorite country songs.

"Joe told me your Mom has a boyfriend," said Eddie.

"Mark," said Sarah. "He's nice. He takes us camping. I think he was a boy scout or something."

"Sounds like he's become a regular part of the family. What does he look like?"

"You saw him. He was mowing our lawn when you picked me up."

"Does he always mow your lawn?" asked Eddie.

"Since he moved in," said Sarah.

Clare didn't tell me someone moved in with her and my children, thought Eddie. *I have a right to know that.*

When he pulled into Clare's driveway, Sarah jumped out of the car before he had a chance to give her a hug.

"Bye," she said as she slammed the car door and flew up the steps two at a time.

32

The SVP of *Girl Glam*, a popular fashion and beauty website for teenaged girls owned by Andover Media, had asked Pamela, her VP of Sales, to come to her office.

"I need you to meet with someone selling a software product that *supposedly* would help our sales team increase productivity. Let me be clear, I'm not interested in buying his product but he's an old friend and frankly, he's a little desperate."

"What do you want me to do?" said Pamela.

"He's had a run of bad luck," said the SVP. "I don't have the heart to turn him down. Since you don't know him, you can do it for me."

"Thanks a lot," said Pamela blowing out a breath. "Fine. What time and where's the meeting?"

"Two thirty tomorrow. He'll meet you in your office."

Pamela nodded and started to walk out when she stopped and turned. "What's his name?"

"Eddie Gamble. I forget the name of his company. Doesn't matter. We're not buying it."

"I *know* Eddie Gamble. He was my boss at *Vacation*," said Pamela, her eyes widening.

"I forgot you worked there. Is this a problem for you, Pamela?" said her publisher, mildly irritated.

"Not a problem. I liked Eddie. He was good to me most of the time and especially kind during a difficult period," said Pamela, remembering when he had taken her out to lunch after she lost her first baby. Her SVP was already absorbed in an unrelated document on her desk and had moved on to another subject.

"Everybody liked Eddie," said the SVP not looking up from her papers, "but he cut too many corners and pissed off the wrong people. He couldn't get a job in this business if his life depended on it."

"I always wondered what happened to him," said Pamela. "One day he was everywhere and then he disappeared, dropped totally off the radar. What if I like the product he's selling?"

"Give him thirty minutes and then get rid of him," said the SVP reading something more interesting on her computer screen."

The next day, returning from a big client lunch with one of her salespeople, Pamela had only a few minutes to spare before her meeting with her former boss. Despite him taking all the *Vacation* sales account info to the competition, she still had a soft spot for him. When he took her to lunch at La Côte Basque, it had meant a lot to her during a terrible time. She had never forgotten the empathy and kindness he showed to her that day and she never would. She hoped whatever he was selling was something she could get behind and convince the SVP to buy. She wanted to return his kindness.

At 2:40pm the front desk rang through to Pamela saying she had a visitor in reception. Pamela looked at her watch. *He's ten minutes late. When we were at Vacation, he would have been furious if I had arrived ten minutes late for a sales call.* Reaching into her desk drawer, she pulled out a comb and mirror to smooth her hair, check her makeup and reapply a fresh coat of plum-colored lip gloss. It had been years since she had seen him and she wanted to look good.

Seconds later, a small gray man in a rumpled suit appeared in her doorway.

"I can't believe it."

"Eddie!" said Pamela forcing a smile after noticing how different her old boss looked.

In the many years since she had last seen him, the change in his appearance was startling. His once wavy blond hair was gray and mostly gone. He wore glasses now and was hunched over. Smaller and thinner than she remembered, and his face was blotchy and puffy. *What the hell happened to him?* thought Pamela. The Eddie Gamble she knew had been larger than life, strong, decisive and always ready with a quip, a nod and a smile. His bright blue eyes were still there behind his glasses but the twinkle had vanished. An unspoken understanding was exchanged between them.

With a smile plastered on his face, Eddie took a deep breath, walked towards her and gave her a big hug.

After they took their seats, Pamela remained poker-faced trying not to stare at the broken man sitting in front of her who at one time had been the embodiment of charisma. Through the grapevine she had heard his career had tanked. She had also heard his wife found out about one of his numerous girlfriends and divorced him. *He thought it was a secret, but everyone at* Vacation *knew*, she thought as she looked at his hands: no wedding ring. *Guess the rumors were true. He used to be so handsome. What the hell happened?*

"Great to see you, Pamela," Eddie said with a genuine smile. "You look exactly the same. You haven't aged a day."

"Still a charmer. You always know exactly what to say."

"I speak the truth. You look fantastic."

"You do too," said Pamela looking down at some papers so her eyes wouldn't give away her lie.

"I've got a little less hair than I used to," said Eddie sheepishly, smoothing the follicles still left on his head.

"You look wonderful," said Pamela with a little too much enthusiasm. "Tell me what you're selling and why we need it at *Girl Glam*. Sell me something, Eddie Gamble."

While he dug through his leather satchel for his presentation book, Pamela had a chance to examine him. He wore a gray suit that was old and she detected a few light stains on his lapel. His tie was slightly askew. His white shirt had a grayish hue and the collar was too loose and swam around his neck. Through the glass top of her desk, she could see his shoes were scuffed and the heels worn. He needed a haircut and possibly a shave. It was difficult to see the old Eddie with one exception: his aqua-blue eyes. They were still bluer than blue.

"I'm working for this cool little technology company," said Eddie. "We have this amazing sales management software that will make your life as a manager so much easier. How does that sound?"

"We already use a program that works really well for us. Tell me what makes yours so different and why it would warrant changing and retraining everyone," said Pamela encouragingly.

"You bet. It's called Sales Genie and it does most of the things your current sales management programs do but our product is much less expensive." Eddie paused for a moment looking around her luxe office. "I guess cost isn't really that big an issue here at Andover. Everyone knows Thomas Andover has deep pockets. I will admit, the program you're currently using has some advantages over mine. If you switched, it would require additional training for your team, but you would save a fair amount of money annually." Pamela looked at him but did not speak and there was a pause in the conversation. "I'm guessing saving a little money on software isn't that important to you. It's probably not worth your time. I understand."

Pamela stared at him, her mouth slightly open. Was this the same guy who led *Vacation* to a record-breaking year of sales? The man who never took no for an answer and broke more new business than anyone in the history of the magazine including its publisher, Julia Bowman? She remembered on more than one occasion him saying, 'When they slam the door, you knock again. If they don't open up, you go in through a window. If the window is locked, you scale the house and climb down the chimney. If they don't have a chimney, you grab a shovel and dig a tunnel into the basement. You never ever give up.' The tired man in front of her had just talked his way *out* of a sale, and Pamela hadn't said one word.

Eddie smiled ruefully and looked down at his lap. He knew he wasn't going to make a deal that day. A wave of empathy swept over Pamela. She thought of the Maya Angelou quote: "People will forget what you said, people will forget what you did, but people will never forget how you made them feel." On that long-ago lunch, for two hours Eddie Gamble had made her feel whole again and she had never forgotten it.

"Eddie, you just talked yourself out of the sale. What happened to banging on the door and climbing down the chimney? You basically told me not to buy from you."

"The product you're currently using is better. Mine is cheaper though."

"Sell me," said Pamela. "I'm begging you. Come on, you were the master of the close. Remember ABC, always be closing?"

She wanted to help him the same way he had helped her. She suspected he needed her now even more than she needed him back then. Encouraging him to try again, she implored him to dig deep and find the old Eddie, the one who took no prisoners.

"Come back to see me again, and bring the guy who always brimmed with cocky self-confidence," she said. For the next thirty minutes, Pamela, now a seasoned sales director herself, gave Eddie very specific instructions on his presentation and how to pitch his product. She gave him the very same direction he would have given years earlier. The irony did not elude her. He had been the master of the universe, the golden boy of Andover Media, the prince of Madison Avenue, and everyone's favorite son. Senior management loved him, and the support staff adored him. His salespeople did backflips when he asked and clients and agencies couldn't get enough of him. Even Hedwig, the fat German lady who ran the concession stand in Andover Media's lobby and didn't like anyone touching her merchandise, loved him. He was the only Andover employee besides Thomas Andover that Hedwig would let thumb through her magazines. No one else in the building was allowed to do that, only Eddie.

Desperate to rescue him, Pamela told him they would try the Sales Genie software for a few weeks as a test. "If it works as well, is easy to learn and use and we could save money, I'll consider it." She didn't think her boss would approve the change, but she didn't have the heart to turn him down that afternoon. He was too fragile.

"Thanks so much for your time. I really appreciate it," said Eddie as he got up to leave. "And, you really do look great."

"You too," said Pamela as she got up to give him a hug. "Let's talk in a few weeks after I've had some time to play around with Sales Genie. I want you to remember how good you are. You were the best. There was nobody better in the ad sales business than Eddie Gamble. You were one of the youngest publishers in the business. Every media company wanted to steal you. Find that person again. He's in there and trust me, he's amazing."

Eddie forced a smile and nodded his head. It was good to be reminded that he had value. It had been a long time since old Eddie had been around. His meeting with Pamela gave him hope that maybe he could find his old self again, but he had no idea where to look.

33

By the end of his sixth month at Sales Genie, with little business coming in from his accounts, Eddie was terminated. He hadn't made many sales and on top of that, word on the street was that Sales Genie was having financial problems. When news of that got out, nobody wanted to buy a subscription to their product fearing they wouldn't be around long enough to support it. Unemployed again, he pared down his expenses and tried to live as simply and cheaply as possible. With the proceeds from the sale of his house nearly gone, late nights out at restaurants with friends was now fully in his rearview mirror.

Now nearly fifty, Eddie scoured employment listings but got far fewer responses than in the past. He was tired. A few people from the old days took his calls and went through the motions but in the end, someone else got the job. He still had a couple of loyal friends but they were busy with their own lives and careers. They offered a supportive ear, but not a job and it was a job that he needed. Weekend invitations to summer houses had stopped long ago. Having Eddie around made successful people uncomfortable. They remembered the guy they used to know and wondered if it could happen to them, too.

As Eddie scrolled through another online job board, one caught his eye. A local lifestyle website called *South Jersey Life* was looking for a salesperson. They covered the six counties in South Jersey and reported on local news, elections, happenings, and festivals. They had 200,000 monthly users and carried local advertising, everything from restaurants to dry cleaners to car dealerships. *I could do this,* thought Eddie. *It's based out of Jersey, so I wouldn't have to spend money commuting into the city.* The position was way below his experience level. The compensation was $40,000 a year plus commission. He was sure he could do the job with his eyes closed. He let out a self-effacing laugh recalling that he had a $40,000-a-year clothing allowance while publisher of *American Traveler. How the mighty have fallen,* he thought. Still, it was a job and Clare had been cranky about the late child support payments.

Unconsciously tapping her foot on the wood floor in her office, Ilene Kostikian looked at her watch and frowned. It was 7:15pm and he was supposed to be there at 7. Looking out the window, she noticed the heavy rain outside weighed down the thick green leaves in the trees. *He's not going to show,* she thought. *He sounded awful when he called. I hope he shows.* Minutes later, the door in her waiting room creaked. "Eddie," Ilene called out, "is that you?"

"Sorry I'm late," said Eddie as he stood in the doorway of her office soaking wet. "It started raining and the traffic was terrible."

Ilene willed herself not to show surprise at Eddie's appearance. *He used to be so good-looking.* "Good to see you,

Eddie, you look... good," said Ilene, artfully lying. "It's been a few years."

Eddie sat in a chair while attempting to straighten out his rumpled suit and smooth his thin wet hair.

"It has been a while," said Eddie with a crooked half-smile, looking over her head and glancing at the art on the walls. "You look great, Ilene. I see you've got some new safari pictures."

"Always a charmer," said Ilene, blushing. "Good of you to notice my new photos. Since we're short on time, why don't you tell me why you reached out to me after all these years."

Eddie looked at his feet. "I guess it's because I wanted some advice on how to communicate with my kids."

For the next few minutes Eddie updated Ilene on what he had been doing since she last saw him. He mentioned the divorce and rattled off a litany of jobs and activities.

"I see," said Ilene. "Sounds like you've had a bit of a rough patch."

"You could say that."

"What's going on with Clare and your kids now?" said Ilene.

"It seems that Clare has a... boyfriend. Mark. He's apparently moved into her house with my kids."

"How do you feel about that?"

"I don't know. They seem to like him and it sounds like he's nice to them," said Eddie. "So I guess I should be happy." There was a long pause. "I guess he's replaced me."

"I can understand you feeling that way. But he hasn't replaced you. You're still their father. Nothing changes that."

Tears welled up in Eddie's eyes. "He's doing a better job than I ever did." A single tear escaped from Eddie's left eye.

Ilene swallowed. She had a hunch when she got the call from him that this was going to be an intense session. "Why do you say that?"

"Because he's there. I never was," said Eddie, a tear now

trickling out of his right eye. "I was always off chasing something. The joke is, I was looking for what I already had. In the process, I lost my wife, kids, career, and most of my friends. And here's the kicker, I still don't understand how it all happened."

34

Two years later, Eddie packed up his last box, carried it outside and loaded it into the back of his car. As he shut the back lift, it occurred to him that his entire life fit into his ten-year-old Jeep Grand Cherokee. Making one final trip back up the stairs into the empty apartment that had been his home for nearly three years, he acknowledged there hadn't been many good memories made there. Now, he was moving to an even smaller place above some old lady's garage in Clayton, NJ, over in Gloucester County. It was a dump but it was cheap and these days cheap was all he could swing.

The move to the smaller place had been necessary after he was let go from *South Jersey Life*. The VP of Sales had told him it was a "budgetary thing, nothing personal".

"Sure," Eddie had said trying to save face. "I understand. I've been in your shoes myself. When the money's not there, you've got to make cuts." The VP let out a breath of relief. Eddie had made it easier for him to cut the cord. They shook hands and agreed that his last day would be in two weeks.

The night he was fired, he examined his dwindling bank account which convinced him to look online for a less expensive place to live. Within the next few days, he found the inexpensive apartment above a garage and also secured a job selling cars at Bernie's Used Cars not too far from his new apartment. The position only paid $24,000 a year but he also would get an additional monthly draw of $800 against commission. Money would be tight but if he was careful, he could make it work. Medical or dental wasn't included and he hoped he had no health issues until he could get back in the game in a better job. A bum tooth would screw up his whole budget.

As he stood in his bathroom above the garage shaving one morning, he moved the razor across his cheek and examined his aging face and scalp in the mirror. *Not much hair left in the front,* he thought. *But not gonna do that combover thing. Never a good look.* He finished shaving, put on a button-down shirt and a jacket, grabbed his car keys and phone and was about to leave when his phone rang. It was Clare. He knew why she was calling, he was behind on the child support again.

"I know I'm late," said Eddie answering the phone. "I've had a few unexpected expenses and..."

"I'm not calling about that," said Clare. "It's about your visits with Joe."

"What about them?"

"He doesn't want to stay over with you anymore," said Clare.

After a long silence, Eddie finally spoke. "Are you putting him up to this?"

"Don't be ridiculous," she snapped. "He said he's uncomfortable in your new place and that it smells. Where are you living now anyway?"

"It doesn't smell," said Eddie getting agitated. "What does 'he's uncomfortable' mean?"

"I don't know. He said it's very small and it feels like you're on top of each other. He's a teenager, he wants to be with his friends on weekends."

"I'm his friend," said Eddie.

"I knew you were going to react this way," said Clare, an edge in her voice. "Most teenagers don't spend entire weekends with their parents. They're social beings and our son is not unlike you. Remember how you were in college? You were the mayor of the campus. Joe likes to be the life of the party too. Hanging out in a stinky apartment above a garage in South Jersey with his father for the weekend is not his idea of a good time."

"I'm sorry my accommodation doesn't meet his high standards."

"Get over yourself. He doesn't hang out with me either," said Clare. "The way to keep him is to let him go. Then, he'll want to see you, but on his time, not yours."

After further discussion, Eddie agreed to curtail the weekend visits with his son for a while and wait for Joe to come around on his own. It was decided Eddie would take his son out for dinner once a week instead.

People shopping for a car at Bernie's Used Cars were looking for one thing—a deal. Eddie spent most of his time on the lot lowering the price to make a sale rather than pointing out the features of a particular vehicle. His commissions were based on a sliding scale. The lower the price, the lower his percentage of commissions. If he took it down too much, he made nothing. Sometimes, he did that just to make sure he kept his job. A low sale without commissions was better than no sale at all.

On a cold, damp December Saturday, Eddie was alone at the dealership. Outside, a man wearing a hat and scarf walked with a teenaged boy around the far end of the car lot. Watching them through the window, Eddie waited inside to let them roam for a while before he approached and began his sales spiel.

"Hey there," Eddie shouted with a forced friendliness a few minutes later as he crossed the parking lot. "You looking for a new car? You came at the right time. We've got some really good deals going on right now." Eddie put his hand out as he got closer to the older man. "I'm Eddie, what can I help you find today?"

The teenager wandered down another row of cars as Eddie faced the older man.

"Eddie Gamble? This is a surprise," said the man with a distinct Australian accent. Eddie looked at his face half covered by a scarf and noted something familiar. It was Jonathan Barker, the nastiest man in the ad business.

"Jonathan," said Eddie forcing himself to smile, "Been a while. How've you been?"

"I've been great. I'm the chief revenue officer at Westport Media now," said Barker with a smirk as he looked Eddie over.

"Westport, great company. Good for you," said Eddie nodding.

"Ad business got a little too rough for you?" said Barker looking around at the dilapidated car lot. "Advertising isn't for the faint of heart. This looks like a good fit for you, selling used cars. A real meat and potatoes kind of sell."

"It's just temporary," said Eddie waving at the cars. "I had been working for this great little media company, *South Jersey Life*. The owner ran into some money problems and had to let the more senior people go. You know, get those high salaries off the payroll. I only took this job because it's near my house and keeps me busy, until I land a senior position somewhere. For now it's good. Who doesn't love cars, right?"

"Yeah, who doesn't love cars?" said Barker. "Maybe I'll think about chucking my job and doing the same thing. I'm going to do you a little favor. Maybe you can make a sale today." He called out to the teenager. "My son here has been saving up to buy his own car. We're on a tight budget. It's him buying, not me, so keep that mind."

"I completely understand," said Eddie. "I'll fix you up with a very good deal."

Two hours later after much haggling, where Jonathan beat Eddie to a pulp in order to get the best deal for his son, Eddie sold Jonathan a three-year-old Honda for well below the asking price. He knew he'd make no commission on the sale but at that moment it was more important for him to look like a big deal in front of his old colleague.

"Nice to see you again, Gamble," said Barker as he and his son walked towards the exit. "I run into Julia Bowman at industry events from time to time, I'll tell her you send your regards."

"Sure, that would be great," said Eddie as Barker and his son walked out the door.

Later that day, the owner of the car lot came in and saw the certificate of sale on his desk. "You sold the Honda?" he said as he picked up the contract and looked it over.

"To a father and son. They'll be back on Tuesday to pick it up."

Reading through the document the owner slammed his fist down on the desk. "You sold that car for $9,000? Are you fucking kidding me? What the hell is wrong with you? That car would easily have sold for 14,000. We just got it in. Why did you do that? Do you have rocks in your head?"

Over the next twenty minutes the owner worked himself into a frenzy and started shouting. By the time their loud one-sided conversation concluded, Eddie was out of a job. "You're a fucking loser, Gamble," shouted the owner as Eddie walked out the front door.

Numb, Eddie stopped at a cash machine to get some money. He checked his balance; only $3,000 left and his $900 monthly rent was due in ten days. Stopping at a strip mall, he went into a liquor store and bought three large bottles of bourbon. Once in the car he turned on the engine, opened the bottle and took a big swig. Sitting in the parking lot, he played out the events at the car dealership in his mind and looked into his eyes in the rear-view mirror. "You are a fucking loser," he said out loud and took another sip. "You lost a job as a fucking used car salesman. Even your kids don't want to see you. You're pathetic." He put the car in drive and headed for his apartment with the bourbon bottle nestled between his legs.

For the next two days Eddie was in an almost permanent state of intoxication and finished several large bottles of alcohol. It was nearly 4:30pm on the second day when he woke up on the couch and remembered that he was supposed to have dinner with his son that night. Still drunk, he got up to take a shower and nearly fell.

Later, after a long hot shower, he felt a little better. He shaved, brushed his teeth and put eyedrops into his bloodshot eyes. Above all else, he didn't want to be late picking up Joe for their weekly dinner. Whenever he was late or canceled last minute, Clare got on his case and he really didn't have the strength to deal with her shit that night. He took one last short drink for the road and threw the empty bottle into the trash.

Driving extra slow to his ex-wife's house, Eddie pulled his Jeep into her driveway and honked twice. The light outside the front door flickered on and a few minutes later his handsome teenaged son walked out, the storm door slamming behind him.

"Hey Dad," said Joe as he got into the car.

"Sorry I'm late, kiddo, got tied up doing a deal."

"Mom said I can't stay out long. Got a big test tomorrow so

we'll have to make it quick, okay?" his son said while texting on his phone.

"School always comes first," said Eddie as he attempted to back out of the driveway but sent the car up onto the curb. Straightening the wheel, he pulled forward and tried again. Several maneuvers later, he finally got the car out on the street.

"Dad, are you okay?"

"I'm fine, kiddo, had a long day," said Eddie squinting at the road in front of him as he slowly drove down the street.

"You're acting weird."

"Just tired," said Eddie while making a right-hand turn. As his car went around the corner, it drifted slightly over to the wrong side of the road.

"Dad, what are you doing?" shouted Joe. Eddie jolted back, sat up straight and steered the car over to the right side of the road.

"Maybe we should do dinner another night," said his son.

Eddie turned his head to look at Joe. He wanted to tell him that everything was fine and he loved him, that he'd figure things out like he always did. But before he could get the words out he ran a stop sign. A car that had the right of way slammed into the passenger side door of Eddie's Jeep. The sound of the crash was loud, there was crunching of metal on metal followed by shattering glass as the air bags inflated. Stunned and in pain, it took Eddie a minute to comprehend what had happened. Something was in his eyes. He rubbed them and saw blood on his hands and looked in the rear-view mirror. He had a big cut on his forehead. He called for his son. "Joe, are you all right? Joe?" Leaning over, he found blood on the teenager's face and the boy was unconscious. Sounds of sirens grew louder. The driver of the other car had not been injured and called 911.

By the time the ambulance arrived, Joe had opened his eyes and was talking. On-the-spot triage by the EMT team concluded that Joe had a broken collarbone, possibly a broken rib or two and several of his deeper cuts would require stitches. They also suspected he had suffered a concussion. Eddie's arm appeared fractured and he, too, would need stitches for several of the cuts on his neck and head. As the EMT team lifted a disoriented Joe into the ambulance, the police officers at the scene asked Eddie some questions about the accident. Whether it was the look in Eddie's eyes or the way he incoherently rambled when answering, the cops suspected he was on something.

"Every year we have a couple of accidents at this intersection," said the officer handing Eddie back his driver's license. "The driver of the car that hit you said you went right through that stop sign."

"I don't know," said Eddie, obviously shaken. "It all happened so fast. Is my son going to be all right?"

"Have you been drinking, Mr. Gamble?" said the officer.

"I had a drink several hours ago but I'm fine now."

The officer pulled out a breathalyzer kit. "We need to check that out, Mr. Gamble. Would you please breathe into this tube so we can have the numbers for our records."

Still shaken and worried about his son, Eddie complied. "Looks like you have a blood alcohol level of 1.0 percent," said the officer. "That's over the legal limit. Maybe you had more than the one drink?"

"I only remember having one," said Eddie.

"Let's get you to the hospital and have your arm looked at," said the officer. "You're lucky neither of you were killed."

In the ER, the father and son were placed in beds across from each other. Joe was examined, his collarbone packed in ice and several deep cuts stitched including seven stitches over his right eye. Riddled with guilt, Eddie watched the doctor stitch up his child.

"He's going to be okay, right?" said Eddie to the physician as he passed Eddie's bed.

"It's a simple break. The lacerations aren't too bad. In a few months, you won't even see the scars," said the doctor. "He's young, he'll mend. Now let's have a look at your injuries, Mr. Gamble."

When they took Joe to another floor to do a head scan, Eddie called Clare.

"Is he okay?" shouted Clare before Eddie finished the whole story.

"He'll be all right. He has a broken collarbone and a few cuts," said Eddie starting to cry.

"What the fuck, Eddie. You were going for pizza."

"There was a stop sign," he said, starting to sob, "I didn't see it. There were bushes in front of it."

"It's never your fault, is it?" Clare hissed. "I'll be there in twenty minutes."

While they waited for the orthopedist, Joe was given painkillers. Eddie sat next to his bed, the disappointment of the universe on his shoulders. He covered his eyes with his good hand.

"Dad?"

"How are you feeling?" Eddie said as he looked up at his son, his eyes wet.

"It still hurts but the pills help."

Looking down at his feet, unable to look his son in the eye, Eddie started to speak. "Joe, I'm so sorry, I didn't mean..."

"It's all right, Dad."

"No, it's not."

By the time Clare got to the hospital, she was in a frantic state. She laid into Eddie when she smelled him and guessed he had been drinking. "How could you?" she said under her breath so her son wouldn't hear their conversation. "You could have killed him."

"It was an accident," said Eddie, "I didn't see the stop—"

"Save it for someone who might believe your shit."

As the words left Clare's mouth, the police officer who had been at the scene of the accident walked up to them. "Mr. Gamble, the attending doctor says you can be released. We'll have to take you into the police station now. We're going to charge you with a DUI. Do you understand what that means?"

Eddie nodded slowly. "Can I say goodbye to my son?"

"Stay away from him," said Clare. "You've lost your right to be his father."

"I only want to say goodbye," said Eddie with no spirit left in his soul as he walked over to his son's bed. "Be good, kiddo. I'm sorry about everything. I'm so sorry."

"I don't want you to be sorry," said his son. "I want you to get it together. I want you to be my dad again."

Eddie nodded weakly. "I'm not sure I know how to do that anymore."

That night, Eddie Gamble, once the rising star of the media world was booked on a DUI, appeared before a night court and spent the night in jail. Released the next day on his own recognizance, he had to appear in court later that month.

With financial help from his parents and an earful of criticism, Eddie hired a lawyer. Since it was Eddie's first offense, he received the minimum sentence—six-month license suspension and forty hours of community service.

35

The deafening train whistle blared again, its lights growing larger each passing second. Three feet in front of Eddie, sitting on the tracks, the little black-and-white dog with the lopsided ears barked as the train whistle blew three times in rapid succession.

"Get out of here. Get the fuck out of here!" Eddie pleaded as he tried to push the dog out of the way with his foot. Unresponsive, the little dog laid his head down on the tracks near his new friend. "I said get out of here. You can't be near me; did you hear me?"

The little dog only looked up at him as four more deafening train horns sounded. "Get out of here, you damn dog," screamed Eddie. "Please!" Another loud horn pierced the air. At the last second, with the train almost upon them, Eddie grabbed the dog. The two rolled off the tracks at the moment the train was about to make contact. They tumbled over in the snow and onto some rocks as the locomotive screeched by. Lying on the ground sobbing with the dog in his arms for nearly two full minutes, Eddie remained still until the train passed. When he saw the taillights of the last car, he sat up, the dog still in his arms.

The dog didn't move so Eddie reached for the flashlight in his coat pocket. When he flicked it on, blood was everywhere—on him, on the dog, in the snow around them. The dog had been injured. Eddie hadn't been fast enough. *Is he dead?* He put his head down on the animal's chest. *There's a heartbeat. He's still alive.* He didn't know if the little dog had been clipped by the train or if their fall had caused the injuries. The unconscious animal's leg appeared to be broken and his skin was torn and bleeding in several places.

"I told you to leave, you stupid, dumb dog," said Eddie sobbing as he looked down at the broken animal. He pulled the bleeding dog into his chest, got up and ran across the snowy field towards the lights of the town. Out of breath when he got to the main street, he stopped for a moment to get his bearings. His Jeep was parked several blocks down the road. With the dog's blood dripping from the gashes on his legs, Eddie held him tight as he ran leaving a trail of red dots on the snowy sidewalk.

Opening the passenger door of the Jeep, he gently placed the injured animal on the seat. The dog moaned as blood oozed from a big gash on its leg . With his heart pounding in his chest, Eddie pulled out his phone and searched for a twenty-four-hour animal hospital. There was one three miles away on the same road. Though his driver's license had been suspended five months earlier because of the car accident, Eddie didn't care and drove double the speed limit. In minutes he arrived at the hospital and carefully lifted the limp dog out of the car.

"Help," shouted Eddie to the woman behind the front desk as he burst into the reception area holding the animal covered in blood, "my dog is hurt. He's been hit."

"I'll get the doctor right away, wait here," said the attendant jumping up. Eddie held the dog in his arms as blood continued to pool on the dog's fur. Fully awake now, the animal looked up at Eddie with innocent pleading eyes.

A young male vet ran into the waiting room wheeling a small transportation cart and the two men placed the injured dog onto it.

"Hang in there, amigo, this doctor will fix you up. You'll be all right," said Eddie to the dog.

While the vet took the dog into the back room, Eddie sat in the waiting room, trembling. *It's all my fault. That dog wouldn't have been there if it hadn't been for me. Everything I touch dies.*

He looked at his watch. *I missed my train tonight but there will be another one tomorrow.*

While he waited he thought about his parents, his colleagues at Andover and Fleming. He visualized his old skiing buddy, Chili, squinting from the sun, cigarette smoke billowing around his head just before he hauled his ass down a double black diamond mogul run. He thought about his kids and how badly he had screwed up and, of course, the car accident with Joe. He thought of Clare, the beautiful wife who was no longer his and now married to Mark. He shook his head. Everything had always gone his way and then one day it all stopped. Nothing ever worked again.

Numb since the car accident with his son, this was the first time he had felt something in months. When he ran across the snowy field carrying the bleeding dog, Eddie had a faint flicker of emotion—he wanted that little dog to live. Closing his eyes, he said a little prayer to the universe that the dog would survive and that his son didn't hate him. After almost an hour, the vet came out and signaled for Eddie to follow him. In a small examining room, the dog lay sleeping. Bandages covered one of his legs and the other had a cast.

"I gave him something for the pain and it put him right to sleep," said the vet. "He'll be out for the next twelve hours."

Eddie nodded.

"Was he hit by a car?" said the vet.

"Almost," said Eddie. "I yanked him out of the way but I think it clipped him and we both fell. Will he be okay?"

"I think so. He needs time to heal," said the vet. "I'd like to keep him overnight so we can keep an eye on him."

Eddie looked down at the floor. "I'm a little tight on funds at the moment. I can take him home and look after him myself." The vet nodded and wrote out detailed instructions on caring for the animal.

"Amigo will be fine," said the vet reassuringly. "He's got a fracture on his hind leg and there were several lacerations on the other leg so I had to put in a few stitches. But he's young, he'll mend."

Eddie nodded: the vet's words sounding eerily familiar.

"He should be as good as new in about four weeks. You'll need to keep a cone on him when he wakes up tomorrow or he'll bite at the bandages. I've put one in the bag for you along with his medication. Try and get some food into him tomorrow and make sure he's hydrated." Ashen, Eddie picked up the bag. "Don't look so worried," said the vet. "In a few weeks he'll be as good as new."

Carefully carrying the dog to his car, Eddie gingerly placed Amigo on the passenger seat. Then he began the long trip back to an apartment he never expected to see again.

36

For the next couple of months, Eddie did nothing but tend to the injured animal out of a sense of obligation. Once the dog's bandages were off, his limp soon turned into a normal walk. Within a few weeks, the dog was running and followed Eddie wherever he went.

"What do you want?" said Eddie gruffly to the dog sitting at his feet.

Jumping on the couch, Amigo settled into Eddie's lap. "You picked the wrong guy," he said to the dog as he pushed the animal off. "Don't you get it? I'm a loser. I even fucked up killing myself." Undaunted, the dog dove into his lap again, looked up at Eddie expectantly and licked his face. "Stop looking at me like that. I can't take care of you. I can't take care of me. I almost killed my own son." The dog rolled on its back exposing his stomach and waited to be scratched. Unconsciously, Eddie rubbed the dog's belly. "I can't keep you." The dog barked. "There's a park near here with a special section for dogs. It's probably filled with crazy dog lovers. You're reasonably cute. I'll take you over there and convince somebody to take you home with them."

The next day, Eddie walked Amigo over to Veterans Park. He planned to leave that day without the dog. Once in the dog meadow, Eddie took the leash off and let the dog go. Amigo bolted like a rocket across the open field towards a bunch of other dogs frolicking on the freshly mowed lawn. Soon, Amigo came racing back with a red ball in his mouth and placed it at Eddie's feet.

"Where did you get that?" said Eddie as he picked up the ball and threw it across the field. Charging after it, the dog moved so fast he overran it and flipped over twice. Soon on his feet, he retrieved the ball and galloped back to Eddie dropping it again at his feet.

"So this is how it's going to go?" said Eddie with little emotion as he picked up the ball and threw it again. Over and over, Eddie tossed the ball and Amigo retrieved it.

On the ninth throw, the ball soared further than intended and landed in the distance next to a bench. The dog raced at high speed across the field after the ball that now lay directly in front of a young man in a wheelchair. Sniffing furiously, Amigo circled the chair, finally stopping directly in the young man's sightline and barked twice. As if he had been awakened from a trance, the young man glanced downward but then quickly looked away.

"I suppose you want me to throw that ball," said the man without a smile. "That's about the only thing I can still do." With his right hand, he leaned over slightly and took the ball from the dog's mouth and tossed it across the field. Amigo tore after it.

"Don't get him started," said Eddie flatly as he approached. "He never gets tired, but you will."

The man in the chair looked down at the dog already back with the ball and eagerly awaiting another toss. Throwing it again with his one good arm, the dog ran off after it. Sitting on the nearby bench, Eddie watched the man in the wheelchair and Amigo continue their game. With each throw, the young man who at first hardly spoke, became more animated. After nearly thirty minutes, and finally winded, Amigo planted himself at the foot of the wheelchair and lay his head down. At first, the young man in the chair ignored the dog but eventually he leaned over and scratched Amigo behind the ears with his right hand.

"Nice dog," said the young man in the chair, speaking to Eddie for the first time. "I used to have a dog."

"You want this one," said Eddie.

The man leaned over a second time and ruffled the top of Amigo's head and smiled. It wasn't a big smile but it was definitely a smile. "I haven't seen you here before," said the young man not looking up, eyes on the dog.

"It's our first time. I live near the center of town. He was a stray. I think being untethered feels better to him."

"I can understand that," said the man without expression looking down at his chair.

"You seem to like the dog," said Eddie. "I'm looking to find a new home for him. My work and my kids take up so much of my time so I have to get rid of him."

"I can't," said the young man pointing with his chin to a big brick building on the other side of the field. "I live over there, VA rehab hospital."

Amigo barked and wagged his tail causing the young man to half-smile again and throw the ball to the far side of the immense green lawn. When Amigo sprinted after it, the young man laughed ever so slightly. "He sure can move," he said, following the dog with his eyes.

Eddie nodded as a dark-haired woman in her fifties wearing blue scrubs approached. Her name tag said "Monica".

"There you are, Justin," said the nurse slightly out of breath. "The aide who brought you out here said you were by the bench. I thought she meant the bench on the other side of the pond. I've been looking all over for you. Did I just see you throw a ball?"

"It's my fault," said Eddie.

"I've never seen him talk to anyone in the park before let alone throw a ball," said Monica.

"I wasn't talking to him. I was talking to the dog," said Justin as Amigo sat down at the foot of his wheelchair again. Justin leaned over and scratched the animal under his chin and behind his ears. When the young man sat up, he was smiling, a big smile.

"Good Lord, somebody catch me," said Monica pretending to fall backwards. "Did Justin Carver just smile?"

Justin grinned again.

"Lordy, that's twice in a row," said Monica signaling for Eddie to follow her as she walked several yards away while Justin played with the dog. "I don't know what you did. The nurses and staff at the hospital have been doing cartwheels trying to get that kid to crack a smile. He was at Walter Reed for half a year and then they brought him here for rehab a few months ago. He's barely talked to anyone since he arrived. These kids come back from Afghanistan and Iraq and the doctors patch them up, but their souls are still broken. You may not realize this but you and your dog performed a little miracle today."

"Wasn't me," said Eddie looking over at Amigo. "Was all him."

"All I know is, my patient is smiling for the first time," said Monica as she walked back to the wheelchair and kicked off the foot brake. "Justin, honey, I hate to do this, but I have to take you back for physical therapy; we're already late."

"Will Amigo be at the park again?" said Justin.

"I don't know," said Eddie.

"Would be nice to see him again," said the young soldier.

"Would be real nice if you could," said Monica giving Eddie a hopeful smile. "Justin comes out here every afternoon if it's not raining."

"I'll have to check my schedule," said Eddie.

"We'll be here tomorrow," said Monica.

Surprising himself, the next day Eddie took Amigo to the park and headed back to the same spot. The young soldier in the wheelchair was there and smiled broadly when he saw them walk across the lawn. As they got closer, Amigo recognized the young man and raced across the grass towards him.

"How are you, boy?" said Justin with a smile as he pet the dog. "I told the nurses all about you. I even brought you some treats." With his good hand, Justin pulled out a plastic bag filled with dog biscuits from his pocket and looked at Eddie. "One of the nurses got these for me in case you came back. Is it okay if I give him one?"

"Sure," said Eddie as he sat on the nearby bench. "He loves to eat." Justin smiled and gave the excited dog a green biscuit shaped like a bone. Eddie handed Justin the red ball. When the dog saw it in Justin's hand, he stood at attention and the young man hurled it into the sky.

"You've got a good arm," said Eddie watching the dog tear after the ball. "You threw that clear across the field. Ever play baseball?"

"I was a pitcher in high school. Then I joined the army and that was the end of my baseball career."

"You mind if I ask what happened?" said Eddie.

"Truck went over an IED outside of Kabul. There were three of us. I was the only one who survived," said Justin, his face suddenly slack. "They were my best friends. That was almost a year ago. I was in the hospital in DC and then they moved me here because I'm from Jersey."

Back with the ball, Amigo barked to get Justin's attention.

The young man's face lit up again and he scratched the dog's neck and threw the ball. For the next hour and a half the scene remained the same. Justin tossed the ball, Amigo fetched it, and was rewarded with a treat. Eddie sat silently on the bench. At a little before four, Monica appeared.

"You made it," she said to Eddie. "Justin's talked of nothing but you and your dog since he met you. You've done a really good thing, you know that?"

"Wasn't me, was the dog," said Eddie.

"I was thinking," said Monica, pausing a moment before she continued. "Would you be open to bringing Amigo over to the hospital? We've got a lot of young soldiers in there who could use some cheering up. Many of them can't go out. Maybe Amigo could work his magic on a few more of our kids?"

"I don't know," said Eddie. "I've got a lot going on right now."

"I'm sure you're very busy. I know it's a huge ask but now that I see how you and the dog have affected Justin, I thought..."

"I'll think about it."

A week later, not sure why he was doing it, Eddie and his dog walked into the veterans' medical facility. Wounded soldiers in wheelchairs lined the hallways. Some played with their phones if they had hands, others only stared into space.

"You must be Mr. Gamble and that little guy must be Amigo," said an elderly woman seated at the concierge station. "You made quite an impression on Justin. He's been talking about your dog all week. There's a group waiting for you in the rec room on the sixth floor."

When Eddie pushed open the doors to the rec room, there were eight young soldiers there, most in wheelchairs.

"They're here," shouted Justin from across the room. All heads turned in Eddie's direction as Amigo strained on his leash. Walking over to Justin, Eddie shook his right hand and then waved to a smiling Monica.

"Thanks for coming, Eddie," she called out. "We've been looking forward to your visit."

Justin reached down and scratched the dog's neck. "Guys, this is Amigo, the one I was telling you about. You should see him run." The young man pulled a treat from his pocket and fed it to the pup.

Scanning the room, Eddie's heart was heavy. *They're all so damn young. Not much older than Joe.* He walked around the perimeter of the room and introduced himself and his dog to each young man. Some responded, others didn't. For a moment Eddie wondered why the hell he had agreed to do this until he heard Chili's voice in his head. *Don't be a fucking baby, Gamble. You had tougher audiences when you were pitching advertising.* He took Amigo off the leash. The little dog circled the room, stopping and sniffing each soldier. A few stroked him tentatively on the head. With each touch the dog wagged his tail. His enthusiastic reaction to them made a few of the men smile a little.

Justin held up the red ball. "Amigo," he shouted as he threw it across the room. The little dog tore after the ball as if his life depended on it, getting tangled in chair legs and boxes.

"He's fast!" said one of the soldiers. "Look at him go." A few of the others chuckled and called out to the dog to bring the ball to them. After an hour, five of the eight men had interacted with Amigo, and Eddie had learned all of their names.

"You did great today," said Monica patting Eddie on the shoulder as she walked him to the elevator. "I saw some sparkle in some of their eyes today. I hope we didn't wear your dog out."

"He's got energy to burn. Looks like you were a hit," said Eddie to Amigo as they stepped onto the elevator. As if on cue, the dog barked and the elevator doors closed. Walking to the parking lot, Eddie had a strange sensation, something he hadn't felt in a long time—hope.

Running out of cash, Eddie walked his dog through town and saw a help wanted sign in a hardware store window. He mustered up his last ounce of determination and went in.

"This is a sales job, pure customer service. You ever work in a hardware store before?" the owner had asked him after he filled out the employment application.

"I've been in sales my whole career," said Eddie with a half-smile. "I used to sell ads for magazines and more recently I sold advertising for *South Jersey Life*. They had some financial difficulties, so now I'm in the market again."

The store's owner showed Eddie around and they conversed about the hardware business and some of the product lines they carried. "I don't pay what a magazine pays, not even close, but it's a fair wage. You seem like you know what you're talking about," said the store owner. "You have a nice way about you. I think my customers would feel the same way."

Given another chance, two days later Eddie Gamble started work selling paint and plumbing supplies for fifteen dollars an hour.

Settling into his new routine, whenever Eddie wasn't working at the hardware store, he'd take Amigo over to the rehab hospital. After a few months all of the wounded soldiers they had met on that first day now regularly engaged with Amigo.

"You hear that sound?" said Monica to Eddie on one of his visits. "It's laughter. Until you and your dog came along, we didn't hear that around here too often. Wish we could clone your dog. Look at the smiles on those young men. You did that. Next time you come, I'd like to take you to another wing and introduce you to some more of our patients."

Time passed and though his son had fully healed, the car

crash and what led to it had a lasting effect on Eddie. Still working at the hardware store, each day was a struggle but he hung on because he had to take care of the dog.

"I got this steady job at a hardware store," said Eddie on the phone to his now sixteen-year-old son.

"Good for you, Dad."

"It's been a long time since we've seen each other and I was hoping you might come over and meet my dog Amigo," said Eddie. "He's funny-looking but you'd like him."

"I'm sure I would."

"Since you've got your junior license now, maybe we could pick a day and you could come over and we could take the dog for a walk and..."

"Mom doesn't want me to see you right now."

"Sure. I understand. We can get together another time."

A week later while lying on his second-hand couch with Amigo beside him, Monica's words from that first day at the hospital reverberated. "Wish we could clone your dog." The old Eddie Gamble, the man who ran big magazines and websites, put together huge international promotions, raised millions and made things happen, had pushed his way to the surface. Neurons fired and for the first time in a long time he allowed himself to dream and dream big. Plotting and parsing hundreds of thoughts and ideas, he was suddenly filled with energy, determination and most importantly, hope. *I can do this. I really think I can pull it off.*

Excited for the first time in a long time, Eddie called his son again and left a message. "Hey Joe, it's Dad. I'm working on a new project and was thinking about you. Would be nice to see you one of these days. Love you, Joe."

On his next day off from work, Eddie went to a nearby animal shelter. A medium-sized brown-and-black dog caught his eye when he passed the animal's crate. The sign on the outside said "Ocean", a one-year-old terrier-retriever mix. Ocean had long floppy ears and looked up and wagged his tail as Eddie stopped in front of him. When the dog turned his head, Eddie noticed his left eye was damaged.

"I wanted to find out about Ocean," said Eddie to the young, female front-desk attendant. "What happened to his eye?"

"That Ocean's a sweetie," said the attendant as she looked through her binder and pulled out the dog's bio. "It says here they found him unresponsive down by the shore. Nobody knows where he came from or what happened to him. He had cuts and scratches all over him and his eye was bleeding when they brought him in. Our vet couldn't save it. We didn't think he was going to make it but after a week or so, he started to come around. I walk and feed him every day. He's a bundle of energy and has the nicest personality. Losing his eye hasn't slowed him down one bit."

Eddie nodded and went back to the kennel to have another look at the dog. After thirty seconds, he was sure Ocean was the right one. The brown-and-black dog was a survivor just like the soldiers in the hospital.

When Eddie brought Ocean home and placed him on the floor, Amigo approached the new dog slowly. The two dogs circled and sniffed, eventually curling up next to each other. To celebrate their first night, Eddie cooked some cheap cut of steak in the broiler for all of them and the three ate dinner together. Later, when Eddie climbed into bed, Amigo jumped in next to him as he always did and was soon followed by Ocean. Looking at the menagerie around him Eddie laughed. "If I'm going to do this," he said to the dogs, "I may need a bigger bed."

37

For weeks Eddie trained Ocean in preparation for the dog's first visit to the VA hospital. Like Amigo, he registered Ocean as a service dog and took him everywhere; parks, malls, and main streets to see how the dog responded in crowds and how he'd ultimately react with the soldiers. Over and over, the one-eyed dog proved to be friendly and gentle. Despite whatever cruelty Ocean may have endured, he was not the least bit skittish. He loved interacting with anyone who would give him a pat, a hug or a scratch behind the ears.

When Eddie decided Ocean was ready, he called Monica. "I've got a little surprise for everyone on our next visit," he said. "I'm bringing a guest."

"Who?"

"You'll have to wait and see."

Pulling into the hospital parking lot a few days later, Eddie turned off the Jeep's engine, took a deep breath and looked over at his two passengers. "Guys, this is our big day. Everyone needs to be in top form. No slackers allowed."

Monica was waiting for them by the sixth-floor elevator and smiled when she saw two dogs. "Lordy! You brought another dog," she said as she stooped down to pet both, setting their tails wagging.

Ocean sat directly in front of Monica so she could more easily scratch his head. "What happened to the poor baby's eye?" she asked.

"Don't know, he's a rescue."

"There are some sick people out there," said Monica grimacing, and then smiling at Ocean as she bent over to pet him again. "You look nice and healthy now. Come on, let's go meet everybody. Wait until they see you brought another dog."

When Eddie pushed through the doors of the rec room he let go of both leashes and Amigo and Ocean raced into the room. Most of the young men smiled and cheered when they saw there was a second dog. Amigo ran to all of his old friends while Eddie slowly brought Ocean around to some of the patients so he could sniff them and become familiar. By the end of the hour, Ocean was officially a part of the gang.

"Monica said they found Ocean at the beach," said Justin, giving the new dog a neck rub.

"They couldn't save his eye but he's doing fine now," said Eddie as Ocean flipped on his back and waited for a belly rub.

"He's kind of like us," said Justin. A few of the other soldiers nodded in agreement. "He got hurt but he pushed through it and came out on the other side."

When it was time to leave, Monica walked Eddie and the dogs to the entrance of the facility.

"Today was a great day," she said. "Did you see their faces when you showed up with two dogs? Your visits have really boosted the morale around here. Next time, would you be up for visiting some of the rooms where patients are more medically and emotionally compromised? Some of our soldiers can't or won't go to the rec room. A bedside visit from the dogs might do them a world of good."

"I'm game," said Eddie flashing a genuine smile. "Monica, I wanted to run something by you. I've had this idea brewing in my head. It's been getting bigger and louder until finally I couldn't ignore it anymore."

"This sounds serious."

"Being here with Amigo was purely accidental," said Eddie. "But over time, even I can see the difference in the soldiers. Amigo, and now Ocean are somehow able to light a spark within them, something they thought they had lost. I know how that feels."

Monica nodded as Eddie continued.

"I have this idea. I want to create an organization that rescues and trains dogs and the people to handle them specifically for facilities like yours. These dogs can help our veterans recover. Now that I see what they can do, I want to do more."

"I love it. There are so many rehab centers and hospitals that could take advantage of a program like that," said Monica.

"That was my thought too. There are loads of animal rescues and shelters but what if my organization was specifically designed to train people and dogs to visit wounded soldiers?"

"That would be incredible, but wouldn't it cost a lot of money?"

"It would, but in a previous life, that's what I did," said Eddie. "I pitched and sold products, built relationships and partnerships and made a lot of money for my employers. I think I could pitch companies and foundations, get some sponsorships and grants and roll out a regional program to start. If things go the way I hope, eventually, we'd go national."

"It sounds amazing," said Monica.

"There are wounded soldiers all over America. I want to provide this service to any soldier who wants or needs it. It might even lead to pet adoption down the road so it would be a win-win for everyone."

"It's a great idea."

"I'm thinking big," said Eddie getting excited, sharing his vision for the first time. "I'm thinking of calling it *Comrades in Arms*."

When he wasn't working at the hardware store or visiting the soldiers, Eddie was trying to figure out the next steps of his plan. Feeling the old positive productive power that he used to have, he fine-tuned the *Comrades in Arms* mission statement, organizational roll-out and partnerships plans. All the while, he communicated regularly with Clare leaving messages for Sarah and Joe with the hope of reconnecting with his children again.

"I know I don't deserve a second chance, Clare," said Eddie over the phone one day when his plan was nearly complete. "I've done more stupid and selfish things than I can count. I've sunk pretty low but somehow, I've been given another chance."

After he told Clare about his work at the veterans' center and his plans for *Comrades in Arms*, she softened slightly. As her ex-husband talked about the dogs and the soldiers and the changes in the men, Clare heard tinges of the old sparkle in his voice.

"I've finally figured out what's important and I want my kids in my life," said Eddie. "I'm not drinking anymore and I'd like to be a better father. I'm trying to turn things around."

Hearing genuine sincerity in his voice, Clare agreed to mediate with the kids. She talked to Sarah, but the young woman wanted nothing to do with her father. Joe, on the other hand, a softer touch, agreed to meet his father for lunch.

The day Joe came for his first visit, Eddie was a bundle of nerves peeking out of his upstairs window every five minutes. He hadn't seen his son since the accident and when he saw a car pull into the driveway he ran down the steps followed by Amigo, Ocean and a new three-legged chihuahua named Puck.

Getting out of the car, Joe approached his father warily, opting to greet the friendly dogs first. "When did you get all these dogs?" said Joe smiling while petting the frisky group jumping around his ankles.

"It's a long story," said his father as the two exchanged an awkward hug. "Come on. I want to take you somewhere. There's something I want to show you."

While the father, son and the three dogs walked over to the Veterans' Rehab Center, Eddie told Joe about the program he was trying to launch. Joe was skeptical, thinking his father was playing another angle until he saw the reaction of the injured soldiers at the hospital.

"It's nice to finally meet you," said Monica. "Your father's told us all about you. I hear you're an amazing guitar player."

"I play in a band," said Joe blushing as his father left the rec room with Puck to visit a bedridden soldier on another floor.

"Your father is a wonderful man," said Monica. "I can't tell you how much he's done for our patients. He's breathed life into bodies that had just about given up."

Soon after that day, Eddie got a fourth dog. Over time, he galvanized animal rescue volunteers and dog trainers to help him develop a comprehensive program for both volunteers and dogs. Seeing his father in a new light, Joe started regularly accompanying Eddie to the rehab facility. Together, working with the dog trainers and soldiers, the father and son forged a new relationship. Impressed with Eddie's turnaround, even Clare agreed to adopt a rescue dog and be part of the first class of dog-handler graduates from *Comrades in Arms*.

After constant badgering, Joe convinced his sister to come to the rehab center with him. Sarah hadn't seen her father in years. When she arrived, she was wooden and distant and Eddie gave her the space she needed, glad that she was there. As the afternoon unfolded and Sarah observed her father interact with the patients, dogs and new volunteers, the ice started to melt... a little.

"Will you come here with me again?" said Joe to his sister at the end of that day.

"I still don't trust him," said Sarah, "but it looks like he's doing something good so I'll wait and see. If this is some kind of a scam or..."

"It's not. Dad's really into it," said Joe, looking over at his father talking in earnest with a newly arrived patient, Amigo on his lap. "He figured out that helping other people feels better than helping himself."

After months of phone calls and corporate pitches, Eddie was awarded two charitable grants. One from a humanitarian organization and one from a group that supported veteran services. He secured a partnership with the largest regional animal shelter in the northeast and set up the *Comrades in Arms* volunteer network for local high school and college students.

By the end of the second year, Eddie Gamble's dream became a reality. With an army of nearly 300 people with service dogs, *Comrades in Arms'* human and canine volunteer program was instituted in seven veterans' facilities in four states. By his third year, Eddie received additional grant money and launched a high school and college training program across the United States. With that piece in place, he reached out to some of his old advertising clients and got his organization into several corporate charity initiatives. With his son by his side, he met with the US Veteran's Administration officials in Washington DC and got sign-off on a nationwide *Comrades in Arms* program that would be underwritten by the US government. From then on, every wounded American soldier, every veteran who ever served at any time would have access to a *Comrades in Arms* dog.

38

Eddie Gamble had searched for something his whole life. His natural gifts of persuasion, charm, and wit had engineered a flashy and successful media career. They brought him power, women and money. He had the perfect life—the big house, the wife, two kids and all the trappings. Even with all that, happiness eluded him. It wasn't until he used his talents to help people who thought they had nothing to live for, that he ended up saving his own life.

The commuter train out of Philadelphia would have hit Eddie Gamble and the little black-and-white dog with the lopsided ears at 6:46pm. No one would have arrived home on time that night; not the passengers, not the police, the EMS workers nor the Amtrak people who had to pick up the pieces. Hundreds of waiting cars would have been backed up at train stations all along the Pennsylvania line with nothing coming in or going out. Dinners cold; bedtime stories unread.

But it didn't happen that way. An accidental acquaintance—a lost man and a forgotten dog united by a mutual desire to belong found each other.

THE END

ACKNOWLEDGMENTS

A Familiar Stranger is my sixth novel and it's been a wonderful journey. This story was quite a bit different from my other books which were mainly psychological thrillers. It's a tale of redemption and one that I couldn't get out of my head.

I've been fortunate enough to have terrific friends and family supporting me with each new book and am very grateful. I'd like to thank my always first reader, my husband Peter Black, who reads my manuscripts in their roughest, barely coherent form and somehow gets through them and comes up with great insights and suggestions. Next, I'd like to thank Diane McGarvey, Marlene Pedersen and Jamie Holt, all voracious readers, who identify plot holes, character inconsistencies and dialogue that falls flat. They are almost always right.

On the publishing end, I'd like to thank my wonderful publishers, Bloodhound Books, who have given me the opportunity to get my stories out to the world. Many thanks to Betsy and Fred as well as my wonderful editor, Clare Law, who edits with a tender yet decisive hand. Also, thanks to Tara Lyons, who makes the production and editing process positive and seamless. Also, thank you to the proofreaders who catch all of my punctuation faux pas. I definitely enjoy commas a little too much.

I hope you liked this story and if you did, please leave a review on Amazon, it's such a big help. Now, on to my next manuscript...

A NOTE FROM THE PUBLISHER

Thank you for reading this book. If you enjoyed it please do consider leaving a review on Amazon to help others find it too.

We hate typos. All of our books have been rigorously edited and proofread, but sometimes mistakes do slip through. If you have spotted a typo, please do let us know and we can get it amended within hours.

info@bloodhoundbooks.com

Made in the USA
Middletown, DE
14 July 2022

69298001R00168